POSED FOR DEATH

POSED FOR DEATH

KENZIE KIRSCH MEDICAL THRILLERS
BOOK SIX

P.D. WORKMAN

 **PD WORKMAN**

ISBN: 9781774684108 (KDP Paperback)
ISBN: 9781774684115 (KDP Hardcover)
ISBN: 9781774684122 (Large Print)
ISBN: 9781774684153 (Kindle)
ISBN: 9781774684146 (ePub)
ISBN: 9781774684139 (Lulu Paperback)

ALSO BY P.D. WORKMAN

Dosed to Death

Gentle Angel

Rushin' Death

Posed for Death

Death of a Corpse (Coming Soon)

Parks Pat Mysteries
Police Procedural Set in Canada
Out with the Sunset

Long Climb to the Top

Dark Water Under the Bridge

Immersed in the View

Skimming Over the Lake

Hazard of the Hills

Knows the Hills (Coming Soon)

Spanning the Creek (Coming Soon)

Sanctuary in the Stream (Coming Soon)

High-Tech Crime Solvers Series
Virtually Harmless

Stand Alone Suspense Novels
Looking Over Your Shoulder

Lion Within

Pursued by the Past

In the Tick of Time

Loose the Dogs

AND MORE AT PDWORKMAN.COM

*For those who care
in every way*

The phone rang as Kenzie was in the bathroom getting ready for her day. She looked at it in irritation. Unless it was Dr. Wiltshire, no one else should be calling her before work. And if it were Dr. Wiltshire, he usually just left her a message on her work phone to let her know where he was going or if something in his schedule had changed for the day, rather than calling her on her cell. Unless he wanted her to attend to the scene of a death.

But the name on the face of her phone was not Dr. Wiltshire; it was Walter Kirsch. Kenzie considered ignoring it. He wasn't likely to be calling her about anything urgent, and she would feel better prepared to talk to him after she'd had a fortifying cup of coffee and some breakfast.

But she was trying to work on a better relationship with him, so she just closed her eyes briefly to gather her thoughts and try to relax, and then swiped to answer.

"Hi, Dad."

"MacKenzie!" His voice boomed, much too loud and cheery for the first thing in the morning. "How are you this lovely morning?"

"I'm good. What's up? It's pretty early for you to be calling."

She hoped that the gentle nudge would get through to him and he would remember the next time not to call her quite so early.

"You always did like to sleep in," he remembered fondly.

Kenzie had liked to sleep in as a teenager and a young adult, but she didn't think that sleeping until six-thirty or seven o'clock should count as "sleeping in."

"Yes, I did back then," she agreed. "But I'm up this morning. I need to get ready for work." Rather than pushing him to hurry up and tell her his business and get him off the phone if he was just calling for a friendly chat, she tried an offer. "Did you want to get together for dinner, and we can have a visit then?"

"Oh, no, you don't have to worry about that. I don't have time to drive down. But your mother has some papers she wants you to sign for the foundation. I thought I would give you a heads-up."

Kenzie frowned and shook her head. "If she has some papers for me to sign, then why isn't she the one calling me?"

"I offered. Thought it would give me a chance to say hello to you. She'll email you the documents. Just make sure you check your email sometime this morning."

"Are they urgent? It has to be this morning?"

There was a slight hesitation before his response. "It would be best if you could get to them this morning, yes."

Kenzie sighed. She really didn't want to know all of the details of why it had to be done right away. It seemed like the more she got involved with the Kirsch family foundation, the more urgent everything became. When she had been shirking her duties, some documents had waited weeks for her signature. But now that she was trying to step up and take an active part, everything needed to be done immediately. She supposed she should be grateful that her mother wanted to involve her and that they were helping so many other people, but she felt a little like Lisa was taking advantage of her.

"Sure. I'll make sure I check sometime this morning and will sign them and send them back."

"Great. That will make her happy. She says hello."

2

"Are you there right now? In Burlington with Mother?"

Walter and Lisa had divorced a number of years before. Kenzie was happy that they were still on good terms and didn't see a problem with Walter stopping in to sleep at the family home or using the office he had there if he happened to be in the area. It was good that they got along together and didn't fight and put Kenzie in the middle of things. But it always made her feel a little bit strange and she didn't quite know how to take their continuing relationship. She had never asked for details of whether they were still romantically involved. That would be too weird. She didn't want to know.

"Yes, I have a meeting here this morning, so I stayed over last night. Always nicer to start the day off relaxed, rather than having to drive out here."

Kenzie nodded. She didn't like to be rushed in the morning either. And looking at the time, she realized she needed to get off of the phone if she were going to get to work on time without having to hurry.

"Okay, Daddy. I've got to go now. I'll talk to you later."

"Say hello to Zachary for me. And for your mother."

"He says hi back," Kenzie said automatically, and she ended the call.

As she put the phone down to finish her hair and makeup, she felt Zachary move in behind her. "Walter?" he asked as he put his arms around her for a quick hug.

Kenzie wondered whether he had heard her call Walter "Dad" or if he just recognized the note of exasperation in her voice when she talked to him. She hoped that her annoyance with him wasn't that obvious. She didn't want Walter to realize how much of an effort it was to talk to him and be civil, though she did want him to know that it was a bad time of day to call her to talk.

Of course, Zachary was a private investigator, so, even if he hadn't heard Kenzie call Walter by name, it would probably only take a sentence or two for him to figure out who she was talking to.

"Yes," she sighed. "Way too early in the morning to be talking to him."

Zachary nuzzled her and kissed her neck, then released her, knowing that she would want to get ready. He was grinning.

"It may not be early for you," Kenzie said, acknowledging that he had probably been up since before sunrise, "but it's too early to talk to him."

Zachary nodded. He never had much to say about Walter. The two of them didn't exactly get along, but Kenzie understood that Zachary didn't want to say anything negative about him to Kenzie, so he was tactful and kept his thoughts to himself. But she knew that he too found Walter taxing and wouldn't want to be talking to him early in the morning—or late in the morning.

"I'll go put the coffee on," Zachary offered.

She patted his sandpaper cheek. "That would be great. Thanks."

He left, and Kenzie looked back at the mirror to tame her long, curly dark hair into some semblance of order and finish putting on her makeup.

Not that her patients would care what she looked like. Since they were already dead.

2

With Zachary taking care of the coffee and getting the rest of their breakfast arranged, Kenzie didn't feel too rushed and could sit down and take a breath before heading straight out to the Medical Examiner's Office. She glanced over the table to see what Zachary had missed and got the marmalade out of the fridge. Her bread was already in the toaster, the coffee was just finishing dripping, and Zachary had his granola bar and yogurt out.

Now that he was on a new medication protocol, he would probably be able to eat both the granola bar and the yogurt when, previously, it would have been a struggle to get either one down with the side effects he had experienced. He saw her put the marmalade on the table and rolled his eyes at his oversight.

"Whoops. Sorry."

Kenzie shrugged. "It's okay. Looks like you got everything else."

Which meant that the ADHD meds were doing their job. Overlooking one thing was easy for anyone to do. Without the meds, he would have been lucky to get the bread in the toaster and the coffee brewing at the same time without getting distracted. He didn't like taking all of the pills he did, but they did make a difference.

Zachary poured them each a mug of coffee and they sat down.

"Everything okay with your dad?" Zachary asked.

"Yeah. Just saying hello and that Lisa has some stuff for me to sign."

He raised his brows and Kenzie shrugged. "I don't know why he was the one to call instead of her. I guess he spent the night there and just figured he'd tell me to watch for them. I don't know what it is all about."

Zachary nodded. "Fair enough."

"But it sounds like everyone is fine. Just some foundation stuff to take care of."

"Good."

"How about you? What are you expecting to do today?"

"Pretty routine. No big cases right now. Might help Tyrrell with looking for work."

Kenzie nodded slowly. She wasn't sure exactly how Zachary would help his younger brother, Tyrrell. Mostly, their getting together to job hunt seemed to consist of a cup of coffee and the newspaper and the two of them chatting while they looked at their computers or phones for any new job opportunities to manifest themselves. Tyrrell was competent enough to look for his own job. He had a college degree, was better at reading, and had fewer challenges than Zachary. It seemed to be more moral support than anything. Tyrrell was at least working part-time with a door-to-door sales company, but he was looking for something better.

"I hope something turns up for him."

Zachary shrugged and grunted. They both knew that it would be challenging for Tyrrell to land a good job with his history of alcoholism and leaving employers in the lurch without any warning. But if he kept working at it diligently, maybe something would turn up.

"How has he been?" Kenzie asked.

"Seems to be pretty good. No warning signs that I've noticed."

Zachary was cautious in expressing this opinion. They had both been surprised by Tyrrell's falling off the wagon previously. While they were both alert for the signs, Tyrrell was an old hand at hiding his drinking and would probably be able to cover up the fact that he had started drinking again until it got really bad.

"Has he seen the kids?"

"I think he's got them this weekend."

"Good. Say hi for me if you see him."

"Will do. How will your work be today?"

Kenzie sipped her coffee and smiled. "I expect it to be pretty dead today."

Kenzie was glad that she had taken the time with Zachary to have their coffee and breakfast and prepare for the day. She felt much more relaxed and focused and ready to take on the day than she would have if she had just headed over to the Medical Examiner's Office after the call with Walter.

She opened up the office, took the phones out of night mode, and started the coffee pot in the kitchen brewing. It would probably be an hour before Dr. Wiltshire got in, which would allow Kenzie the time to check her voicemail, email, and any deliveries or overnight check-ins before he arrived. She would have everything set up for him, ready to go. The late spring brought with it alcohol poisoning and post-prom DUI deaths, but it was not busy like December and January were. They had a few postmortems lined up, but on the whole, things were pretty quiet.

Carlos had called ahead that he had a couple of bodies to bring in. Dr. Wiltshire had already attended the scenes or reviewed them remotely and said that the bodies could be released for autopsy. Kenzie filled in the check-in sheets with the initial information she had and met him just inside the loading dock as he off-loaded the first delivery.

"Which one is this?"

"Joseph Howard."

Kenzie checked the clipboards and picked up the appropriate one. "Okay. Unattended death. Elderly man. Being cared for in his home. Is that right?"

Carlos nodded his agreement. "Pretty simple; died in his sleep at home."

There wouldn't be a lot for Kenzie to do on that file. Unless someone had flagged the circumstances of death as suspicious, an unattended elderly person dying would not require a full autopsy. They would examine the body for any signs of violence or anything that seemed out of place, but would probably not need to open him up. Release the body to the funeral home, and they would be done with their part in Mr. Joseph Howard's death.

She directed Carlos where to leave the body and handed him the clipboard to scribble a few more notes into and then sign it. Kenzie countersigned as having received the body, and Carlos was off again to pick up the next one.

Before Dr. Wiltshire got in, Kenzie remembered that she needed to sign the foundation documents that her mother had emailed her. At her desk computer, she opened her personal email account into a new tab and skimmed down the list of unread messages. There was one from Lisa at her foundation address, so Kenzie opened it up and clicked a couple of times to print the attachments.

Dr. Wiltshire came in at that point, so Kenzie turned back to her work and gathered the physical notes and messages that Dr. Wiltshire would need to begin his day.

"Hello, Doctor."

"Hi, Kenzie. How are things shaping up today?"

"Nothing out of the ordinary. A couple of requests from upstairs for answers on completed postmortems." She flapped the pink slips at him. "Some lab reports back for you to review. I didn't see anything unexpected on any of them, but I only skimmed. Carlos brought in one of the unattended deaths from last night that you already authorized. He's gone back for the other. It didn't sound like either of them was anything to be concerned about?"

"Nope. Not as far as I could tell from what I saw," Wiltshire agreed. "We'll have a look at the bodies this afternoon and, if there isn't anything of concern, we can release them right away to the funeral homes. Let their families get on with their lives."

Kenzie nodded. "Okay. Sounds good."

"You aren't too backed up with paperwork, are you? You have some time to join me on the postmortems?"

Kenzie smiled. "You bet."

"Perfect. We can each take one of the new arrivals. And then catch up on the others in the cold room. I think we can get caught up on any backlog."

Since they didn't generally do autopsies on the weekend, there were sometimes weekend deaths waiting for them when they returned to work on Monday. Prom season meant that there were more than usual. Kenzie shook her head, thinking about the young people celebrating their graduation from high school, only to have their lives cut short due to drinking, drugs, and cars.

Wiltshire nodded, giving her a sympathetic look. He knew better than Kenzie the tragedy of the yearly uptick in deaths during a time that should have been filled with happy, bright futures.

Kenzie would take an eighty-year-old man who had died in his sleep over an eighteen-year-old whose life had been tragically and unexpectedly cut short any day.

3

Kenzie approached the table that was generally set at the appropriate height for her to do a postmortem so that they didn't have to constantly raise and lower the tables. George had placed Mr. Joseph Howard there, a fact Kenzie verified by checking both ID tags before she began. Mixing up bodies was something that they did their best to avoid. Every body, every sample, and every file needed to be checked twice to ensure that the paperwork did not end up in the wrong place.

Kenzie tapped the floor button with her foot and began her dictation with her name, Joseph Howard's name and file number, and the date and time. She began with the gross examination, which was probably all that would be required.

"Mr. Howard was in home care. There are no IV's or catheters attached," Kenzie observed. He looked to be in his seventies, gray-haired, thin but not emaciated. She noted the height and weight on the dictation. There were no obvious traumatic injuries. Kenzie began a close examination, working her way from the head to the feet on first the patient's front, and then his back. She looked for any changes or discolorations to the skin, needle marks, or perimortem bruising.

She paused in her recording and turned to Dr. Wiltshire, waiting until she was sure his recorder was not on either.

"Doctor, there are some petechia."

"Not unusual," Wiltshire assured her. "They can be caused by a lot of different things, including coughing, sneezing, or vomiting. Just note them and see whether there is any indication of what might have caused them."

Kenzie nodded and continued with her examination. She used a magnifying lens to look closely around the mouth and nose of the patient, and then at his neck. She increased the magnification and put the image up on the screen.

"Mild abrasions to the throat," she observed, taking a couple of pictures. She hadn't raised her voice to inform Dr. Wiltshire of this, but he heard and paused in his examination. He turned and walked over to Kenzie's table, looking at the image on the screen and then at Mr. Howard's throat himself.

"Very minor. Easy to miss."

Kenzie nodded. Dr. Wiltshire stayed by her side as she continued the examination. Kenzie examined the hands carefully. There appeared to be some mild bruising on his fingers. She tried the Alternate Light Source and the bruising on his fingers became more clear. So did bruising around his wrists. Kenzie frowned in concentration as she took pictures, trying to get the best images possible.

"Restraint bruises?" Kenzie suggested.

Dr. Wiltshire nodded. "Not unusual for a senior. He might have been in soft wrist restraints to keep him from climbing out of bed. There is certainly nothing that obviously indicates cruelty or abuse."

Kenzie still found her breathing to be too shallow, a knot in her stomach as she considered each finding. While she understood that patients in the hospital sometimes had to be restrained for their own safety, this man had been in his own home.

She checked all of the usual IV locations to confirm that he had not been on intravenous fluids. If he had been in the hospital recently, one of the first things they would do would be to start an IV to make sure that he was well hydrated and to give them access to his veins if they needed to give him something. There were no recent IV punctures. Kenzie checked his hips for any indication of bedsores and rolled Howard a little to check his buttocks and shoulders, but didn't find signs of any. If he had been restrained, it must only have been for a short time, or else someone had moved him to another position regularly to make sure that he did not develop any. That, at least, made her feel a bit better.

Dr. Wiltshire stayed beside the table while she continued with the examination. Eventually, Kenzie had completed her head-to-toe, front-and-back gross exam. She looked at Dr. Wiltshire.

"So... what do you think? Do I just say that's it? Release him to the funeral home?"

"You don't sound sure."

"Well, I'm not," Kenzie admitted. "There are enough questions raised by the gross exam that I would like to do more... but I don't want to open him up for no reason. I don't want to cause the family extra grief by doing an unnecessary procedure."

"Of course not," Wiltshire agreed. "But you cannot be guided by what the family wants. Your role here is a search for the truth. Do you feel that you have established natural causes? Or do you need to investigate further?"

Kenzie vacillated, not wanting to put it into words. She wasn't really *really* worried about the case. It seemed fairly straightforward, and she would probably find nothing more if she did a full autopsy. But there were enough niggling doubts that she wanted to be sure that there was nothing more.

"You have already made a decision," Dr. Wiltshire said, meeting her eyes and smiling encouragingly. "You're trying to find a way to bolster your decision and make it more palatable, but you have already decided whether you need to investigate further or not."

Kenzie sighed, looking down at the body before her. "Yes." She rested her hands on the table in front of her. "You're right."

"You'd better get started, then. I'll finish my gross exam and then assist as needed. Document what you have learned so far and your reasons for doing a full autopsy. Get some more pictures of the throat under the ALS."

"Okay. Thanks."

Kenzie followed Dr. Wiltshire's directions and dictated an explanation that was probably much longer than necessary to justify her choice. By the time she was finished making the y-incision and exposing the organs for examination, Dr. Wiltshire was finished with his gross exam and had signed off on his patient as a natural death. Kenzie started to examine, weigh, and dissect each organ.

"Can you bring up the statement by the son?" Dr. Wiltshire asked.

Kenzie left the heart on the scale and gave the computer verbal commands to display the statement made by the man's son as to what had happened. Dr. Wiltshire read through it, brows drawn down.

"Found dead in his bed in the morning. Looked like he was asleep. Discovered he wasn't breathing." Dr. Wiltshire shook his head. "Nothing to indicate that he was restrained or explaining the mark on his neck."

"You think he left things out?"

Dr. Wiltshire nodded. "I would say so. Does that mean that it is a suspicious death?" He shrugged and shook his head. "No. People *do* leave things out. They worry about what other people will think. They don't want to have to explain anything. So... sometimes we have to probe a little bit further." He raised his eyes from the body and gave Kenzie a look. "That is, we have to get the police to probe a little further."

Kenzie nodded. "Right. Our job is to prepare the autopsy report. It's their job to follow it up."

Dr. Wiltshire nodded his agreement. "Exactly. We don't get involved in that part."

"Though... we can ask a few questions," Kenzie suggested.

"We can ask for clarification if something doesn't fit or is ambiguous. We don't have to go to the police before getting clarification."

"Well... no." Dr. Wiltshire's tone was cautious. "But you're skirting the line, Kenzie. We do build a picture from a combination of the witness statements and what we discover in the autopsy. We can't always tell everything from the body. Heart failure, severe anaphylaxis, positional asphyxia... There are a lot of things that can look exactly the same on the examining table. It isn't until we get all of the details from the police, the site survey, and the witnesses that we can begin to build a complete picture of what happened."

Kenzie nodded. "This isn't an episode of *Bones*." At Wiltshire's questioning look, she clarified further. "One of Zachary's favorite shows."

Wiltshire smiled. "Of course. Mine too. But we aren't always blessed with all the clues, sophisticated equipment, and personnel they have. In real life, we have to do the best with what we've got, and we don't always have all of the information we would like to have."

Kenzie didn't carry on a conversation while she examined the heart and lungs. "They're congested with blood," she said eventually, a fact that Dr. Wiltshire had surely observed himself, but said nothing about, letting Kenzie work through her own investigation. "All of these things suggest...strangulation or asphyxiation." Kenzie went back to the pictures of Mr. Howard's throat. "With the mark on his throat... I think probably strangulation."

"I would agree," Dr. Wiltshire affirmed quietly.

He said nothing as Kenzie tapped the record button and added supplementary notes about what she had discovered during the autopsy.

"What do you think happened?" Kenzie asked after a period of silence.

"It doesn't appear to be a deliberate ligature strangulation. Or manual strangulation. The marks are indistinct and are not even. I think... it was probably accidental. Maybe he got tangled up in his sheets. A scarf or cord for the blinds. Something like that. People are not always aware of the hazards until it is too late. They don't realize how quickly someone who is confused, who maybe has mobility challenges, can get themselves into trouble. And if you cannot react immediately…" Dr. Wiltshire motioned toward Mr. Howard's body. "There can be tragic consequences."

"How should we proceed? Just kick it upstairs?"

"I will submit it to the police as soon as possible. But I think that first, we need to talk to the paramedics who responded to the scene. See if there is anything they might have missed once we bring it to their attention. And get clarification from the son as to what position his father's body was in when it was discovered. We might be able to coax a little more information from him that way."

4

W hat position was the body in when you arrived at the scene?" Kenzie asked Baden, the paramedic who had been first in the room after Howard's son had made his 9-1-1 call.

"Lying on the bed," Baden responded, his voice casual. "Uh... supine. Arms at his sides. He seemed quite peaceful. Just died in his sleep."

"There wasn't anything around his neck?"

There was a pause before Baden answered. "If there had been something around his neck, doc, I would have told you. Of course we would have noticed and reported that."

"Even if the son didn't want it to be reported?"

"Of course. We don't make our decisions based on whether the family members like it. I don't want to end up in trouble with the Attorney General."

"No," Kenzie agreed. "But sometimes... we might move something without even realizing it. Pushing blankets away from the throat and chest to be able to examine him. Something that fell from the bed or was pushed under the pillow or covers that you didn't realize the significance of."

"I wouldn't have missed something like that," Baden said. "Are you accusing me of missing something?"

"I'm not accusing anyone of anything. I'm just wondering if there is any possibility that something *was* missed. Or maybe… an indication that someone else had changed things… cleaned things up before you arrived."

A longer silence this time. Kenzie didn't hear Baden discussing it with his partner, so she didn't think the other paramedic was there with him. But it was possible that Baden had the phone on speaker or his partner was leaning in close to listen to the call. That they were writing notes to each other, making motions, or mouthing words.

"I can't think of anything that seemed out of place," Baden said finally. "I'm sorry. I would tell you if there was, of course. But everything seemed to be just as I said. The old guy died in his sleep. His son found him that way in the morning. He looked peaceful. Not like there had been any kind of struggle. No drugs on the bedside table. No blood or signs of violence. Just like a hundred other people who died in their sleep the night before." He gave a small laugh. "Sometimes, we're not so lucky. We don't always find them the next day. Sometimes there isn't someone checking in on them each day and a body goes a few days or a couple of weeks without being discovered. You do not want to see what that kind of scene looks like. Or smells like!"

Kenzie had to shake her head at that. "Where exactly do you think they go after you see them?" she asked. "There is no fairy that magically transports them to the funeral home. After you find someone who has been dead for a couple of weeks, they come here so that I can have a look."

"I know *that,*" Baden said irritably. "But it's not the same as when you walk into a room where a body has been putrefying for that long. At the morgue, you have big fans to pull the air out of the room and out the exhaust. So you don't have to smell it like we do, in a room filled with noxious body gases that have been building up for days."

Kenzie didn't bother to argue with him. He was probably right. They kept the air circulating as much as they could in the morgue, kept the bodies in the cold room to keep them from decomposing too quickly, and could walk out of the room for a breath of fresh air when needed. They didn't just let the bodies stew for days on end.

"So when I ask your partner, he'll report the same as you? That there wasn't anything suspicious in the room. Nothing that appeared to have been altered or tampered with?"

"Sure, of course. We're not trying to cover anything up. Why would we?"

"I don't think you would," Kenzie assured him. "I just want to make sure we've got all of our bases covered and are getting the same story from everyone."

"I don't understand what the problem is. What makes this death any different than any other elderly person dying in their own bed? I understand that they have to all run through your office, but that's just the routine. It isn't because there is anything suspicious."

"No. All unattended deaths are processed through our office. But there are a few things in Mr. Howard's case that make us take a closer look and ask some more questions. There wasn't anything that seemed off to you or made you suspicious?"

"No."

"You didn't think that the body might have been repositioned?"

She was expecting another quick "no," but didn't get one this time. She waited for Baden to consider the question. Much better that he stopped to think about it than just snapped back an answer because that was what he wanted to believe.

"Nothing particular," Baden said eventually. "I certainly couldn't have put my finger on anything. Livor mortis was on the side rather than the back, but I didn't think anything of it. He was sleeping on his side, and the son pulled him over when he checked on him in the morning. Repositioned him to check whether he was breathing or to try to get his attention. Didn't even realize what he had done."

Kenzie had noticed this discrepancy between the body and the story that had been told to her as well. Howard had died on his side; there was no question that the body had remained in that position for long enough for the blood to have settled in his side rather than his back. And Baden's explanation also made sense. It didn't prove or disprove any of the son's story.

"I have another question, and you're not going to be happy with me," Kenzie said. "So let me answer you first—no, I don't think you're stupid and I don't think you're lying to me. I just need to ask to verify the information we got. Mr. Howard was not in restraints when you found him?"

"Restraints? No. We would have mentioned that, you know, we're not—" Baden stopped himself and chuckled. "Okay, you already said we're not stupid. Yeah, if the body had been tied up, we probably would have mentioned that to you from the top."

"And were there any restraints there? Attached to the bed, on a table nearby, anything like that? Any sign that restraints had been used before you got there."

"No. Nothing. If there was anything... the son had enough sense to remove it from the room."

"Yeah."

"People do that sometimes, you know."

"Remove evidence?"

"No, I mean... tie up—restrain old people who wander or do things that could hurt them. You can't have them climbing out of bed, hitting themselves in the head, or pulling out stitches. Sometimes these folks have dementia and you can't explain it to them. You have to do what you can to keep them quiet and safe."

"But you don't see that in homes, do you? Only in hospitals where the more seriously ill patients are sent?"

"No. You see it in some of these home care patients too. A lot of them, actually. I couldn't give you any kind of percentage because people usually remove them before we show up on the scene. But I've had to take enough grandmas and grandpas out of restraints myself to know that it's not just the odd case. And sometimes, it's not full restraints like a hospital would use. Maybe just a sheet tied around the person's middle to keep them from getting up on their own. Homemade straps or a torn sheet to tie their wrists to the rails of their bed. Toy handcuffs, even. Whatever they can think of to help them to keep Mom or Dad from wandering."

"I thought that once things got to that point, they would take them to the hospital or have them put into a home."

"No. People want to keep them at home until the end if they can. Maybe they can't afford any other kind of care or they're afraid of their loved one being abused or lonely. So they do whatever they can to ensure that the person stays in their own home."

Kenzie jotted down some notes as Baden talked.

"But you didn't see any of that in this case. Just that livor mortis was in his side."

"And he could have normally slept on his side. It doesn't mean anything. The son might have tried to wake him or revive him. He might have even attempted CPR before they decided there was no point. He was on his back when we arrived."

"Okay. I'll talk to your partner to confirm… I'm sorry to bug you with more questions. We just want to be sure."

"You think that something else happened? Something suspicious?" Baden asked.

"I don't have any theory at this point. Just exploring all of the possibilities. But it looks like there was something around his neck at some point."

"Something around his neck. Well, not when we got there. If he got himself tangled up in something, the son had the sense to remove it and sanitize the scene."

"I guess so. Thanks for putting up with my questions. I'll let you go now."

"Okay…" Kenzie got the impression that he was going to follow up with one of those platitudes like "Call me if you have any other questions," but then decided that he didn't, in fact, want

Kenzie calling him back with any more questions. "I guess that's it, then. Goodbye."

Kenzie terminated the call. She stared at her notes and jotted down a few more things they had covered in their discussion.

It was probably nothing. Certainly, no one had set out to kill Joseph Howard. But he had, in fact, died. And it looked as though his son had not been entirely honest with the paramedics and professionals about exactly what had happened.

Kenzie's phone rang while she was in the car, and she answered it automatically on hands-free without looking to see who it was.

"Hello?"

"MacKenzie."

"Oh," Kenzie glanced at the phone. She should have looked before answering it. "Mother. How are you?"

"I'm fine, dear. How about you? Busy day at work today?"

"Yes. Oh—" Kenzie swore. "Those papers. Yes, I got them, printed them off to sign them, and then I got interrupted. I'm sorry. Things did get a little crazy. I meant to have them back to you."

"I know that you are a busy person, MacKenzie..."

"I am, but that's no excuse. I'm sorry. I'll do it when I get home, okay? I really did mean to get to them. I'm not trying to be passive-aggressive. I know that you needed them. You even had Dad call me to make sure that I was on top of it."

There was a silent pause.

"I didn't tell Walter to call you about them," Lisa said.

"Oh? Well, he did. I thought that was because you were worried about it. In getting them back right away." Kenzie tried to remember exactly what her father had said about them. Had he said that Lisa had asked him to call? Or had he just said that they needed to be done right away and Lisa would be emailing them to her? Why had he gotten involved with something that was in Lisa's wheelhouse?

Of course he was a member of the foundation. He was, in fact, the namesake of the foundation, but he had always left it to Lisa to run. Even though it was the Kirsch family foundation, Lisa Cole Kirsch was the one in charge.

"So, you'll get them back to me tonight?" Lisa asked tentatively.

"Yes. As soon as I get home, I'll take care of it."

"Thank you. I do appreciate it, MacKenzie. It's nice to see you being more involved with the foundation lately. I have always hoped you would take a bigger interest in it."

5

"How did things go with Tyrrell?" Kenzie asked Zachary as they sat down for supper that evening.

Zachary shrugged. "There aren't a lot of new listings from one day to the next. It is usually the same places over and over again. Or the same type of jobs, and Tyrrell is hoping for something that isn't just construction or casual labor. It would be nice if he could get something where he could put his college degree to use."

Kenzie nodded as she opened a bag of salad to dump into a bowl. "It would be nice... but you can see that most people aren't going to want to hire him with his history. Disappearing on a binge is not really something that employers look for in an employee."

"If alcoholism is a disease, then they shouldn't be able to discriminate against him for it."

"That's not realistic, though. You might not be able to fire him for being an alcoholic, but a potential employer who checks references and the first thing that he finds is that Tyrrell has been an unreliable and absentee employee... that's exactly the kind of behavior that references are supposed to cover, that's why we check references. So it's not discrimination if you won't hire him based on what his references have had to say about his work and dependability."

Zachary sighed. He filled a jug with water, added a layer of ice, and put it on the table. "I know. It would just be nice if there was a way he could get past that. And if he could use his degree."

"I hear you," Kenzie agreed. "And there are programs to help get someone back on their feet. Places that hire convicted criminals, people living on the street, or who have other black marks against their names. There may be some programs out there that could help him."

"But those are not the kinds of jobs that he wants. Driving around stocking vending machines. Painting cars. Holding traffic signs. I know they are entry-level jobs for a reason... but it would be good if there was something he could feel like... he had earned it. That he was valuable to them."

Zachary had already hired Heather, his sister, to help with the private investigation business. So he probably didn't have the capital to hire Tyrrell too. And Tyrrell wasn't necessarily suited to or interested in private investigations. He thought that Zachary's job was cool, but he'd never acted like it was a business he would like to learn himself.

"Maybe something will turn up," Kenzie said. But she didn't feel too confident that something would. Whether alcoholism was a disease or not, Tyrrell had burned a lot of bridges by just taking off when things got overwhelming and he needed to drown himself in drink. He had cut himself out of a lot of opportunities.

Zachary stood looking at the table as if he didn't really see it and couldn't think of what to do next. Kenzie opened the cutlery drawer and motioned to it. He moved slowly from his reverie and took out the knives and forks to continue setting the table.

"How about you? How was your day?" he asked, moving the conversation away from Tyrrell.

It was probably a good thing to take the focus off of Tyrrell and his difficulties and move on to other things.

"Well, we worked on a couple of autopsies today. Had a bit of a backlog that we're trying to catch up on."

"Anything interesting?"

Kenzie didn't answer for a minute, dicing a tomato while she thought about it. "One that's sticking with me. Didn't look like anything at first. Thought it was just an old man who died in his sleep, natural causes."

"But it wasn't?" Zachary prompted after a few seconds of silence.

"No. Doesn't look like it. I mean, it probably still is just an accident. But I don't think he just died peacefully in his sleep."

"Yeah? What did you find?"

"A mark on his neck. Bruises on his wrists. Congested heart and lungs."

"And that means...? You think there was violence?"

"Congested organs suggest asphyxiation. Something cut off his breathing."

"And with the mark on his neck... you think he was strangled?"

"Yes. But it was probably just an accident. Twisted up in his bedsheets or something like that."

"That could happen," Zachary agreed slowly. "With elderly people... you know with babies, they say not to give them blankets. Just to dress them warmly enough in their pajamas."

Kenzie nodded, though this wasn't something she had thought very much about. She had no children of her own and it had been a long time since her sister Amanda had been a baby. Kenzie had helped raise her, but she hadn't been informed on things like whether to use blankets or a sleeper to keep Amanda warm. She hadn't read any baby care books. She'd just followed Lisa's example when demonstrating how to do things like changing a diaper, feeding Amanda, or putting her to sleep.

"It would be the same for people who are elderly and don't have much mobility, wouldn't it? If they are active enough that they might get tangled up in the sheets but not strong enough to get out of them if they did… then they should just be dressed in warm clothing, not be given sheets and blankets that could be a hazard."

"I never really thought about it," Kenzie admitted. "Everyone goes out of their way to babyproof a house and to do everything they can to avoid a toddler accident or injury. But do we do the same thing for our elderly? You don't hear of people elder-proofing their home."

"Maybe because they're too tall," Zachary suggested. "You can put things in upper cupboards and put padding around low counters, but how do you put *everything* out of the reach of a grown adult?"

"You'd have to lock things up. Locks on cupboards, drawers… what about the stove? How do you prevent someone from turning on the stove and burning himself?"

Zachary looked at the knobs. "I don't know."

Kenzie looked around the kitchen and shook her head. "I think you'd have to keep them out of the kitchen altogether. But most kitchens don't have doors that can be locked. Usually, there's just a doorway, without any physical door."

"You'd have to get one put in."

"I guess so."

Kenzie thought about all the other things a confused elderly person might get into. The list was endless. Not just household appliances, but poisons, stairs they could fall down, and all of the slippery surfaces in a bathroom. Getting in and out of the tub might quickly become impossible for someone with limited mobility. It would be a nightmare trying to foresee all of the risks.

"You think that he just strangled on a blanket?" Zachary asked. "He just got twisted up in it or something?"

"I don't know yet. I need to find out more from his son and anyone else who was at the scene before he was removed. See if they can tell me more about what position the body was in and whether they removed anything from the scene."

"Not a blanket?" Zachary guessed.

"Well… I don't really think so. It doesn't really fit the abrasions and bruising that I saw."

"What would?"

"Still looking at something that was fabric, I think. I don't know. I'm having trouble picturing what happened, so that makes it impossible to visualize what the object that strangled him might have been."

They finished setting the table and sat down. Kenzie dished herself up some salad and pasta. Zachary's pile of salad was much smaller, but at least he took some. She actually found him to be pretty good about taking some of whatever she prepared. Years in foster homes and institutions had probably trained him to accept whatever was on offer.

"You said that he had bruises," Zachary said after chewing and swallowing his first bite of pasta. "That would be pretty common in older people, wouldn't it? Just like toddlers and six-year-olds who run into everything. Old people have thin skin and bruise really easily."

"Yeah, sure," Kenzie agreed. "And he had his share of spots on his shins where he might have tripped over or run into something. But he also had bruises around his wrists."

"Oh," Zachary thought about that, chewing slowly. "So he had something around his wrists. Did somebody grab him or was he in shackles?"

"Nothing as hard as shackles. They would have left quite a bit more bruising and abrasion. Maybe even broken wrists," she added, thinking about what she had learned on another case from Dr. Wiltshire. "People in shackles often end up with broken wrists or ankles."

"But something else…?"

"Maybe soft restraints, like a hospital might use. Or maybe just from someone holding on to him, like you said. It's hard to tell. It isn't a distinct mark. You can't see finger marks."

"Just bruising."

Kenzie nodded. "Just a few bruises. They could have been caused by a lot of things."

"Maybe someone lifting him up?" Zachary made a motion as if pulling someone up by the wrists.

Kenzie frowned, thinking about it. "Yes, it's possible. But if he needed assistance getting up, they should have had someone who could lift him the right way or show them the right way to move him. You shouldn't be pulling an elderly person by their wrists. You get your arm behind them…"

"Yeah. But people still do it wrong. They don't even know there's a right and a wrong way to do it." He shrugged. "I wouldn't know the right way to move someone like that. You know about bodies and the best ways to shift them, but I would be useless…"

His face turned a little pink, and Kenzie remembered how a year before, he had struggled to get an unconscious Luke out of the car. For Kenzie, it had been pretty straightforward. She knew all of the ways to lift and balance a body. Luke wasn't nearly as heavy as some of the bodies she had to deal with at the morgue. Of course, she always had the services of Carlos and others who worked around the morgue if she needed help with someone larger, but she liked to just handle it herself, if she were able. Zachary had been blown away by her ability to move and transport Luke, even in the midst of a very highly stressful situation.

"Yes," she agreed with Zachary, smiling at the shared memory, "some people are more educated in how to lift or move people than others."

6

K enzie was working through her task list and figuring out how to use her afternoon as efficiently as possible. She had gotten through a lot of administrative tasks in the morning, but she hoped to get the reports written and finalized for the postmortems she had led over the last few days. It wasn't good to leave them waiting for too long. They would get buried and she wouldn't be able to remember everything she wanted to. Having to go back to the recording and notes to refresh her memory several times was not efficient and she was never sure that she had remembered everything she could to write a complete report.

The phone started to ring, and Kenzie picked up the receiver without looking at the call display. "Medical Examiner's Office, Kenzie Kirsch speaking."

"I want to know why you haven't released my father's body to the funeral home yet," a man snapped. "You guys can't have that much work to do."

Kenzie raised her brows. What did he know about how much work they had to do or how much work a single postmortem might entail?

She didn't react emotionally, though. This was not an

uncommon occurrence. People often thought that they should be able to turn around autopsies much more quickly than they could, so even though their website and other public information said that people should be prepared to wait several days to a week for even the most routine autopsies, people often called feeling aggrieved because it had taken two days and they were running up against a deadline for the funeral date they had set. Kenzie could never understand why anyone would set a funeral date before they even had the body.

"Can I ask who you are calling about?" she asked in a neutral tone, encouraging the caller to be more professional in his attitude.

"Joseph Howard. He died in his sleep; just what exactly do you need more time for?"

"Postmortems sometimes take a few days to turn around," Kenzie told him flatly. "I'm sorry that we are not able to promise next-day service. We are still working on the investigation and report for your father's autopsy report."

"What is there to do? He died in his sleep. He was an old man. He just died of old age."

"There are some findings that we are looking into further. We will release the body as soon as we are finished."

"You don't have any further findings," Howard's son sneered. "You're just being lazy. You probably haven't even started on it. Where is the service we were promised? You *said* it would only take a day for the autopsy."

"I'm not sure who told you that, sir. They were mistaken. We are rarely able to have everything finished in just a day."

"*Have* you even started it?"

"Yes, sir. We have done the initial examination and are waiting for transcription back on the notes, and a few slides have been sent to the lab. I have followed up with one of the paramedics who attended the scene but am still waiting to hear from the other one. I had some follow-up questions for you too, if you have the time."

The man spluttered for a moment. He couldn't very well take back what he had already said and say that he had no time with them to ensure that they had all the information they needed. If he wanted his father's remains back as soon as possible, he had to cooperate with their investigation and any questions they might have.

"What questions?" he demanded finally, when he had gotten his tongue untied.

"I didn't catch your name, sir. What was it…?"

"I am Joseph Howard's son. Kyle. Kyle Howard."

"Great." Kenzie typed the name on a fresh note. "And what is your birth date?"

"Why do you need that?"

"I need some identification and confirmation that you are who you said you are. I'm sure you wouldn't want me to give out information to just anyone who called claiming to need information in this case."

"I don't know what information anyone else would want," Kyle muttered, sounding a little mollified.

"Your birth date? And your driver's license number?"

"My driver's license?"

"If you wouldn't mind," Kenzie agreed. "We do need to make sure that you are who you say you are."

He muttered under his breath, and Kenzie could hear him moving around as he presumably took his wallet from his back pocket and tried to separate his operator's license from the tight pocket it was lodged in.

Then he gave her his birthday, the driver's license number, and, when she asked for it, the expiry date. He was, at least, someone who kept on top of his driver's license and hadn't let it lapse. A lot more people than Kenzie would have expected ran around without a valid driver's license.

Kenzie logged into the DMV database and copied the number he had given her into the appropriate field. Kyle Howard's information popped up on the screen. He was in his sixties, with a florid red face and white hair. He had a round face and thick shoulders and looked like a heart attack waiting to happen. If he weren't careful, he wasn't going to outlive his father by very much. She checked the address against the file and checked the rest of the information on the screen against what he had given to her. He appeared to be legit.

"Great. Sorry for the bother, but you can understand the need for proper security around here."

"So? What can you tell me about why it is taking so long to get my father's body back?"

"It is not taking a long time. How long has your father been living with you?"

He didn't answer at first, but then, as the silence drew out, he decided that he'd better answer her if he wanted any answers himself. "A few months."

"And are you his primary caregiver?"

"Yes."

"How has that been? What has his health been like lately?"

"Pretty good. He's had a cold and a UTI, but mostly he's been okay for someone his age."

"That doesn't sound too bad. What about his mental state?"

"What do you mean?"

"Was he depressed? Anxious? Agitated? Did he know where he was and why he was there? Any trouble remembering you or dealing with the day-to-day stuff."

"He did all right. People that age forget sometimes. It didn't matter. We still got on okay."

"And was he agitated?"

"I don't even know what that means. No."

"Did he get confused? Did he ever wander? Get violent? Have a meltdown and you didn't understand what had upset him in the first place?"

"No," Kyle said. "Nothing like that."

"Did he always remember your name and who he was talking to?"

"Yes. There wasn't a problem with that. He wasn't senile."

"Did he get out of bed by himself? Was he able to get around on his own? Get from one room to the other? Use the toilet by himself?"

Kenzie knew that Mr. Howard had been wearing a diaper. He clearly didn't get to the toilet on his own all the time.

"He had trouble sometimes," Kyle said cautiously. "With his balance or whatever. Old people don't lift their feet high enough. Trip over things. He did that. Would go down suddenly without warning. He was supposed to be using a walker. That way, he could get around without us worrying that he was going to fall."

"He never fell with the walker?"

"No."

"Did he always remember to use it? Agree that he needed it?"

"He was stubborn. He didn't always want to, even when I would remind him that it was important. He would think that he was feeling okay, say that he wasn't that old, and then he would start walking and go down. Old people are stubborn."

"They certainly can be," Kenzie agreed.

"You sound too young to be taking care of a parent of your own. I bet yours are still getting along on their own."

"You're right," Kenzie agreed. "I'm lucky that I don't have to worry about that quite yet. They are both still able to manage things on their own." Kenzie thought about Walter and how he would behave when he started having medical problems due to aging. The man would not go gracefully; Kenzie was sure of that. There would be a big stink when he had to cut back on activities because of his health.

"Lucky is right. Cherish this time because it won't last forever. One of these days, you are going to be the caregiver for your parents. Why didn't anyone ever tell us that this was going to happen? We were fed the myth that our parents would be healthy into their nineties, and then when they needed help, we would have our choice of nursing homes and their pension and RRSPs would cover whatever we found, along with government grants and subsidies. Well, do you know how many nursing homes were ready to take him right away?"

"Not a lot, I gather," Kenzie hazarded.

"Nowhere we wanted to go. And the places where I could get him a bed, do you know what they were like? Do you have any idea what those places look like? He didn't want to go there. I didn't want him to go there."

"So you decided to keep him at home."

"What other choice did I have? Where else was I going to take him? There was nowhere else."

Kenzie was sympathetic. She hadn't visited a lot of nursing homes, and the ones she had been at had been pretty nice, but she knew that they weren't all. The ones that took on high-end clientele were not bad. But the ones available to people who didn't have the money to afford something nice? Or that government programs funded? Kenzie had a feeling they wouldn't be nearly as nice as what she had seen. And that was a scary thought. Would the patients in those nursing homes be able to complain or tell their family members what was going on? And even if they could, what were their family members going to do? What could they do if there was nowhere else to take them? Not everyone could keep his father at home as Kyle had.

"Do you work from home?" Kenzie asked. She assumed that he would have to have something he could do from home if he were going to be his father's full-time caregiver.

"No, I have to go to the office. I get someone to look in on him to make sure he's okay. It's still as expensive as hell, but not as much as full-time nursing care."

"Do you mean you have a neighbor go in, or a nurse, or...?"

"There's an agency. They send someone over a couple of times a day to help him with whatever he needs. Whatever he needed," Kyle modified his tense. "Now... he doesn't need anything at all."

"No. I'm very sorry for your loss."

"What we need is for you to release his body. I don't care how sorry you are."

"We will release it as soon as we can."

"What are you waiting for?"

"When he was left by himself, how could you be sure that he wouldn't fall down and hurt himself? Or light the stove or something else that might be dangerous for him to do unsupervised?"

"He was fine. I don't need you checking up on his care. He had everything he needed. I took good care of him. He was in good health. If you looked at him at all, you could see that. He was in good shape. He wasn't starving or neglected. He had everything he needed."

"Yes," Kenzie agreed. "I can see that you cared about him and took good care of him. There are just a few other things that I'd like a little bit of insight into."

"Like what?" Kyle asked in exasperation.

Kenzie sighed. She wasn't sure how to introduce the topic tactfully. She had already tried it from several different angles. She was going to have to be blunt if she wanted him to actually answer her questions.

"Mr. Howard. I need to know whether your father was ever restrained."

7

W hat do you mean?" Kyle asked.
"I think you know what it means to be restrained. There are bruises around his wrists. Did you have him in soft wrist restraints so that he would not get out of bed or wander around your house?"

There was a silence while Kyle considered this question. He knew now what Kenzie was after, and he was probably considering how much would be safe to tell her. He didn't want to get in trouble or have her judge him. He wanted people to know that he had taken the best possible care of his father, not that he'd had to restrain him to keep him from hurting himself or burning the house down.

"There were times… when he wanted to get out of the bed on his own, and it wasn't safe. He would fall down if he was left to walk by himself. He needed someone right there with him to make sure that he used his walker and that he went slowly and hung on to it so that he wouldn't fall. Obviously, I couldn't be there twenty-four hours a day to be sure of that."

"I see. Thank you for confirming that for me. Was he wearing the wrist restraints when he died?"

"No."

"There was also a mark on his neck. Did he get tangled up in the sheets or did something else happen that could have left a mark on his neck?"

"No. I told you that he just died in his sleep."

"And you don't know where the bruises on his neck might have come from?"

"I'm sure if he could tell us, he would, but no one knows what he might have done to hurt himself. I never saw him fall and he was never tangled up in any sheets. I never saw any bruises on his neck."

"You didn't notice anything."

"No. There wasn't anything that he could have hurt his neck on."

"You're sure."

"Nothing."

"And you don't know what he might have gotten wrapped around his neck, either on purpose or by accident."

"Why would he have wrapped something around his neck on purpose?"

"He could have, if he liked having something wrapped around him." Kenzie remembered a case that Zachary had investigated where an autistic boy had liked to have his blanket wrapped tightly around him. It could have been something like that. "Or he might have put a necktie on, thinking he was going to get dressed up for something. Or, unfortunately, we do end up with some cases of seniors who have intentionally harmed themselves or tried to commit suicide. As much as we would like to think that it doesn't happen, seniors can get very depressed. Especially when they are taken away from their home and all of their possessions and don't feel welcome anymore."

"My father did not commit suicide."

"Was there any reason you can think of that he might have wrapped something around his neck?"

"No, and he didn't wrap anything around his neck, so that's a stupid question. It never happened."

"I think that there are things you are not telling me."

"I've told you everything. Now get that report written and release my father's body to the funeral home so that we can have the funeral and mourn him. This... not being able to move ahead is maddening. He wouldn't want to be lying there in the morgue."

"I realize that. We will get him released to you as soon as we can. Thank you for taking the time to answer my questions."

She didn't have to find a way to terminate the call, because Kyle did. At least he wouldn't be calling her again any time soon. People tended not to like being accused of neglecting or abusing their loved ones. Kyle wouldn't want to have to face her questions a second time.

One thing that Kenzie had neglected to do was to find out who was helping Kyle to take care of his father. What agency was providing the personnel to look in on the elderly man a couple of times a day while Kyle was at work to ensure that everything was okay?

She had a pretty good idea that Kyle would not answer the phone if she called him back. He was finished with talking to her. He wouldn't be answering any more questions.

Instead, Kenzie looked at her notes and found the name of the other paramedic who had been with Baden when Kyle had called 9-1-1 to report discovering his father dead. Williams. It took a couple of calls to the fire station before she managed to get his contact number.

He answered the phone when Kenzie called, but he didn't seem too excited about it. Kenzie couldn't blame anyone for not being excited to see "Medical Examiner's Office" on their call display. It wasn't likely to be good news. But at least Williams would have an idea what it was about.

"Williams here."

"Hi, Mr. Williams. I'm sorry to disturb you, but this is Kenzie Kirsch from the Medical Examiner's Office and I had a few questions to ask you about Joseph Howard, a senior who had passed away."

"I know what you're calling about," Williams said. "I already talked to Baden."

"Okay, so you're already up to speed. That's great. Did you have any thoughts on the situation, rather than me plying you with questions?"

"Not really. Everything seemed fine when we got there. Nothing out of the ordinary. Nothing that worried me."

"What position was the body in when the two of you got there?"

"Supine. On the bed. Like he'd been sleeping."

"And neither of you moved the body?"

"No, of course not. That was the position he was in, so we could see that he didn't have any respiration and his eyes were dull. He was dead when we got there. All we did was verify the fact and call for the medical examiner."

"Did his son say anything about having touched or moved the body?"

"No, nothing. Ask him."

"I already have. He wasn't in a very cooperative mood."

"I guess not, since you're practically accusing him of having caused his father's death."

Kenzie breathed in quickly and held her breath, thinking about that. "I never said that. I never said that he'd had anything to do with his father's death. We're just trying to get all of the details. Then we can sort out the contributing factors."

"If you're asking about restraints, then you're accusing him of having something to do with his father's death."

"No. I haven't said that. There are all sorts of circumstances where someone has to be restrained. If he was doing it safely, I'm not concerned about it. I think that if he needed restraints, he should have been in a hospital or nursing home to take care of him professionally, but he wasn't killed by wrist restraints. I'm not sure what caused his death at this point. There are still questions to be answered. But he wasn't killed by his wrist restraints."

"Whatever. It doesn't matter because we never saw anything there—no restraints of any kind. If there were, then the son had already gotten rid of them. There's nothing for us to see."

"That wasn't my only question."

"I didn't see anything that he might have gotten tangled up in. He wasn't wearing a necklace. There was no rope around. The sheets were not wound around his neck. Not when we got there."

"Okay. I wondered if you noticed what agency was supposed to be helping with Mr. Howard's care. Kyle said he had hired someone, but I didn't ask who that was and he's not answering the phone now."

"You already scared him off?"

"I just need to know who was in there to help with the caregiving. Did you see any mention of who it might be?"

Williams was quiet for a moment, thinking about it instead of harassing Kenzie. "There are only a few agencies in town that do that kind of thing. He might have had a neighbor or friend, though. Sometimes it's done under the table. Might be getting help from illegals as well, you know, paying cash under the table."

"He said he'd hired an agency, so I thought I would start there. If there are only a few, it shouldn't be hard to find out whether anyone took the job or not."

"I think… '*You're Family*' *Home Care*. I think I saw a magnet on the fridge. But I'm not sure; don't take that as gospel. We go to a lot of different homes that use home care."

"I'm sure you do," Kenzie said. She noted the name of the agency. "Thank you, that's a starting point, at least. I appreciate it."

"That's all you need from me?" he asked suspiciously.

"That's all I need right now. That and your confirmation that there were not any restraints visible or anything that might have gotten wrapped around his neck. And you've already answered that."

"I don't think you're going to find anything out, but if there is something to find out... well, good luck with that."

"Thanks. I appreciate the help."

8

I t took more than one call to find out from the home care agency whether they had been the one to provide care for Joseph Howard and, once they had confirmed it, which of their workers had been there to see him recently. There was apparently a fairly large turnover with home care staff, and a number of their nurses had been involved in Howard's care. Dolly had been identified as the nurse who had seen him the most often and most recently, and Kenzie eventually managed to talk her into sitting down for a cup of coffee together. Dolly did not want to go to the Medical Examiner's Office, and she did not want Kenzie going to her place of work to talk with her there. A compromise of some neutral ground seemed like the best solution.

The only thing about Dolly that made Kenzie think of Dolly Parton, the only other Dolly she knew of, was her blond hair. But she was older, and it was not just blond, but interspersed with gray as well. She did not have Dolly Parton's well-known figure, or her voice or mannerisms. Maybe she'd had some of those attributes as a younger woman, but that had been a long time ago.

The woman was overweight and slow-moving. Her posture suggested a strong back and shoulders, which Kenzie supposed was what allowed her to bring home a paycheck from the home care business. Kenzie wasn't sure how often Joseph Howard had fallen, but, if he needed assistance getting up from the floor, he would need someone with muscle to get him back on his feet.

Dolly stirred her tea, looking anxiously at Kenzie as she tried to put Dolly at ease with some small talk. It clearly wasn't working. Dolly was getting more anxious about why she had to meet with someone from the Medical Examiner's Office and what she would have to tell Kenzie.

"Don't be worried," Kenzie assured her. "I don't think that you've done anything wrong. It isn't that kind of meeting. I haven't had any complaints about your care of Mr. Howard. His son, Kyle, didn't say he had any questions or concerns about your care. He didn't suggest that it might have been because of something that you or anyone else at the agency did."

"They're still going to think that I did something," Dolly complained a little breathlessly, as if she had just run up a flight of stairs. "It doesn't matter if I tell them that I didn't, they're going to think so anyway, and I'm going to be let go."

"If you need me to assure them that you didn't do anything wrong, even put it into writing, I'd be happy to do that. I'm not trying to mess things up for you."

"Well..." Dolly picked at a cuticle. "Okay. It would be good if you could tell them that it wasn't anything I did."

"Sure. Of course. They're the ones who told me that you were taking care of Howard the most often. They know that I wasn't looking for someone who had done something wrong."

The woman nodded but didn't seem reassured by that fact. Maybe there was someone at the agency who had it out for her, and that was why they had sent Dolly in Kenzie's direction, assuming that she would be in trouble for something to do with Howard's care so they would be able to get her fired. Who knew what kind of politics went on in the place.

"How long had you been working with Mr. Howard?" Kenzie asked. "Did you enjoy working for him?"

"He was a nice old gent," Dolly said with a shrug. "There are good and bad things about every patient. You just try to focus on the positives and forget about the negatives."

"He was competent? He could carry on a conversation and was nice to you?"

Dolly pursed her lips. She was the one who had used the word "nice" to describe Howard, but maybe that wasn't the best descriptor, since she seemed to be regretting it now.

"I didn't mean that he was nice to me," Dolly waffled. "I doubt he even knew who I was. But he wasn't nasty like some of them are. I know that it's just degenerating brain cells that make them that way, it isn't their fault, but it's hard not to take it personally when someone is railing at you and calling you every obscene name under the sun. It's not their fault..."

"No. There can be personality changes that go along with dementia, and they don't seem to get nicer, for some reason."

Dolly nodded her head in agreement. "They do not!"

"But Howard wasn't like that? Not one of the ones who called you obscenities?"

"No. He wasn't like that. He was just... vague. I don't know if he always knew what was going on. He would get confused. Sometimes his mind was somewhere else, like he was just turned off. But I'd rather be like that when I'm old—napping in the sun. Not thinking of anything, or else remembering things the way they were fifty years ago. Just... fading."

Kenzie nodded. She played with her coffee cup, rotating it in a circle, trying not to make too much eye contact or make Dolly feel like she was under the microscope or being judged.

"That sounds nice."

Dolly nodded. "That was what I meant."

"So he wasn't able to hold a conversation most of the time? Was he able to communicate his needs?"

"I could usually tell if he needed to move or wanted to get up to go for a walk around the house. If he needed a painkiller. He had a prescription, and Mr. Kyle said I could give him one whenever he needed it. Within the dosage instructions, of course. So if he seemed like he was having a rough day, or if he was groaning or restless, I would give him one and he would perk up. Just because you're old, it doesn't mean you should have to be in pain all the time."

"No. I think it is important to keep people comfortable, even if it does have the effect of eventually shortening their life—not that I think giving him a painkiller had anything to do with Mr. Howard's death," Kenzie assured her, holding up her hand to quell any protests. "I'm just saying, quality of life is more important than gaining a few more days in length. We should treat people how we would want to be treated."

"Yes. I did everything I could to keep him comfortable. Some people have a favorite robe or blanket; I've even had patients with teddy bears. Whatever it takes to make them feel happy and at home. Why stay at home if you're going to be treated like you're at an institution?"

Kenzie nodded. "Have you worked in a nursing home? Or only in home care?"

"Only in home care. I wouldn't go to a place like that, where the elderly are just warehoused. Treated like they don't even matter. They just want people to be out of sight, so their families can say they are doing everything to take care of their parents, but they don't have to actually do it themselves." Dolly shook her head and tsked. It was clear that she had definite ideas about how nursing homes were run.

"Is that what you told Kyle? That a nursing home would be a bad idea? Did you tell him that Mr. Howard wasn't yet to the point where he needed professional care 24/7?"

"Mr. Kyle didn't want Mr. Joseph going into nursing care. He had visited a few of those places and said there was no way he was going to send his father to one of them."

Kenzie thought back to Champlain House, a seniors' home that she had visited when investigating a viral outbreak. It had seemed like a pretty nice place. The residents all had their own rooms. Meals were provided, and housekeeping looked after bedding, laundry, and whatever else needed to be done in the rooms. There were doctors and nurses on staff.

But she had only been to the independent living unit. She had not visited the dementia unit or hospice. She hadn't seen the seniors who had been severely afflicted—only those who were still mobile and in possession of their faculties.

"Did he look at a lot of places?"

"How many places do you think there are in a town like this?" Dolly countered. "He even went into Burlington and Montpelier, but he knew that if he put Mr. Joseph there, he would only be able to see him on weekends. He couldn't make that trip every day. He wanted to have his father close to him. He wanted Mr. Joseph to be with his family, not isolated somewhere hours away."

"Of course. He was in a very difficult position."

Dolly sipped her coffee and gave a little shrug. "He wasn't that bad yet. Mr. Joseph was still okay staying at home. He didn't need nursing care all day."

"What were his needs? What services did you provide?"

"I would come twice while Mr. Kyle was working. He gave him breakfast. But if Mr. Joseph was having a bad day and had still been sleeping when Mr. Kyle left, then he would leave me a note and I would feed him. I cleaned up any accidents. He could still toilet himself, but sometimes he couldn't wait until I got there or had problems. I changed his bedding. Got him dressed if Mr. Kyle hadn't already. Put on a movie or TV station that he liked." She shrugged. "Just whatever I could to make him comfortable and happy."

"And then you came back again about when? Midday to give him his lunch and another bathroom break?"

"Yes. One o'clock, usually. And then he would go down for a nap. And Mr. Kyle would be home to give him supper and spend the evening with him."

"You felt like the arrangement worked out pretty well?"

Dolly gave a brisk nod. "Yes, I think it was the best solution. He could still stay at home with his family and got the care he needed. He just needed a little help," she explained. "He didn't need someone there all the time."

"What did he do while you and Kyle were both gone?"

"Watched TV or had a nap," Dolly sounded annoyed, having just explained this to Kenzie.

"And can you tell me what… safety measures were in place?"

9

D olly looked down at her coffee. Even though she had already been drinking it, she suddenly discovered the need to add more sugar and cream, and stirred them studiously.

"What do you mean, safety measures?"

"Well, I would assume that there were some procedures in place to make sure that he could not hurt himself while you and Kyle were gone. Even if he usually just sat in front of the TV, he might get it in his head one day to… go for a walk or cook dinner, like he used to do when he was younger. Sometimes people get it into their heads that they can do something that they used to do all the time, even though they aren't that physically capable anymore." Kenzie smiled. "I have a friend who broke her wrist when she decided to show her daughter how to do a cartwheel. We used to do them all the time as a kid, but I don't think I would be up to trying it now as an adult. And I know that she shouldn't have!"

"Sometimes people forget their limitations," Dolly admitted. "But Mr. Joseph was very good. He wasn't attempting any cartwheels."

"So there wasn't any need to adapt his environment? To pad

sharp counter corners, or lock the door to the garage, or give him a bed with rails so that he wouldn't fall out of bed during the night?"

"Things like that… yes, I suppose so. Mr. Kyle didn't want his father to get hurt. I didn't want him to get hurt. Especially not while he was by himself and there was no one there to help him."

Kenzie nodded and waited for Dolly to describe what some of those safety measures might have been.

"We couldn't have Mr. Joseph trying to use the stove or trying to go down the steps from the house to the street for a walk. He had a longer staircase. Not one of those houses that just has one step up to the door, or three steps. It was a long, concrete staircase with a rail, and Mr. Joseph could get badly hurt if he fell down that."

"It sounds like it. So what did you do to prevent him from getting out?"

"In the beginning, there was a child safety thing on the front door. You know, a piece that goes around the doorknob, and you have to squeeze it the right way to turn the doorknob. Otherwise, the person will just keep turning the plastic bit around and around and can't turn the actual doorknob to get out."

Kenzie nodded. She had seen such things at her friends' homes when they started having babies. "That sounds like a reasonable precaution."

Although what if there was a fire or other emergency that would require Joseph Howard to leave the house? If he couldn't get out on his own, was there some kind of evacuation plan in place where a neighbor would help him? Did the local fire department know that there was a senior living there who would need to be rescued? Or was that all left to chance, praying that it would never come to that?

"But later on, something more was necessary, right? Because a plastic doorknob wouldn't keep him from going into the kitchen and turning on the stove."

"He was getting worse. Very slowly. He still had good days and bad days. But you could see that he was declining… overall."

Kenzie smiled and nodded encouragingly, waiting for her to provide more details. She knew that she couldn't get aggressive about it. If Dolly thought that she was being interrogated or that Kenzie thought one of them might have done something wrong, she would clam up. If she could just keep it as a casual conversation, she would be able to find out what she needed to.

"Mr. Kyle moved out of the master bedroom to one of the smaller bedrooms so that Mr. Joseph could have the master bedroom as his apartment, with the attached bathroom. It was all set up like a small apartment or hotel room. He had his bed, and a table and chairs, and a mini fridge. And the bathroom. We just had to lock the bedroom door, and he was limited to the bedroom and bathroom, where he couldn't get hurt."

"So he had his own little living space inside of the house. Somewhere you had made safe for him."

"Yes, exactly."

"And that worked for a while."

Dolly didn't look like she was going to tell Kenzie anything else about Mr. Joseph's gradual decline. She would like to leave it at the time when Mr. Joseph could still get around the bedroom suite by himself. Yes, he was locked in, but he had everything he needed. Food, bathroom facilities, entertainment, and his bed. Everything he needed to be happy and safe.

"You said that sometimes Mr. Howard could not wait until you got there to take him to the bathroom."

"Yes. Sometimes. It was very occasional. He had good control, it's just that sometimes it would take me a little longer to get there, or he'd had more to drink in the morning than usual... it's like that as you get older, you know. You think that once a child is toilet trained, that's the end of it, but accidents happen as you get older too."

"I understand that."

"So, sometimes he couldn't wait."

"That tells me that he couldn't get to the bathroom without you."

Dolly chewed on her lip. "I suppose."

"He couldn't get to the bathroom on his own, even if he was capable of using the toilet without assistance."

Dolly hesitated, unable to come up with an answer to this. Kenzie waited a while and then prompted her further.

"Kyle said that his father could get around. That he used the walker sometimes, but he didn't like to. He was stubborn about it."

"Yes." Dolly gave a slight smile, fondly remembering the old geezer's stubbornness.

"So why did he have to wait until you got there?"

Dolly shrugged. "Well… there was a railing on his bed to keep him from falling off."

"And he couldn't get around or over it when he wanted to?" Kenzie knew that railings were not always just a safety measure for restless sleepers or children. They were also used to keep people from wandering. Sometimes combined with other methods of restraint—handcuffs for prisoners or soft restraints for psych patients or the elderly.

"It was very difficult," Dolly hedged. "He could get around it himself, but…"

"But he wasn't supposed to."

"No. He was supposed to wait for one of us to come and put the railing down and help him out of bed. So that he wouldn't fall."

"So when you left him alone watching TV or having a nap… he wasn't just sitting in his chair. He was in bed with the rail up."

Dolly nodded with some reluctance. "Well… yes. So that he wouldn't get hurt."

"Because he would walk around without the walker and fall down?"

"Yes. He was okay ninety-five percent of the time, but one fall at that age is too much to risk. He could break his hip or wrist, hit his head, anything… Elderly people are frail. Something like that can be devastating. Do you know how many of them die after breaking a hip? It's the beginning of the end."

"Mr. Howard hadn't broken any bones before?" Kenzie had already seen Howard's x-rays. She knew that he hadn't had any hip or wrist fractures. Some very old, healed fractures, an arm and a rib, from when he had been a younger man, maybe even from childhood, but nothing recent.

"No. But that didn't mean that he couldn't. We had no way of knowing how strong his bones were or what fall might take him down. You can't take risks like that."

Kenzie nodded her agreement, hoping it would calm Dolly down and keep her talking. Kenzie was making inroads into what had happened to Howard, the type of situation he had been in. If she just kept Dolly talking, she was sure she would get to the bottom of it. How Mr. Howard had ended up strangling in his bed that night.

"So you kept him in the bed with the rails up when there was no one there to watch him."

"Yes." Dolly looked pleading. "That was what Mr. Kyle wanted. Care workers like me… we take our instructions from the family. They are the ones who know the person in need of care, what is best for them. If a client says that we need to keep him in bed, or to lock the door, or whatever, we do it. If I didn't do it, and Mr. Joseph got hurt because of it, what do you think would happen to me? Mr. Kyle would sue me, and I would get fired. Maybe the cops even decide to charge me with assault or something like that. I don't want to end up in prison because I didn't think Mr. Kyle was right about needing to lock the door!"

10

---

nd it didn't bother you that he was basically being kept a
prisoner there?"

"He was not a prisoner!" Dolly said immediately. "It
was not like that! He had to be protected. If I let him out of the
room, out of the house, and he walked out onto the road and got
hit by a car, I couldn't live with myself. I really couldn't. I would
never want one of my charges to get hurt like that. I always follow
the instructions of the family."

"What are some of the things other families ask you to do?"
Kenzie asked. Maybe if she took Joseph Howard out of the equa-
tion, Dolly would be more forthcoming. She wouldn't be worried
about being found at fault for something to do with Howard's
death. She could just discuss what restrictions home care patients
were put on in general, with no names given.

"Well…" Dolly drew the word out, thinking about what she
wanted to share. "There are a lot of different things. With some,
you have to be careful of what you feed them. They might have
allergies or choke easily. Some people can only have liquids. Some
have to have stool softeners to keep things moving properly."

"Yes…?" Kenzie was impatient with the discussion of food

when she wanted to talk restraints. But she needed to stay with Dolly in the conversation and not push her too hard too fast.

"Some of the patients we deal with are bedridden. Or they have low mobility and must stay in a wheelchair."

"Sure. You must get a lot of exercise moving them around. That's a lot of lifting."

"If they are very heavy and cannot help move themselves, we have to use a sling and mechanical lift. I couldn't move them without it. But Mr. Joseph, he could stand and walk. He just needed someone to steady him, help him to move his feet into the right position. Most of the old folks, they aren't paralyzed. They just have a hard time moving around."

"Mr. Howard could get off the bed himself if you put down the rails."

"Yes..." The word came out hesitantly as if there were a long story behind it. A long explanation of what he could and couldn't do and why they had to keep him in the bed the rest of the time.

"And what about other patients?" Kenzie again tried to ease Dolly's anxiety by focusing on another nameless patient. "You must have had some that the bed rail would not be enough for. I know when I was a resident, there were plenty of elderly patients who couldn't be wandering around unassisted, but they could get out of a bed with a rail in a heartbeat. It wasn't enough to keep them in bed."

"Yes, you have seen that. You know that it's for their own good."

Kenzie nodded her agreement. All it took was seeing one grandma fall flat on her face and bust her nose wide open. A resident didn't forget that lesson. With dehydration or a UTI, even a person without dementia could end up confused, wandering, and getting themselves into trouble.

"Wheelchairs sometimes have a belt to keep the patient from falling out," Dolly said.

"But they can take it off themselves if they want to. Assuming they have use of their fingers."

"You can get a restraint belt too, that ties or buckles behind the wheelchair so that they cannot do it themselves. It keeps them in the chair so they can't slide or climb out. So they won't try to walk off and fall down."

"Sure. That makes sense."

"And beds… if the rails are not enough, there are wrist restraints. Ankle restraints too. So that they can't climb over the rail and get out of bed."

"But they don't always work, do they?"

Dolly took a sip of her coffee, which Kenzie thought was probably cold by now, oversweetened and full of creamer. Her eyes returned to Kenzie several times as she thought through what she wanted to say.

"No, not always. Some patients are like Harry Houdini. They can get out of anything."

"And some of them try and fail, but get stuck in a position that puts them at risk."

"There have been some cases," Dolly said, her voice low and reverent. Respecting the patients it had happened to or the caregivers who had been blamed. "Patients slip down, get stuck in a head-down position, or with their neck at an angle, and something can happen…"

"Positional asphyxia."

Dolly nodded. "They can smother, even though there isn't anything against their face. Just because of the awkward position they are in."

Kenzie wanted dearly to ask, "Is that what happened to Mr. Howard?" But she refrained. Dolly didn't want to talk about Mr. Howard. Kenzie would eventually circle back around to him, but the time was not right. There was more information to be gathered.

"A posey is better than wrist and ankle restraints," Dolly offered.

Kenzie frowned, looking at her. "What is a *posey?*"

"It keeps them lying down flat. They can't get partway up like they can with loop restraints. That's a much better solution."

"But what is it? I haven't heard that term before."

"It's… a vest. You dress the patient in the vest, and there are long ties or straps with buckles that you fasten around the bed or the wheelchair—you can use them in wheelchairs too—and they keep the patient's body positioned so that they can't pull up from the bed or away from the wheelchair and end up in a position where they are at risk."

Kenzie pictured it in her mind. "Like a straitjacket?"

"No, no," Dolly waved her hands as if to erase this picture from their minds. "Not like a straitjacket. It is a vest, no sleeves. It leaves the patient's hand and arms free. Wrist restraints don't. If you leave someone in wrist restraints, they can't knit or read a book or do anything else to entertain themselves. All they can do is wait for you to come and get them out. But with a posey, they can do other things. They just can't get out of the bed or wheelchair. It's much better."

Kenzie nodded slowly. A *posey*. She would have to look them up and do some research. Was it possible that was what Mr. Howard had strangled on?

"Did Mr. Kyle ask you to use wrist restraints or a posey on Mr. Howard? To keep him from climbing out of the bed when neither of you was there?"

Dolly sighed. "Yes. We used both for Mr. Joseph."

"Both?" Kenzie asked sharply. Dolly had just said that the posey would leave Joseph Howard's hands free, but the wrist restraints would not. She couldn't see what the point would be in using them both together except to completely immobilize the patient. And how was that humane? How did that protect them from harm?

"Not at the same time," Dolly said hurriedly. "No, no. I'm sorry, I didn't mean to make you think that. The posey is good, it keeps the patient in the bed, but you can't have them lying flat on their backs all the time. They'll get bedsores. Same with using a posey to keep someone in a wheelchair. You can't leave someone in the same position for that long. It's bad for the circulation, digestion, and bed sores. It's very important to avoid bedsores. The patient needs to be moved regularly."

"Oh, okay."

"So you put the posey on sometimes, and other times, a wrist restraint that allows him to lie on his side or to choose another position. They can't just stay in the same position all day."

Kenzie nodded, understanding and agreeing. And that would explain why Howard had marks on his wrist and had strangled on something. They didn't both happen at the same time. Wrist restraints sometimes, a posey vest in his bed or sitting in a wheelchair. Dolly coming twice a day to get him walking around, to feed him and help him to use the bathroom. Kyle had not just let his father lie on his back on the bed all day. *That* would have been negligence.

Kenzie still wasn't sure what she thought of him leaving his father at home while he worked, without direct supervision for several hours a day. But what other options did Kyle have? It seemed like he had done his best to find a situation that worked for his father but, in the end, it had not worked out. As much as he had tried to help his father to live his last few years with dignity, in his own place rather than in a nursing home or hospital, he had ultimately been unable to give him what he had needed.

11

Fitting in interviews around her other work had taken Kenzie a couple of days and, before she knew it, it was the weekend and she was trying to figure out how to get a few loose ends tied up at work, her errands done, and relax a bit before heading south to Lorne Peterson's and Patrick Parker's house for Sunday dinner. They didn't get there every Sunday, but tried to get there at least once or twice a month to see the two men. Lorne was an old foster father of Zachary's who had kept in contact with him over the years, even though Zachary had only been in his home for a couple of weeks. They shared a passion for photography, and Zachary had also given Lorne—who he still had trouble referring to as anything but Mr. Peterson—emotional support through his divorce from his wife and blossoming relationship with Pat during a time when being gay was not acceptable or cool. Couples like Lorne and Pat were probably subject to more discrimination and violence than either Kenzie or Zachary understood. It wasn't a topic that they dwelled on.

Zachary had been separated from his brothers and sisters when he was put into the system and had only been reunited with them recently. Between the time that he was ten and just a year ago, Lorne and Pat had been his only family. So it was important for him to nurture that relationship. Kenzie had her parents, and she knew she should spend more time with each of them. She was trying to, but it was hard sometimes. She didn't get along with them like Zachary got along with Lorne and Pat. Even though Kenzie loved them, Lisa and Walter drove her crazy and she wasn't inclined to spend more time with them than she had to.

But she was learning to live with the discomfort and just do it anyway. How long were her parents going to be with her? Not forever. Hopefully, for a long time, but not forever. When they were gone, Kenzie didn't want to have regrets about not having taken the time with them.

"It's my turn to drive," Kenzie told Zachary as they grabbed anything they needed to take with them. Zachary looked up, his mouth already opening to argue the point with her. They both liked the highway drive, Zachary because he felt most calm and focused while driving, and Kenzie because she loved any opportunity to take her "baby"—her red convertible—out on the open road. She didn't speed like Zachary, despite her baby being a sports car, but liked to just put the top down and let the wind blow through her hair, feeling free and exhilarated. Her hair would be a complete mess by the time she got to the Petersons', but it was worth the resulting tangles and grit to enjoy that freedom.

"I think you drove last time," Zachary tried.

"No way, Jose. You drove last time. It's my turn."

Zachary frowned, thinking about it.

"You know it's my turn," Kenzie said. "You're trying to think of a way to talk me out of it, but you know it's my turn. I'm driving my baby down."

"We could go in separate cars, in case I want to go over to see Joss too…"

"We're not staying overnight this time. You won't want to try to squeeze a visit with Joss in after dinner. It would be too much. You know you need at least two days if you are going to visit your sister."

Maybe he wouldn't need two days if Joss were a little easier to get along with. But his eldest sister was sharp and acidic, and dealing with her took more mental energy than he had on a day when he'd already been traveling and visiting with Lorne and Pat. She was challenging to deal with and, as far as Kenzie could tell, didn't attempt to get along with Zachary or be tactful when dealing with him. Their visits left him raw. Kenzie admired him for still wanting to go back to visit her regularly. Even if it was just because he wanted to talk Kenzie into letting him drive this time.

Zachary grinned as he picked up his equipment bag, stuffed with his laptop, photographic equipment, and peripherals. He and Lorne would probably spend a few hours reviewing each other's most recent work and sharing the best pictures.

"You're probably right," he admitted.

"And you know it's my turn."

He shrugged, still smiling.

It was nice to see him healthy. In good spirits, his face thin but no longer gaunt; he'd even managed to get a bit of a tan over the last few weeks as he intentionally worked in more time to walk and take pictures instead of only leaving the house when he had a surveillance job or errands to run. Or a date. Or therapy. The point was, his skin was no longer pale as a ghost, but lightly tanned, and she liked the healthy glow.

Kenzie picked up her purse and a shoulder bag with some files in it that she had promised herself she would review after supper when she had a few minutes to relax. She probably wouldn't, but she'd have them with her, if she could talk herself into it.

"What?" Zachary asked, catching Kenzie's eyes on him.

"Nothing. You're just looking... happy."

"Why wouldn't I be?"

They both knew about his depression and traumatic past. How seriously depressed he got before Christmas and all he had been through over the past year. There were plenty of reasons for him not to be happy. But at the moment, his medications were working, it was nowhere near Christmas, and he was going to visit his family.

"I just mean… I think your nature walks and photography are really helping. You look good. Healthy."

"Amazing what happens when you leave your lair and venture out into the sun." Zachary's words were light and playful, not sarcastic. Kenzie smiled in response, happy that he was in such a good place.

And happy that it was her turn to drive.

Lorne and Pat were always glad to see them. Lorne was the elder of the two, a white fringe of hair around the top of his head, smiling round face, and a comfortable body that was definitely not what anyone would call athletic. Pat was younger, closer to Zachary in age, and was careful about diet and exercise. Despite the delicious meals he would always whip up when he knew that Zachary and Kenzie were coming, he didn't overeat and managed to keep his body trim and muscular. Gray was creeping into his hair around his temples, making him look more distinguished, but he was still fit and vigorous. He didn't share in Lorne's and Zachary's love of photography, but he kept a beautiful house and garden and their home was always comfortable and inviting.

"Zachary! Kenzie!" Lorne hugged them both tightly, as enthusiastic as if it had been months since they had last visited. "It's so nice to see you. How was the drive here?"

"It was good," Kenzie told him. "Perfect weather."

"Get your enjoyment out of that car while you can. The summer will be gone before you can even blink and you won't be able to drive with the top down."

Pat stepped out of the kitchen to greet them, towel over one shoulder and something that smelled delicious bubbling on the stove behind him. "I hope you're hungry!"

"We always come hungry," Zachary declared.

Of course, it wasn't true. He'd often been on medications that killed his appetite or made him nauseated. But the current cocktail was better and Kenzie knew he would have a good-sized portion of whatever Pat had cooked up.

"Well, visit for about ten minutes and then it will be on the table."

They sat down to visit while Pat went back into the kitchen.

"How has your week gone?" Lorne asked, ready to hear about what they had been doing.

"It went by fast," Kenzie observed. "I don't feel like I'm any further ahead this week than I was last. I was hoping to clear a few more cases."

"But you can't control what new files come in or whether you can find all of the clues you're looking for..." Lorne suggested.

"That's true," Kenzie agreed.

It was funny that Lorne referred to them as files rather than bodies and refrained from referring to the postmortem examinations. But then, most people were like that. They didn't think it polite to talk about bodies and pathology in polite company. And especially not at the dinner table. Just one of the reasons Kenzie loved and admired Zachary. He was always interested in hearing the gory details of her cases. Especially if they were anything interesting or puzzling. He liked mysteries, and that included intriguing autopsy discoveries.

"I have one this week that I've been having trouble with," Kenzie said. "A senior who was brought in as an unattended death. We both thought it would just be 'natural causes,' but there were some disturbing signs."

Lorne swallowed, and Kenzie gave him a reassuring smile. No, she wasn't going to get into graphic details with him.

"Just... it was probably still accidental death, but it doesn't look like his heart just stopped during the night."

"So... an accident. You don't think it was homicide. You don't think it was anyone's fault."

"No... but I am having some trouble in that... I think it could have been avoided. But I don't think it was done intentionally, and probably his son was *trying* to keep him safe, even if it did backfire and end up causing his death."

Zachary looked at Kenzie questioningly. They had discussed the Howard case briefly, but most of that had been before Kenzie had interviewed Kyle Howard and Dolly. Kenzie had learned a lot more during that time.

12

S oup's on," Pat announced from the kitchen doorway, and he began bussing dishes to the table. Everyone got up and made their way over to either sit down or help Pat bring the remainder of the dishes in. Once everything was in place, Kenzie sat next to Zachary, across from Pat and Lorne.

"This looks wonderful, as always. I always feel like I can't eat for a week after I've been here, if I'm going to avoid putting on the pounds! I just want to eat everything. *Lots* of everything."

Pat smiled. "I wouldn't suggest eating only once a week. But I don't think you've put on any weight since I first met you, so you don't have to worry."

"That's only because I've been holding back."

They dished up. Zachary was watching Kenzie.

"So are you going to tell us more about this case, or was that it? You're just going to tease us?"

Kenzie looked at Pat. "I don't know about talking shop at the table. Not when it is about my work."

"Nothing graphic," Lorne said. "You're usually a pretty good judge of that."

"So?" Zachary persisted. "Is it one we can talk about?"

"I'm not sure it will be that interesting to you. Just an older man, a senior, who died in his sleep. Only I think he strangled; I don't think it was just old age."

"Strangled. But not homicide?" Zachary asked.

"No. I'm pretty sure it was accidental. I don't think anyone had any reason to kill him intentionally. He lived with his son, who is pretty broken up about the whole thing. I don't think there was a huge inheritance or anything like that. I think it was just an unfortunate accident. I want to do a little more research to establish what happened before I do my final report."

"How did he strangle?" Lorne asked cautiously. "I wouldn't think he would let his father go to bed with anything around his neck."

"I couldn't figure out what it was at first. There wasn't anything at the scene. It had been sanitized before the paramedics got there. But I've been talking to one of his care workers and that conversation led me to look at poseys."

"Posies?" Pat repeated, his brows drawing down. "As in flowers?"

"No. Not flowers. A posey is also a kind of vest designed to keep a patient from wandering. To restrain them to their bed."

"To tie them down?" Zachary looked at her, his expression darkening.

"Well, yes. To tie them down. The posey is designed to keep their arms and hands free so that they can still do things while sitting in a wheelchair or lying in bed, but to prevent them from getting up. Some patients with dementia or other conditions can wander and get into trouble. Hurt themselves."

Zachary didn't say anything, poking at the food on his plate. Kenzie got the feeling that he was not happy hearing about this. Maybe it was too close to a case that he'd had, looking into the death of an autistic boy in a residential school. She hadn't thought about it, or she might have chosen not to mention Howard's case.

"If I ever get to that point, you can take me back behind the barn and shoot me," Lorne told Pat. "I don't want to be a burden on anyone. I don't want to live that kind of life. Just shoot me and bury me under the wood box."

"We don't have a barn or a wood box," Pat pointed out. "Or a gun."

"Well, you get the picture. I don't want to end up like that. If I start to lose my marbles, help me to end it before it gets too advanced."

Pat rolled his eyes and shook his head. But he was younger than Lorne and took much better care of his body. Chances were, Lorne would fail long before Pat. And he would be left with the same dilemma as Kyle. How to take care of his partner in the best way possible. A way that respected his human dignity and kept him in a comfortable environment until the end. Kenzie didn't like to think about Lorne making an end-of-life plan. He was still in pretty good shape and didn't show many signs of slowing down. But of course, that could change in an instant, with a virus, a blood clot, or a traffic accident. Human bodies were frail. Kenzie knew better than most how many different ways they could be broken.

"And you think that this man strangled because of the posey?" Zachary asked, bringing the conversation back to Kenzie and her case.

"It is beginning to look that way. I could tell that he had been restrained and that there had been something around his neck and that he asphyxiated. If the son will admit that he was wearing a posey when he died, that would go a long way to tying the case up."

"Aren't these poseys made to be safe?" Pat asked. "Aren't there safety standards? Failsafes?"

"Not really. There has been some talk about making sure that they can open from the front, that the person wearing it can let themselves out in case of emergency."

"Well, that sort of defeats the purpose, doesn't it?" Lorne contributed. "I mean… restrain the patient but give them an easy way to get out?"

Kenzie nodded. "It doesn't really make sense, I know. In some cases, the patient is amenable to wearing a restraint. Because it keeps them upright in the wheelchair and doesn't let them fall over, or something like that. But in the majority of cases... no, I don't think you want to build in an escape feature."

"But you would think that they would construct them in a way that they would not be dangerous," Pat persisted. "Someone can strangle in one?"

"I've been looking at the literature because I thought the same thing. If it's a safety device, then how could it be what caused his death? But..." Kenzie shrugged. "It actually isn't that uncommon. Someone tries to escape from it, or slides down and gets caught up on it..."

"Then they should improve the construction or stop using them."

"I'm going to follow up with some people I know in nursing care and try to get a feeling for what's going on in the industry. How they are viewed, how safe they are if used correctly, that kind of thing. Figure out just what went wrong in this case."

"*If* you can get the son to admit that he was in a posey when he died," Zachary reminded her.

"Well... even if I can't get him to admit it, he appears to have strangled on something. We can still rule it an accident. It would just make it a lot cleaner. And I think it would be less painful for him if he would admit it. If he keeps denying it, he ends up carrying that burden alone. Not being able to talk to anyone about it or receive any comfort or reassurance from anyone else. That would be a pretty heavy load."

13

G etting old isn't for sissies," Lorne intoned.

They all chuckled, except for Lorne. Lorne and Pat looked at each other.

"I get so worried when I forget something," Lorne said. "We've had several friends now who have... had dementia or other issues. It's frightening when people your age are starting to fail."

"You're still young," Zachary protested. "You have a lot of years left."

"Maybe I do and maybe I don't. None of us know how long we have. But I'm the oldest one here. Chances are, I'll be the first to go. And I don't want it to be with dementia." He shook his head. "Not like that."

Pat put his hand on his partner's arm. "I haven't seen any sign that you're failing," he reassured. "Everybody forgets things sometimes. Walks from one room to another and can't remember why. Can't remember a word or someone's name when you're trying to recall it. You haven't had any lapses that I've noticed."

"No... it isn't that I think I have dementia now. But how will I know if I do? Isn't that what they say?" he addressed Kenzie, "That it isn't the person with dementia who notices that they have a problem, it's the people around them? To the person, everything is still normal and they don't realize everything is going sideways. So what if I do begin to fail, but I don't know it? And by the time I'm ready to implement an end-of-life choice, I'm not competent anymore, so they won't let me?"

"You will know before you reach that point." Kenzie swallowed, a hot lump in her throat. Lorne was not *her* foster father, but she had grown close to him in the time that she had known Zachary, and she didn't like to think of him getting older, sicker, or dying. "You'll know about the diagnosis in the early stages and you can make your choices then, make your wishes known."

Lorne shook his head. "It's all very murky. I wish I knew all of the ins and outs. And what if I'm competent mentally, but I'm sick or disabled? Nursing homes... how do you know when it's time?"

"You wouldn't need to go into a nursing home," Pat said firmly. "I would take care of you. You could stay home. I'm strong. It wouldn't be a problem."

"But you'd have to take care of me twenty-four hours a day. You wouldn't have time for anything that you wanted to do. It would be better for me to be in a care facility. You could visit."

"No one knows what you would or wouldn't be able to do," Pat pointed out. "This is all speculation. I don't even know how we got on to the topic. Nursing homes have their place, but I don't think we'll need one. They are more for people who don't have family to look after them."

"And there is the cost!" Lorne said, turning his attention to Kenzie. "Do you know how much money those places cost? Thousands of dollars a month! How does anyone afford that?"

"Some people have insurance or take out a mortgage on their home. There are government relief programs. I don't know all the details, but if something happened and you needed to be placed in a home, we would find a way."

"Look at Roger and Janice," Lorne said to Pat. "They never thought that they would be separated. But when she had a stroke, he had to put her into a place. She can't do anything for herself. And he couldn't do everything."

"There is no point in spending time worrying about it now," Pat said, "We don't know what the future holds."

Lorne nodded and ate a few bites of his dinner, obviously still thinking about it.

"There are some very good facilities out there," Kenzie said. "I know that people try everything possible to avoid having to go into nursing care but, generally speaking, the homes are very good. The staff is compassionate. They got into nursing care because they do care about people. It certainly isn't like it pays a lot. They're there because they want to be and, generally, they take excellent care of the residents. And a lot of them have exercise programs and social activities, art, hair salons, all kinds of things."

"If you're just there because you're a senior. But if you're there because you can't do any of those things…"

"Well, yes," Kenzie admitted. "If you can't do anything for yourself, then obviously you can't get much out of that kind of programming. But I don't think you need to worry about it yet. Like Zachary said, you're not that old."

"Old enough that some of our friends are already going through this. Early dementia. Strokes. Falls. Heart attacks."

"You just do your best to take care of yourself," Pat advised. "And the rest… is up to God, or fate, or whatever you believe in."

They continued to eat. Kenzie was enjoying the meal but was uncomfortable with the silence. She should not have brought up Howard's case. She didn't want to bring everyone down. She glanced over at Zachary, who hadn't said much during the conversation.

"Are you okay?"

He nodded. "Just thinking."

She waited for him to say more and, when he didn't, prompted him. "About anything in particular?"

"About institutions. And restraints."

"Your case at Summit?"

"That," he nodded. "And others… Bonnie Brown. Group homes. Jails. Other places."

Kenzie thought about it as she ate. There were stories of restraints that had led to deaths in a lot of different institutions and circumstances. Even just an arrest could result in a detainee's death due to excited delirium or prone restraint. And it wasn't always easy to tell the cause.

"In Summit, that boy wrapped the blanket around his neck himself."

Zachary nodded. "Yes. Initially."

"That wasn't because of restraints."

Zachary shrugged. "Locked doors are a kind of restraint. And if you can't see people, what's going on behind that door... that can result in someone's death."

"Yes. I guess so."

"They had other forms of restraint too... the skin shocks were a form of restraint. And they had backboards. And isolation cells. The whole thing was... more of a prison than some of the prisons I've seen."

His voice was hoarse, his eyes far away. Kenzie didn't want to pull him out of his musings too abruptly, but she did want to move him on. It had taken him a long time to get over what he had seen at Summit. If getting over it was the right term.

"And Bonnie Brown?" Kenzie raised her brows questioningly. Bonnie Brown was a children's facility that Zachary had stayed at from time to time. Not juvie, but children in need of supervision. Kids who, for one reason or another, could not manage in foster care but needed more structure and supervision. She knew that was where Zachary had gone when he had first been put into the foster care system before going to the Peterson home. And he had gone back there periodically when his behavior became unmanageable. When he couldn't stand being with a foster family over Christmas and needed somewhere that did not remind him of what he had lost that day.

"Bonnie Brown." Zachary took a deep breath and let it back out again. "Yeah. Detention cells if you didn't behave. Security staff. Handcuffs, sometimes. There was one girl who died when I was in there." His Adam's apple bobbed up and down as he remembered. Kenzie had heard parts of this story before, but only pieces. Brief mentions, and then Zachary would veer off on to another subject, avoiding it. "Annie." He named her. Kenzie thought that might be all that he was able to say about it, but she gave him another minute to decide. "She died when they left her in handcuffs overnight." His chin lifted slightly, trying to pull himself out of memories that threatened to drown him. "Positional asphyxia. I guess that's what killed her. They didn't know, back then."

"They should have," Kenzie asserted. How many people—children, mentally ill, high, or arrestees—had to die before people understood and stopped leaving prisoners prone or in restraints? And now add the elderly to the list of people who might be restrained, not because of wrongdoing but because of age and slipping memories, and who might die in restraints because their caregivers did not know anything about positional asphyxia, excited delirium, prone holds, or the danger of strangling on their restraints.

"And drugs," Zachary said.

Kenzie looked at him and tried to connect that comment up with anything else he had said. It was a non sequitur; she couldn't figure out how it related to the conversation.

"Drugs? What about them?"

"Another method of restraint. Chemical restraints."

"Oh. Yes." Kenzie hadn't even been thinking about medications but, of course, it was true. Violent psych patient admitted? Administer Haldol. Someone who was always agitated and angry? Give them something. Prisoners who were constantly getting into fights with the other prisoners and staff? Prescribe them something to calm them down and make them more compliant. She'd heard of children in foster care, or even living with their own families, being drugged with cough medicine, Benadryl, antipsychotics, sleeping pills, whatever it took until they were sedated enough that they could not disrupt their school class. Or their parents, who might want to go out for a nice dinner and date. Chemical restraints were definitely a thing in a number of different situations.

"We're sorry about those experiences you had to go through," Lorne told Zachary, leaning toward him and reaching across the table to touch his hand lightly. "No one should have to go through that."

At first, Kenzie thought he was just talking about foster care and Bonnie Brown. But then she thought about Archuro and the fact that he had also used a chemical cocktail injected into Zachary's bloodstream in order to torture and control him. When Lorne and Pat had first arrived at the hospital, they had been told the drugs in Zachary's system might affect his memory. She didn't know what drugs had been used or how much Zachary remembered. He had refused to talk to her about it, but she knew that he'd described bits of the experience to Dr. B, his therapist.

Anger flared in Kenzie's breast and she wished—not for the first time—that Archuro had been killed during the takedown. Or in the jail he was incarcerated in. Killed by anyone and in any manner, it didn't matter to her. She just hoped that one day it would happen, and Zachary could be reassured that the monster who had tortured him could never do it again to anyone.

"What are they like?" Zachary asked, turning to face Kenzie so abruptly that she jumped. "The nursing homes. They're not like that, are they? If you went to visit someone… it wouldn't be like prison, would it?"

Kenzie shook her head. But the truth was, she didn't have much experience with nursing homes. With hospitals, yes, and she had been learning a lot more about home care. But her only real experience with nursing homes was when she had investigated a viral outbreak at Champlain House the previous October. And she had only been in the independent living wing. It had been nice. Fairly pleasant. The people there seemed happy and the staff easy to get along with. The residents had their own rooms and freedom of movement. But she would have to dig a little deeper if she wanted to be able to answer that question honestly.

"I haven't been to a lot," she admitted. "I need to do a bit more research. Because I want to get some answers about this patient, what happened to him, if he would have been safer at a nursing home, and what his son's options were. I would like to know how we're serving our seniors. Are they falling between the cracks? Being taken advantage of by big corporations that run these places?" She shook her head. "I don't know. I need to do more research."

14

---

enzie had first met Dr. Able during her investigation of the viral outbreak. He was one of the doctors at Champlain House and had seemed very capable. He had not objected to seeing her or acted like she was putting him out by asking questions. He had been lucky that the blame for the infection had not landed on his shoulders when everything hit the media. It hadn't been his fault, but there had been issues with the nurses not accepting the Medical Examiner's orders, which resulted in even more people being exposed to the virus.

Dr. Able couldn't be blamed for that.

In the intervening months since she had last seen him, Kenzie had forgotten how good-looking he was. Tall, with dark wavy hair, piercing blue eyes, and a ruggedly handsome face and strong jaw. Good genes. Or a good plastic surgeon. She suspected the former.

His eyes twinkled when he caught her examining him. He smiled slightly.

"It's nice to see you again, Dr. Kirsch."

"It's good to see you too. Thank you for agreeing to see me."

"Now I understand that this time, your questions have nothing to do with Champlain House, is that right?"

"Well, it's not an investigation into Champlain House. But I am looking for information about how places like Champlain House are operated. So it's about you, but not."

He nodded his understanding. "Well…" He leaned back in his large office chair, getting comfortable. "Tell me what you would like to know."

"This started with the case of a senior who apparently died in his sleep. But on further investigation, we realized that his heart had not just stopped. It looks like an accidental death, but I want to understand all the circumstances around it. Get a real feel for what the mitigating factors were."

"And what does that have to do with Champlain House?"

"I was wondering if you could tell me about how you handle restraints. Or any safety measures that end up restricting patients' freedom of movement. I have no idea what the regulations are or what protocols you normally follow. What you would consider safe or not safe."

Able sucked in his cheeks, thinking about this. "I see. Well… the first thing you should know is that there is a very wide range. And it is all based on a resident's needs. We want to restrict their movements as little as possible, of course. Great pains are taken to ensure that they are placed in the least restrictive environment possible and that their movements are as free as they can be." He pressed his palms together and touched them to the front of his face, tapping thoughtfully. "That said, a resident's safety is paramount. We cannot let people hurt themselves because we are not comfortable with implementing the restrictions necessary."

Kenzie nodded. So far, it felt like all she was getting was double-talk. Nothing at all informative. "That all sounds good," she told him. "But it's theoretical instead of practical. Can we talk about actual practices and examples?"

Able shrugged and nodded. "Fair enough, I suppose," he agreed.

"So far, I've only seen your independent living wing, and all of the residents there are... independent. No restrictions on their movement, as far as I could see."

"Very little," Able agreed. "We ask them to be back in their rooms for lights out and to keep us informed of their movements in case something happens, and we need to track them down. There is the occasional argument or altercation, and then we ask people to return to their rooms. But on the whole, yes, they're allowed to go where they like, participate in the various activities, make friends... We want them to be as independent as possible. We foster that attitude as much as we can. The more independent they are, the more stimulation and responsibility they have, the better it is for their brains. It helps them to make connections and remember things. To fight off depression. Lowers risk of dementia."

"But you have other units as well. You have a dementia unit?"

"Yes." He tapped his fingers on the desk, his mouth pursing slightly. He wasn't as excited to talk about the dementia unit as he was to talk about the more active and pleasant independent living wing. Kenzie could understand that. "Unfortunately, not everyone stays at the peak of health. Our bodies and brains degenerate over time and, even if you are doing all the things that are supposed to be protective, you can't completely eliminate stroke, high blood pressure, viruses and infections, and Alzheimer's disease. There will always be people who can no longer look after themselves or even remember who they are. It is a very sad situation. And I hope that we help our residents' families to feel better about it. To know that they are doing everything they can for their loved ones. That they're being treated with dignity and respect and given all of the physical and mental attention they need."

"I'm sure that the ones that can afford your rates are very happy that you are taking care of their family members," Kenzie agreed, watching Able closely for his reaction to this somewhat backhanded comment.

"Our rates are quite reasonable, all things considered," Able said without apparent offense. "You remember that they are getting twenty-four-hour care, fully qualified nurses, that they are being monitored closely physically and over camera feeds. These things cost money. And there are bursary and assistance programs. We do our best to help families navigate those programs and applications so they can afford to care for their loved ones."

"And then they don't have to worry about what might happen to the person if they stay at home."

Able looked serious. "We sometimes have to speak very plainly to families who think they can continue to care for their loved ones at home. A husband or wife just isn't equipped for the responsibility of caring for a person's every need, especially in complex medical cases. We try to help them see that caregiver burnout and the risks of having someone in their home without that twenty-four-hour nursing care and surveillance are just too high. You can't do it forever. Sooner or later, the patient suffers. And unfortunately, so does the family. And then either there is a tragic end to the situation, or it becomes an emergency and they don't have the time to find the right facility. Instead, they have to go with whatever facility is able to take a new patient with complex needs."

Kenzie nodded slowly. "I guess that must happen a lot."

"It does. People think they can care for their loved ones at home until the end, but they can't. They have in their minds that nursing homes are a modern phenomenon and, before that, everyone took care of their family members by themselves. So it must be possible. But that isn't really the way things were for our forefathers. Yes, they took care of grandma and grandpa because they had no other choice, but there was also no medical care, so those family members did not live very long. And there are cultures where they were simply left on a mountain to die. People with dementia or psychosis were locked up in insane asylums for the rest of their lives, which again, were very short. Modern nursing homes are not taking the job away from the families. They are making it *possible* for them to take care of their loved ones."

"So you don't think much of families who keep the person at home."

"When they require treatment or twenty-four-hour supervision? No. Families need to realize when they can no longer provide the care their loved one needs."

15

They were both silent. Kenzie thought over the Howard case. She still needed answers she didn't have.

"Do you use poseys here?"

"Poseys? Yes, on occasion." He pressed his lips together. "Not very long, though. There are other solutions. Restraint vests do pose certain risks."

"Can you tell me about those?"

"If you can perform an internet search, I assume you already know most of the risks. Poseys are not a secret, even though people generally don't like to talk about them. First and foremost, even when used properly, they can restrict movement too much or hold the patient in a position that is harmful to his health. They might struggle and get twisted up the wrong way. Or try to escape the bed and end up hanging himself. Anyone using restraints needs to know the risks and what to do to alleviate them."

"Are there laws specifying when they can and can't be used?"

"No."

"Or how they are to be used? What needs to be done to lower the risks?"

"Nothing legislated, no. It is up to the facility to figure it out. Or the caregiver, if used in a home care situation."

"And any facility can just make up its own rules?"

Able raised his brows and shrugged. "We have internal policies and procedures to be followed. If we find that a staff member is not following those rules, they are dismissed."

"No warnings, just gone?"

He nodded. "It is that important. If you can't follow safety protocols, you cannot work here. No second chance."

Kenzie wondered if that also applied to nurses who refused to follow quarantine orders. She had never heard what happened to the nurse who had taken Lola to the Halloween Ball and put everyone at risk of contracting an aggressive, potentially fatal virus.

"So you have a policy with regard to poseys?"

"Yes. And any similar physical restraint."

"And that is?"

"When a restraint is first applied, a supervisor needs to either be inside the room or needs to log bed checks every fifteen minutes to make sure that the restraint is working and is not putting the patient's health at risk. Does it fit properly? So that they are not able to get around or through it? Is the patient fighting the restraints? Are they in a safe position? What are their vitals? There is a checklist to go through every fifteen minutes to ensure they are safe and well. If they are fighting the restraints, someone has to stay with them. They cannot be left alone."

Kenzie nodded. That made perfect sense. Those were the people most likely to have adverse health effects. And the most likely to get tangled in a restraint.

"Good. Yeah. That makes sense."

"After the first hour, if there have been no concerns and restraint is still necessary—often within an hour, the need for the person to be physically restrained has been eliminated—then the checks are made every hour. After four hours, they are lengthened to four-hour intervals. But a patient is rarely in restraints for longer than four hours. And the staff will generally keep up fifteen-minute or one-hour check intervals even when they are not required. It's up to their judgment, if they feel they are needed more often."

"Four hours seems like a long time." A lot could happen in four hours. It was a long time to go between bed checks, unless the patient were sleeping.

"As I said, the staff will often stick to fifteen-minute or one-hour checks. But we rarely have patients in restraints for that long."

"Then how do you deal with someone who wanders? Who tries to escape or to do something dangerous to themselves or others?"

"Similar to raising children… distract them. Find them something else to do. Talk with them and engage them. Check to make sure that they are not in pain or dealing with a UTI, two things that can cause an increase in agitation. Unless someone is off of their psychiatric meds, we rarely have anyone who is a threat to themselves or others for any length of time. Some facilities won't use poseys or soft restraints. They consider them too dangerous. More dangerous than the harm that a patient could cause to himself."

"You don't agree?"

Able licked his lips and considered it. "I think that, used the right way, they are a beneficial tool. But used the wrong way… used indiscriminately and for long periods of time… the risk is not justified. I would much rather have my residents handled in another way. The dementia ward is a locked ward. Patients cannot simply walk out. You need a key code to get past the doors. That eliminates most risks right there."

"But some dementia patients are violent."

"Yes. Sometimes. And if they are consistently violent, we will recommend medications to settle them down. Putting them in restraints long-term causes too much harm. Bruising or even broken bones. Strangling. Ending up in a dangerous position that puts pressure on their diaphragm so they cannot take a full breath. Bedsores. Constipation. Loss of energy and appetite.

Better if we can control violent behavior with an antipsychotic or sedative."

"What about falls?"

"What about them?"

"Don't poseys and other restraints help prevent patients from falling? I have one patient who would refuse to use his walker and end up falling. So his son used a posey to keep him in bed when he wasn't there to supervise."

"Unfortunately, they don't prevent falls. They just cause other falls. Patients climbing over bedrails or getting pinned between the bedrail and the mattress. Tipping over beds or chairs. Fighting restraints until they are black and blue. It doesn't stop them from being injured."

"So what would you recommend for someone like that who was caring for a loved one at home?"

"I would recommend that they get their loved one into a proper care facility where they can be supervised, have a fall sensor, and have medical staff available when needed. I would not recommend that someone susceptible to falls and who refused to use a walker be cared for at home."

"You said there aren't any laws about how poseys are to be used in nursing homes. Are there any that prohibit people from using them at home?"

"No. There aren't. There are no laws restricting their use in any way. Or who they can be sold to. If they could only be purchased by a nursing care facility, that would be one thing. But you can pull up Amazon on your phone right now and have one delivered to your house tomorrow, no questions asked. How you choose to use it is totally up to you, and there isn't even a warning in the product listings that they could cause injury."

Kenzie shook her head slowly, thinking about that. Anyone could purchase a posey or another restraint system for use in any situation, without any oversight.

And if something happened, the caregiver could just remove the posey from the victim's body and dispose of it quietly before the paramedics arrived. And no one would ever know the difference.

Except for Kenzie. Kenzie knew. She couldn't ignore the mark on Mr. Howard's throat and pretend that she hadn't seen it. She now understood what had happened to him and that's what would go down in her report.

And how to prevent such a thing from happening again in the future? That was another question altogether. With no regulations, no training required, and no warnings about how dangerous restraints could be, Joseph Howard's death would not be the last that Kenzie attributed to a posey.

16

Dr. Wiltshire stopped at Kenzie's desk and waited for her to finish what she was typing and look up. Kenzie smiled and nodded.

"What's up?"

"I'm wondering how you are doing on the Howard file. We really should finish it up."

"Right. Umm, I just wanted to talk to you about that before drafting my final thoughts on it. I don't want to waste my time on something that you're not going to sign off on."

He lifted one eyebrow. "And why would I not sign off on it? If you have done your job and identified cause and manner of death, there's nothing for me to do but review your findings."

"Yes." Kenzie took her time, thinking about how to best approach her explanation. "I'm sure you will... but I just wanted to make sure. It seems fairly straightforward after the postmortem and talking with Mr. Howard's son and one of the visiting nurses. It looks like he was put to bed in a posey and, during the night, slid down and was strangled by it. A posey is—"

"I'm familiar with what a posey is. This is not my first rodeo. There was no mention of a posey in the police or paramedic notes."

"No. That's the one issue. The son apparently removed it and sanitized the scene before calling 9-1-1. But I have confirmation from the nursing aide that a posey was used regularly to keep Mr. Howard from wandering. He didn't like to use his walker, and they wanted to keep him from falling down."

"The nurse says that a posey was in use?"

"Yes. She didn't say for sure that he was in one that night. It would have been the son that put him down to sleep. But she had instructions to use it during the day when she visited and… left Mr. Howard alone."

Dr. Wiltshire shook his head, sighing. "Society has reached the point where it is no longer considered okay to leave children or animals waiting in the car while you run your errands. I can only hope that we reach the point at which it is not acceptable to leave a senior who cannot take care of himself alone in your house."

"Aren't we at that point yet? If someone called the elder abuse hotline and said that Howard was being left home alone in restraints, wouldn't they intervene? Wouldn't Kyle be charged with neglect or abuse?"

"Possibly. But I wouldn't count on it. He was looking after all of his father's needs. He wasn't malnourished or physically abused. And when he died, it wasn't because he'd been left alone during the day."

"No, it was because he had been left in restraints at night, with no one supervising."

"It could just as easily have happened in a nursing home or hospital. None of those facilities would be watching him twenty-four hours a day. He would be left in his room for several hours without intervention. Certainly overnight. Maybe a check-in halfway through the night, but maybe not if he had a bed alarm or motion sensor in his room so they would know he was up."

"They would not have left him in a posey overnight."

"You don't know that. It would not be unheard of."

Dr. Able had said that at Champlain House, he would eventually be checked on every four hours. That would indicate that a patient could be left in a posey for longer than four hours. Maybe eight or ten or even more. As Dr. Wiltshire said, one bed check during the night to make sure that he was okay. But a lot could happen during the four hours in between.

Kenzie sipped her cold coffee and put it down again. "Okay. I'll get it written up for you today. It's already mostly drafted; I just wanted to make sure that you would be okay with me citing it as accidental death, even though we don't have confirmation that he was actually wearing a posey at the time of his death. There is a mark on his throat, so we know he was wearing or had something wrapped around his neck that was removed after his death."

"Yes, that's fine. You don't have to say it was a posey since we don't know if that was what he was wearing at the time of death, but you can say that he was known to be restrained by a posey at other times and that he died from strangulation. That you believe it to be accidental." He gave a slight smile. "You are saying accidental, I assume? Not that the son deliberately killed him by leaving him in a posey?"

Kenzie chuckled, even though she didn't think it was funny. "No, of course not. I will be saying death by accident."

"That's all we need, then. That he died by strangulation, possibly a posey, by accident."

"Okay. I'll try to get it done by the end of the day."

"Good. The family is eager to hold a funeral."

"Of course." Kenzie nodded. She knew that not just from the call she had taken from Kyle, but by several messages he had left and an email that he had submitted through the *Contact Us* form on the Medical Examiner's Office website. The man was not happy about having to wait for her to finish her investigation. And she had deliberately avoided speaking to him because she didn't want to deal with his demands and anger over the case not being handled as quickly as he would have liked. She hoped she wouldn't hear back from him when he realized that she had performed a full autopsy, complete with y-incision. Hopefully, the funeral home would deal with the dressing of the body for the funeral and it wouldn't be done by Kyle himself. Knowing that she had done an autopsy and actually seeing the sewn-up incision were two very different things, and she was sure he would not be happy about it.

"Thank you. We have a couple more postmortems to get caught up on." He looked at his watch. "Tomorrow for those, I'm thinking. I also have some reports and paperwork to clear today. We can tackle the postmortems tomorrow."

Kenzie nodded. "Thanks."

Her ears were attuned to the ding of the elevator down the hall and around the corner, since it was the only way the public could reach her desk. Hearing it now, she turned her head and watched to see who was approaching—hopefully, just a cop with a routine request.

But she did not recognize the man who came walking down the hallway at a quick clip. Dr. Wiltshire gave Kenzie a nod and turned to leave. "I look forward to receiving that report, then."

Kenzie nodded and swiveled her chair around so that she was facing the approaching man directly. Maybe a public inquiry. Or someone delivering samples from a lab. She was familiar with most of the couriers or deliverymen who came to the morgue, but they could always have employed someone new.

She gave a nod and a friendly smile. The white-haired man did not smile back. He was clean-shaven, with a round face and pale blue eyes. He was broad and heavy, but not paunchy. Maybe he'd been on his high school football team in his teens. He'd stayed in relatively good shape though still a little too heavy. His face was red from exertion or the heat.

"How can I help you?" Kenzie asked. He was not carrying a messenger back or backpack, so he was probably not a courier from one of the labs.

"You can help me by telling me why it is taking this office so long to release my father's body to the funeral home."

Kenzie's heart sank as she realized that this was Kyle Howard. She had not helped herself by avoiding his phone calls. He had given up on trying to reach her by phone or email and had come to see her in person instead. Kenzie swallowed.

"Mr. Howard. Dr. Wiltshire and I were just discussing your father's case." She looked in the direction Dr. Wiltshire was walking, hoping he would turn at the mention of his name. "We expect to have the report complete tonight. Then we should be able to release your father's body tomorrow."

"What is taking so long? This should have been done in a day!"

Dr. Wiltshire had turned around and was returning.

"Postmortems routinely take a few days to complete," Kenzie told Kyle honestly. "And we've had a bit of a backlog over the past week. Believe me, it is not unusual for it to take a few days to a week. Even when we don't find anything unusual or concerning, it can take time."

"Unusual or concerning?" Kyle repeated as Dr. Wiltshire joined them at the desk. "What are you talking about? My father died in his sleep. There is nothing unusual or concerning about that."

Kenzie hadn't meant to imply that there was anything wrong with Mr. Howard's postmortem, but she couldn't think of a way to walk back what she had said. He would know soon enough that they were not classifying Howard's death as natural causes.

"Mr. Howard?" Dr. Wiltshire offered a hand. "I'm Dr. Wiltshire. I am the Medical Examiner."

Kyle turned to him, face darkening even more. "Then maybe you can explain to me what's going on. I can't believe the way this has been handled. Did you know that—" he motioned to Kenzie to begin a rant about how she had handled his father's case.

"I am fully up to speed on Dr. Kirsch's actions and findings," Dr. Wiltshire interrupted. "She has been working under my supervision and has not done anything improper. I'm sorry that you have been inconvenienced, but that is the price we pay to ensure that we have all the facts we need."

"All of the facts? You don't know anything. You have no idea what the past few months have been like for this family. After all that we have gone through, I would think that you would be able to at least do your jobs efficiently and give us some measure of peace!"

"Perhaps you could come to my office. This is not the best place to be holding such a conversation."

Kyle clenched his jaw, then nodded curtly. Dr. Wiltshire looked at Kenzie.

"Dr. Kirsch, will you join us?"

Kenzie was surprised. But she did what she was asked and rose to her feet to follow them. She was not looking forward to getting another earful from Kyle Howard.

17

D r. Wiltshire invited Kyle to sit down, politely asked if he wanted coffee, and fussed over him a bit to make him feel like he was a special guest there rather than just someone who had borne down on them and was determined to make things as difficult as possible for them.

Kenzie sat down in the other guest chair, ensuring that it was a good distance from Kyle's and that she was facing him, angled just slightly toward Dr. Wiltshire. She thought about all the times she had watched Zachary take a chair that faced the room and the door rather than turning his back on other people in the restaurant or whatever place they were in. Maybe she was getting a little taste of what he felt all the time. The feeling that she needed to face the potential threat and not be taken off guard. While she was sure that Kyle had only come to talk to them and vent his feelings, she couldn't help feeling vulnerable, concerned about what could happen if he lost control. He was much bigger than Kenzie and could do some damage if he put his mind to it. She had no desire to be physically attacked. Even his verbal attack was making her anxious and uncomfortable.

Hopefully, he was settling down with Dr. Wiltshire's care and attention, realizing they were not adversaries. Dr. Wiltshire and Kenzie were just two public servants doing their job.

"You're sure you won't have a coffee?" Dr. Wiltshire asked again as he sat down behind his desk. "A glass of water?"

"I don't need anything," Kyle snapped back. Determined, Kenzie thought, not to take any favors from them. Not to let himself be bought by some small gesture.

Dr. Wiltshire looked serious. He laced his fingers together and placed them on the desk in front of him. "I am sorry that your family has been through such a difficult time recently. Was your father's decline fairly rapid?"

"Everything was fine. He was living in his own apartment in one of those senior communities. Where they all have their own places and take care of themselves, but there are a lot of community things, people their age or in their own circumstances living close by. They're supposed to be very close-knit and provide emotional and social support."

Dr. Wiltshire nodded. "And then what happened?"

"He had pneumonia. He was very weak afterward. Needed help. He didn't want to impose on family and was happy living independently, so we found a nursing home for him." Kyle's expression darkened. "Do you have any idea what they are like? The ones that normal people can afford to get into? He had been happy in the senior community. He really liked it there. He liked being independent and around people his age. He had to sell everything to get into the nursing home. Couldn't afford it any other way. All of the money that he and my mother had put into their house. Years of struggling to pay the mortgage. Sold so that he could afford to live somewhere with basic medical care. Sunshine Care."

Kenzie listened to the story unfold. She could predict where it was going. His father had been unhappy at the nursing home. He didn't like being treated like he was incapable, even if he did need help with a few things. He wanted to go back to the senior community, but he couldn't, so he ended up moving back home with his son, where they butted heads over what he could and couldn't do safely. But at least he was at home with family, instead of strangers who just wanted his money.

Kyle stared off into the distance. He was no longer angry, ranting at the two doctors still holding his father's body. He was thinking back to the time before everything had fallen apart for him. When he'd had a life that was his own instead of having to look after his dad.

"I knew something was wrong there," Kyle said. "I could tell after he had been there just a couple of days. The staff didn't listen to me when I told them what Dad needed. They acted like I didn't know what I was talking about. They were the professionals, so they knew what they were doing. Dad was... wrong." Kyle shook his head in a tense, tight motion. "I wasn't sure what it was. Thought it might just be because he was tired after the pneumonia and needed to build his strength back up again. When he was able to get around better, he would be happier. But he wasn't."

Kyle looked around. Kenzie thought he was regretting that he hadn't asked for a coffee or water. He needed something to do with his hands. A reason to take a break from speaking and mull things over and marshal his thoughts properly. He clasped his hands together, searching for something in the room that he would never find—the answers to his questions.

"He was... very dark. When I would go see him, he wouldn't talk to me, wouldn't smile, wouldn't visit. He sat in his room, on his bed or in his wheelchair, just staring at the TV they left on for him. Dad was never a big TV watcher. I knew that they were the ones turning it on and parking him in front of it. He would barely respond when I would walk into the room and try to talk to him."

"Did you take him to the doctor?" Wiltshire suggested. "The ER?"

"They had doctors there. I thought they knew what they were talking about. They said that they'd examined him already and that he was fine. He just didn't have much energy after the pneumonia. They thought that he would get better. In the meantime... I should not worry about it. Just leave him there and let them take care of him."

18

They waited for more information. Kenzie thought about what Zachary had said about chemical restraints. Had they given Howard something to make him so passive? It sounded like he had really been out of it, quite a change from how he had been at his seniors living center.

"This place," Kyle said. "There were always people crying and moaning. Shouting that they needed something. And the staff would sit around and talk and ignore them. I would walk past someone's room and they were on the floor where they had fallen, but the nursing staff had just left them there. What if they broke a hip or hit their head? What if that was my father, and they just left him lying there hurt and suffering?"

"Did you file any complaints? Talk to the owners or someone higher up the food chain, rather than just the day staff?" Dr. Wiltshire suggested.

"I made complaints. I never heard anything back. I don't know if they ever got anywhere or were just thrown in the garbage. How could I make sure that they took care of my dad? He had been so set on going there, still living on his own rather than relying on family. But the things that were going on there... something was wrong. Something was very wrong. He had bruises. And rashes.

He could go to the bathroom on his own, but I'd get there and find that he'd been in a diaper all day. That he had a rash from being left in a dirty diaper. They said he wasn't using the toilet and they didn't want to keep cleaning soiled clothes and sheets. But I know that before that, he was using the bathroom by himself. He didn't need any help."

"An illness can change things. More than you know. A lot of what a person can do for himself is based on energy levels, and something like pneumonia can make it difficult to do anything for months."

"It wasn't just his energy levels. Because he was better than that before he went in there. Even with the pneumonia, he was still getting up, going to the bathroom, and eating breakfast. He wasn't just sitting in a chair or lying in bed all day long."

"So you didn't leave him there."

"I couldn't. If I did, he would just die there. They were ware-housing old people. They weren't there to help them and provide nursing care. This was where people were sent to die! And I didn't want my father there. He was completely helpless. I knew that it wouldn't be long before he was dead."

Kenzie and Dr. Wiltshire both nodded in unison. Kenzie was sure that she would have done the same thing. There was no way she would leave one of her parents—or anyone else she loved—in an environment like that. Sometimes people were severely handi-capped. Pneumonia, a stroke, heart attack, or some other disease could completely change the direction of their life and what they could do. But Kyle didn't believe that was the case, and he could not let his father stay there like that.

"When I told them he was leaving there, they just laughed. Said that I could take him out if I wanted to, but he was already paid up to the end of the year. And he'd made a non-refundable deposit before moving in. They had thousands of dollars of his money. And they were supposed to be the most affordable option. That's all they wanted. Just his money."

"And you never found another facility for him?" Wiltshire asked.

"Are you kidding? There was no way I was taking him back into one of those deathtraps. There was no way I was letting them get their claws into my father again. Maybe it would have been different at a more expensive place, but how was I going to get him in anywhere better? They already had thousands of dollars of his, and I didn't have the money to put down as a deposit on another place. I wasn't going to take the equity out of my own place and end up with *both* of us homeless and with nowhere to stay. I had a friend at work who helped to set me up with home care. She said that it was manageable; I could get the same level of care, or even better, through home care than through a nursing home."

He cleared his throat and looked around again. Kenzie supposed she should offer him a glass of water again, but she didn't want to miss anything that he might say when she left the room to get it.

"Things were pretty bad when I first brought him home," Kyle confided. "I didn't know how I was going to manage it. For the first week, he was always angry, couldn't understand why I had taken him out of there and wouldn't let him go back home. To the senior village, he meant. Back home to where he had been happy. He couldn't even remember being at the nursing home. He couldn't remember how bad it had been and that I had rescued him from it. He thought I had stolen him from his home, where he had been happy. He would hit and kick me, throw things around. Act like a bratty two-year-old, except that he was big enough and strong enough, even after the pneumonia and being at that place, to really do some damage. He gave me a black eye. Almost broke my nose. He didn't want me to touch him or to help him with anything."

Kenzie wondered at the change in behavior. Maybe he'd had a stroke? It was possible to have small ischemic events without anyone realizing what had happened.

"So I left him alone." The man leaned on Wiltshire's desk. "Not *alone* alone. I was still there. Still made his meals and made suggestions and sat with him each night. I took time off of work. Not paternity leave, but something like that. Elder leave. A few weeks to get him settled and to see if it would work out or if I really had to give in and put him someplace else like Sunshine. I just gave him as much space as I could. And he started to come out of it. He said he didn't know why he'd been behaving that way. That he just couldn't control himself. It was like a monster was inside his brain, taking over."

"Do you think he was having psychotic episodes?" Dr. Wiltshire asked. "Did you get him onto a medication that helped?"

"No." Kyle bit his lip. "I think he was withdrawing from whatever they'd been drugging him with."

19

Kenzie felt her eyes widen. "What did they have him on?"

"I don't know. They wouldn't ever tell me—private medical information. And I wasn't his guardian, so they couldn't share anything with me. I would have to go to court to get his medical records." Kyle looked at Kenzie. "And do you think that they would put it on their records? I doubt it. Whatever it was they had him on to keep him quiet and in one place... it wore off, but it was a couple of weeks before Dad started to seem like himself again. He stopped hitting and throwing things and was calm. He said he couldn't remember much about what went on at Sunshine, but... I think he remembered more than he admitted to."

"I'm so sorry that happened to him. And that you had to deal with it too."

"These places have oversight," Dr. Wiltshire said. "You need to find out what the channels were for reporting abuses and file about what was going on there."

"At this point?" Kyle turned his palms up helplessly. "What's it going to help now? He's gone. I thought that I could care for him at home and he would recover from the pneumonia and what they had done to him at Sunshine, and then everything would go back to normal. That he would be back to the way he was before."

"But he was still limited in what he could do?"

"Physically... I don't know. He was a little frailer than he had been before. I wanted him to use the walker so that he wouldn't fall. I was terrified about him falling down and not being able to get back up after seeing what was happening at Sunshine. I didn't want him to be down on the floor and not able to get back up when I wasn't there. Even with a nurse coming in a couple of times a day, something could still happen. But worse than that was his mental state."

He swallowed. Kenzie was reeling over everything that Joseph Howard had had to go through. And how many other seniors dealt with the same things? Not just illness and disability, but nursing or medical staff who were callous or indifferent, families who couldn't be there for them all day, having to be alone for hours, either living on their own or with family who still had to work during the day.

"When I would try to walk Dad to the bathroom to make sure that he didn't fall, he would get frantic. Try to push me away, slap at my hands. It wasn't like the anger and violence when he was withdrawing from whatever they had him on at Sunshine. It was... pathetic. He was afraid. He couldn't tell me why, or didn't want to. But something happened there. I was worried that it was..." Kyle trailed off. "I told myself that it was just because of the way he'd been left in a diaper when he was at Sunshine. That he was afraid I would force him to wear one and take away his dignity. Or cause painful rashes. But we didn't discuss diapers. Never once. He knew that I didn't have any in the house. I'd never told him that I didn't think he could manage anymore. I just wanted to take him to the bathroom to make sure he didn't fall on the way."

"And you think that he might have been abused?" Wiltshire suggested gently. "That someone might have been sexually abusing him?"

Kyle shuddered. "I never thought that was something that you would have to worry about at a place like that. Sure you have to worry with little kids. Watch for red flags. Make sure that they feel safe and that no one is paying the wrong kind of attention to them. But an old man? I've even heard about old women getting raped in places like that. I know it happens sometimes, as horrible as it sounds. But an old man?" He shook his head. "I can't wrap my head around it. I thought... it *must* be something else."

There wasn't any point in telling him anything different. He already realized it was the most likely explanation for his father's behavior. He just didn't want to admit it, to have to deal with it.

"You couldn't tell, right?" Kyle asked, looking at Dr. Wiltshire and then at Kenzie. "Doing his postmortem, I mean. You couldn't tell if something had happened to him."

"I wouldn't have been able to unless it was pretty severe," Kenzie said, shaking her head. "It had been weeks since he had been at that place?"

"Months."

"He would already have healed from any damage in that length of time, unless there was an infection or very serious damage, and you would know that from taking care of him."

He still looked at her pleadingly.

"Rest assured," Kenzie said gently. "I didn't see anything that indicated he had been sexually abused."

Kyle nodded and let his breath out. "I'm sorry. I know I'm being stupid about it. But... I just can't imagine anyone doing that to my father. Things settled down after the first couple of weeks. Mostly, there wasn't anything to remind either of us what had happened there. We didn't talk about it. Just talked about the present. How his day was. What show he wanted to watch on TV. He liked to read. Sometimes he would go through a few books in one day. So it wasn't really a hardship for him to stay in the bed or chair while I was gone."

"But he was in restraints," Kenzie said. "I saw indications of that."

"It was just for safety. He wouldn't remember that he was supposed to stay in his room and not make his own dinner or do the yard work. He agreed to it. He said that he knew it was to keep him safe." Kyle dabbed at a tear in the corner of his eye. "He didn't want to fall either. Sometimes he would wander, and he couldn't remember where he had been or what he had been thinking when I asked him about it. He just had these… episodes that he couldn't remember later. So he agreed that it was best if we just did something to remind him that he couldn't get out of bed by himself."

He had agreed to be restrained? Kenzie would have said that it was nonsense and no one would agree to the kind of restrictions Howard he been forced into. Only she had read a few articles lately about facilities that had tried to go restraint-free, and how the residents had been afraid to do it. They had been sure that they would get hurt falling from their beds or chairs. Staff had worked with them on choosing safety measures they could get out of themselves. A wheelchair belt that they could unbuckle, rather than one that was buckled behind the chair so that they couldn't get out if they wanted to. Poseys that opened in the front rather than the back. Lap desks or chairs that helped them to stay upright and be able to do the activities that they wanted to without being trapped until someone came along to let them out.

Kenzie had never been in a situation where she had been involuntarily restrained. Not since she had been a toddler, long before her memory. Even as a child, when she had worn a seatbelt in the car, that had been a choice, something she could reverse with the press of a button. She'd been okay with seatbelts, knowing they were there to help keep her safe in the event of an accident. She had been happy she was wearing one when, on New Year's Eve two years earlier, she and Zachary had gone off the road and been in a serious wreck. The only reason that neither of them had been killed was that they had been wearing seatbelts.

But what would it be like to be in a restraint that she could not get out of? That she had to rely on someone else's whim to free her? Zachary could tell her about his experiences in Bonnie Brown and foster care. But that wasn't the same as experiencing it herself. The closest experience she'd had was during her kidnapping, when they had put a hood over her head. But they had not handcuffed her. She had been locked in a room with a hood over her head, but she had still had freedom of movement. It had been a terrifying experience even then. She couldn't imagine how bad it would have been if she'd been unable to move.

20

He's been through enough," Kyle said abruptly. "After everything he's gone through over the past year, the illness and being abused in Sunshine Care, and then having to be restrained at home for his own safety... can't you release him now? Can't you just turn him over to the funeral home? He's been stuck in limbo for so long already. I don't want him to be stuck anywhere anymore. I want to know where he is and that he is at rest."

"We'll release him as soon as we can," Dr. Wiltshire agreed. "As early as tomorrow morning, I hope. But we do have to finish our reports, check any additional lab tests that have come in, make sure that we both agree with each other's conclusions. It is a longer process than many people think. It isn't just a matter of looking at the body and being able to tell immediately what happened to him. It's a very detailed process. We don't want to be exhuming people later because we didn't take enough time the first time around." He drew in a breath and shook his head. "No. We don't want that. We want to do it right the first time. And you want to know, when you get your father back, that it's all over. That we aren't going to come back to you with anything else. It will all be finished, and you can go on with your life."

Kyle gazed steadily away from Dr. Wiltshire, who he appeared to be trying to avoid. "I don't know how I will ever go on with my life after what has happened. How does someone do that?"

"As difficult as it is, I think you will find that time does help to remove the sting. That it will be easier to think about your father and this last year without being so sad. But it will take time."

"I made all of the wrong choices. I should have insisted that he move in with me when he had pneumonia. Even before that, when he was looking at moving to the senior community. I could have asked him to come live with me then. Maybe he could have avoided getting pneumonia if he wasn't around all those people. Or once he had pneumonia, if he'd just come to live with me instead of going to Sunshine. I could have taken care of him much better. You think that a big company with all that training and staff will be better qualified to care for a slightly frail man recovering from pneumonia than me, someone with no experience with anything except raising children. And I wasn't even all that good at that if you want the truth. I left it to my wife. I wasn't one of these superdads, involved in every aspect of their children's upbringing. I was just there sometimes, telling them to be quiet so I could watch TV at the end of a long, hard day." He shook his head. "Like my day was any longer and harder than my wife's. Or even my children's. Kids don't have stress? They don't get hurt or have to deal with bullies or demanding adults? What made me deserve quiet time in front of the TV more than they deserved time to play? Or for my wife to put up her feet at the end of the day while I made *her* supper?"

"You did what you thought was the best for your father," Kenzie said. "You did what he told you he wanted to do. And when it turned out to not be an ideal situation, you got him out of there. You did what you were supposed to do."

"I should have reacted faster. Maybe I could have avoided some of the trauma that he went through. I knew something was wrong, but it took time to get him out of there. And at home... I just wanted him to be happy. I didn't want anything bad to happen to him."

"I'd like to hear about what happened when you found him. I know it's painful, but I need the details to finish my report. I know that you moved things before the paramedics got there."

Kyle's face got red and he opened his mouth to object. Kenzie shook her head sternly.

"I know that you did."

Kyle looked at Dr. Wiltshire, his face tight and angry. "You're the Medical Examiner, right? So why am I being interrogated by this woman? Why does she have anything to do with my father's case? You are the Medical Examiner; you're supposed to do it."

Dr. Wiltshire didn't react emotionally as Kenzie feared that she would if she were the one to answer. His voice was calm and reasonable. "I have support staff. Dr. Kirsch performed the post-mortem and is working on the final report. If you want it to be finished quickly, you should answer her questions."

"She doesn't know what she's talking about. You're just going to let her throw around accusations like that? I didn't have anything to do with my father's death. I did everything I could for him."

"She hasn't accused you of doing anything to hurt him. She's asking questions about what happened. How do you expect either one of us to sign off on the report if we don't know what happened? We need to satisfy ourselves as to what it was that happened. All of the events that led up to your father's death."

"It's none of your business! I already talked to the paramedics. I talked to the police. Everyone knows what happened. If they don't have any doubts about what happened, why do you?"

Kenzie wondered if they should call the police on the case and let them know that Kenzie's findings were not consistent with how the scene had been described to them. Maybe *they* could get the straight story from Kyle. He clearly did not intend to tell her about it.

"The police do not have access to the same information as we do," Dr. Wiltshire pointed out. "The reason that we have the body is to investigate, to see what is not readily apparent to the naked eye. I'm sure the look that the police had at the scene was very brief. They would not be able to see all of the marks on his body or the state of his heart and lungs. Those are things that we discovered when he was on the table. Our final report will go back to the police. Maybe they will have further questions for you then."

"You're threatening me now?" Kyle's voice rose angrily.

Dr. Wiltshire stood up. "I'm not threatening you. I'm letting you know the procedure. And now, I think we are finished here. I appreciate the background that you've provided to us. I hope that having gotten it off your chest, you'll feel a bit better about it now."

He walked around his desk and stood beside Kyle's chair until he stood, making a movement as if he were shaking off the accumulated stress of the day, everything that they had put on his shoulders.

"This isn't over. I'm going to be filing a complaint with..." Kyle's eyes darted back and forth, and he shook his head, trying to decide on the appropriate course of events. "With the Attorney General's office. You have no right to hold my father's body hostage, trying to coerce some statement from me. If you're done your autopsy, you have to release him to me. That's the way it works. Don't try telling me that you're still pursuing the truth. I know better. You're just trying to put the blame on someone. And that someone is me. Because I was the closest one to him. I took good care of my father. I did everything I could to keep him safe. He died in his sleep. None of that has changed. Whatever it is you're trying to pull, it's not going to work. Just *give me my father.*"

Dr. Wiltshire motioned toward the door. "This way, Mr. Howard."

Kyle went with him. Kenzie stayed behind in Dr. Wiltshire's office, waiting for him to return. Or if she heard yelling or fighting, she would call for the building security or the police to come and break things up and put Kyle under arrest until he could control himself. It was a couple of minutes before she heard the quiet tread of Dr. Wiltshire's shoes as he returned.

"Kenzie. Okay?"

Kenzie stood up. She nodded. "Yes, of course. I'm fine."

"I'm sorry about that. We don't usually get walk-in complaints here. The patients don't seem to mind the accommodations," he joked gently. "But there are the occasional family members who think that they can bully us into giving a particular ruling or rush procedures. We do what we can to help families deal with their grief, but…" He shrugged, spreading his hands wide. "It is a very emotional time for him. He has a lot of guilt and loss to deal with."

"I know. I feel bad for him. But—"

"But you can't let it affect your job. No. Of course not. And I wouldn't expect you to change any findings based on bullying and outside pressure. He's welcome to go to the Attorney General's office, or the police, or the media. That won't change the outcome of our report."

Kenzie nodded her agreement. "I won't be influenced."

"But it would be good if you could get it done tonight." Wiltshire rotated his wrist to look at his watch. "Of course, if he hadn't taken up so much of our time, we would have been able to finish it sooner. If you don't have time to do it this afternoon, that's fine. Wrap it up tomorrow."

Kenzie tapped the button on her phone to check the time. "I think I can manage tonight."

It would mean working late and taking time away from Zachary. But he understood that there were times when she needed to do that. Just as Kenzie understood, there were times when Zachary had surveillance or other jobs that took him away from her on occasion. They were both professionals; there were going to be times when their work made demands on their time.

21

Kenzie was tired when she finally got home. It had taken longer to finish the report than she had expected, and she had stayed a few extra minutes to wrap up other items on her to-do list and to take one more look at her email and the other reports still on her desk waiting for handling before leaving for the day. She wanted to make sure that everything was ready for her in the morning so that she didn't start the day feeling like she was already playing catch-up. Now, even though she was getting home late, everything would be staged for when she arrived the following day and she could just start with the first item on her list—assuming that there were no emergencies to deal with.

"Long day?" Zachary asked, looking up from his computer as Kenzie entered the kitchen through the garage door. He rubbed his eyes, and Kenzie could tell that he'd been looking at his screen for too long.

PI's on TV never spent any time on the computer. They chased all their leads down in person and were constantly getting in trouble. They were always on surveillance or asking questions in dark bars. Zachary had cases that were active and required him to be away from the house and dealing with things in person as well, but much of his time was spent on his computer researching, running background, trolling people's social media feeds, and other tasks. Reviewing video footage of crimes and accident scenes or reconstructions wasn't exactly something he could put off or decide not to do. But his red eyes told her he hadn't taken many breaks today.

"You need to put in eye drops, not rub them."

He pulled his fingers away from his eyes, chagrined. "I know. You're right. I just forget…"

"Go put some in now, and then we'll figure out something to do for supper."

He pushed himself up from the couch and headed down the hall. "We can just warm up something frozen," he suggested.

"Yeah." Kenzie kicked off her shoes and put her purse down on the table. She opened the door to the freezer to survey what they had on hand. While having easily prepared frozen meals always seemed like a good idea, she didn't like them that much. The occasional pizza was good, but the pastas never seemed to come out the way she liked them, and frozen burritos…

Zachary joined her after a minute. "Anything look good?"

"Not really," Kenzie admitted. She closed the freezer again. "You're working on the couch? I thought you were trying to use the office more. Better ergonomics."

"I did most of the day. I wanted a change of scenery and to see you when you got in."

He was usually on the couch when she got home, so she wasn't sure how much time he actually spent in the office or whether he just *said* that he used it. She had a feeling he liked to be where he could see the doors. He didn't want to be in a position where someone could sneak in without his knowing it.

But maybe he did use the office the rest of the time. She didn't know. And it didn't really matter. She just liked the idea of his putting it to good use, since most of the time when Kenzie was home and using her laptop, it was with her on her bed propped up against pillows, with the laptop on her knees. Not a good ergonomic choice, but she sat in an office chair all day and, when she got home, she didn't want to feel like she was at the office.

"Do you want to order in, then?" Zachary asked. "Or do you want me to go pick something up?"

"I should just make something," Kenzie opened the door to the fridge and looked at the meager supplies. Why didn't she ever cook anything? It wasn't like she didn't know how. But she never seemed to have the energy to do much and, when she did get around to it, didn't have the ingredients she needed. Because she didn't want them to just languish in the fridge, gradually decomposing. Sort of like at work.

"You've had a long day," Zachary told her. "You don't need to make anything. I can go out for burgers. Thai. We can have something delivered."

"Yeah... I suppose."

"Which?"

"Thai sounds good. But you can order it in. You don't have to pick up."

Zachary nodded. He went to the drawer where they kept the menus and pulled a well-worn one out. Despite the existence of many food-delivery apps, he frequently resorted to a physical menu and called their order in. Maybe he found ordering on the web too distracting, getting caught up in reading social media or checking his email and never actually getting around to ordering a meal.

"So, how was it?" Zachary asked when they sat down on the couch to cuddle and wait for the food. "I know it was long. How bad was it?"

Kenzie sighed. "Had a family member actually show up demanding their loved one's body."

"Oooh... I didn't think you could do that."

"You can't," Kenzie agreed with a smile. "And it wasn't like he thought he could. He was just trying to force us to deal with him. Wanted us to finish the report and release the body to the funeral home."

"But you can't finish until you're finished."

"Yeah. Dr. Wiltshire talked to him, luckily. I didn't have to deal with him by myself. I was there, but Dr. Wiltshire is the Medical Examiner. He's in charge. I just can't believe the audacity of this guy to charge in there, making demands."

"Is he *someone*? I mean, a political figure or someone who expects special treatment?"

"No. At least if he was political, I would know how to deal with him. With all of my father's friends, I know people and how to appeal to their egos. But this guy... no, he isn't anyone special, but he really *really* wants us just to release the body."

"Why?"

"I think... he doesn't know how to move on until we do. I don't know. He said that his dad had been through enough, and he didn't want him to be in limbo anymore. That he wanted him to be able to be free."

Zachary nodded slowly. Like Kenzie, he wasn't religious, so positions like this could be puzzling to them. Did Kyle actually think that his father's spirit was bound until his body was buried? Was it just a metaphor for Kyle being able to bury him and move on emotionally? Or was there another level that Kenzie was missing?

"People can be irrational," Kenzie said. "A death in the family can be traumatic, and they don't know how to deal with it, so they resort to magical thinking. Look for a reason it happened. Look for the magical thing that will make them feel better. But... everyone has to process it, eventually, in their own way."

"What did he mean about what his dad had been through? Had he been sick for a long time?"

"It sounds like it was a few months. We'll need to get his medical records to nail down the timeline exactly, but he was in good health, living independently, then got pneumonia, and then needed help. But the nursing home that he ended up in was— according to the son—negligent and abusive, and his father suffered there. So he pulled him out and took care of him at home, but mentally, his father was never back to where he was before his stay at the nursing home. I guess the son feels like he lost him twice. Or three times. Because he never actually got him back again."

22

I want to follow up on the nursing home," Kenzie said. It had been simmering under the surface for some time. She had been thinking about it in the background, all the time she had been doing other work. It made her more distracted and prone to making mistakes in her work, but she didn't know what to do about that. Someone had to do something about the nursing home. If Joseph Howard had been neglected and abused there, then other people were too, and it was one of the few places available to the working class in Roxboro. To find somewhere else, they would have to go to one of the bigger cities, several hours' drive away. They wouldn't be able to visit except on weekends and holidays. If Sunshine Care had that many problems with their staffing levels, training, or people following the correct policies and procedures, then something needed to be done about it.

"Why don't you, then?" Zachary asked. "You can use your position at the Medical Examiner's Office to at least ask them some questions. See what kind of vibe you get."

"I'm not sure I can do that. I have to be careful when I invoke the Medical Examiner's Office. Because if it is for something that isn't actually work, I could get in pretty big trouble. And if I'm asking questions people don't like, they're going to end up calling

Dr. Wiltshire or someone higher up the food chain to look into it. I don't need that kind of scrutiny. I just want to do my job."

"Doesn't your job include making sure that places like that are safe?"

"Not really. I'm supposed to be assisting Dr. Wiltshire, not pursuing other investigations. And seniors are not exactly my wheelhouse. They do eventually come through my office, of course, but... there might be problems with me asking questions when there hasn't been any indication that there is anything wrong at Sunshine Care. I mean, nothing that relates to any death investigation."

"But it does, when you think about it. If he was there a few months before he died, and he never fully recovered, then that might be a contributing factor in his death."

"It's a stretch," Kenzie said. "A pretty long one!"

"Hmm." Zachary sat with his head against Kenzie's, thinking about it.

"I can't just ignore it. Even if it is nothing to do with my office or my case, I can't just pretend that I didn't hear what the son said about the things he saw there."

"But it's second-hand. You need to see something yourself so that you can report it. Or find something that ties into your investigation that means you need to follow up with them."

"Yeah. And there isn't anything. I already know that. So what do I do?"

"I don't know much about the current laws on reporting child abuse, let alone elder abuse. I guess there probably are laws about it now, but there didn't use to be. No one even realized that it was a thing. I know that with child abuse, some people are required to report anything that they see or suspect—doctors, teachers, social workers—and then other people, like me, not a professional, where I'm not required to report anything by law, but I *should*. But they can't fire me or throw me in jail if I don't."

He snuggled against Kenzie.

"But I would never *not* report something," he assured her.

"I know you wouldn't." Kenzie had no doubt about that fact. Zachary was very concerned about child welfare. He had seen what the system could do to them. He had seen how depraved people could be toward society's most vulnerable, and he would stand in the way of a moving train if he had to in order to protect a child—even one he had never seen before.

"I honestly don't know much about elder abuse reporting either," she admitted. "There must be channels. I'm sure I could find out by one of our police contacts. But like you say; first, I would need something to report, and all I have right now is second-hand. The guy could have been making everything up. Trying to make me feel guilty so that I would go ahead and push everything through before I was ready to."

"Then you should go there... visit... see if you think anything is going on."

"I'm not a private investigator. I don't have the expertise to be sneaking around there, spying on people, ferreting out their secrets."

Zachary was grinning. "You're not trained, but you've done some pretty good work up until now! It's not just medical mysteries that you've been able to solve."

"I don't know. It isn't like anyone would do anything in front of me. I can't exactly go undercover as an old lady. They would know I was an outsider, and they would be careful not to do anything illegal in front of me."

Zachary was biting his lip. "I wouldn't be so sure," he said. "I can remember... I was in a lot of places that were supposed to be under regular inspection: Foster homes, group homes, Bonnie Brown, other facilities. Hospitals, even. When they knew that inspectors were coming by, they would tell everyone to be on their best behavior. They wouldn't say that they didn't want to get in trouble for with the inspectors, or donors, or whoever was coming. But we would know. We would know that they didn't want us to give away that they weren't doing something they were supposed to or that they were covering up something they weren't supposed to do. And we always knew what those things were. I mean, if the parents or administrators act one way in front of the social worker and another way when there isn't anyone else around, then you know what they don't want the social worker to know. That they're abusive, or lock kids up, or don't feed them properly. But the thing is… things happen, even when the administrators are doing their best to keep everything quiet. One kid will talk about getting hit. Or will say they sure wished they had something to eat, or whatever."

Kenzie raised a brow and nodded, encouraging him to go on.

"But when it's just one kid, saying one little thing, then it's easier for the inspectors to ignore it. Everyone else laughs, so the inspector decides it's just a joke and there isn't anything to worry about. Because investigating *one* thing that *one* little kid said is way too involved, with too much paperwork, and it isn't worth it. Inspectors will ignore a lot of little things before they decide that it's serious enough to investigate."

"So you think…" Kenzie tried to round up Zachary's thoughts and corral them into a cogent thought. "That if I go have a look around, I *will* see something because they won't be able to cover everything up. If I pay attention to the little things that everyone else would ignore, then I'll have something I can report."

Zachary nodded, satisfied. "Yeah. You will. They can't cover everything up. They can't keep everyone quiet. Somebody will say or do something to tip you off."

"As long as I don't ignore it."

"Right. It's those little things that tip you off."

Zachary watched a car drive up to the house and pulled away from Kenzie to answer the door. They opened the containers of spicy, hearty dishes at the kitchen table and dished them up.

"I can't go under the auspices of the Medical Examiner's Office," Kenzie said. "So what am I supposed to do?"

"You could get a couple of hours off. Maybe tomorrow afternoon. Because you worked late today and you have some things that need to be done."

"Yes. It's not the hours I'm worried about. Dr. Wiltshire is good at giving me time off if I ask for it. I wouldn't need to say what it was for, just that it was personal. But what would I say showing up at the nursing home? I'm just a random person looking into if there is any abuse going on?"

"Well, I don't think I would recommend that approach," Zachary said, laughing as he added some noodles to his plate. "As a private investigator, I would try to be more subtle about it. Think about who would legitimately show up at a nursing home asking questions and would be allowed to walk around to see what was going on."

"Maybe I'm looking for a nursing home to put my mother into?" Kenzie changed her mind. "My father, actually. I'd rather put him in a home where he couldn't cause any trouble. My mother does a lot of good work."

"You don't think that your father does any good work?" Zachary looked at her. "I thought that with the lobbying he does, he effects changes that are pretty important."

"Well... yes. But as you know, he also causes a lot of grief. And I can't guarantee that he'll be on the same side of the fence as me on anything. My mother doesn't get involved in political stuff, really, just charitable ventures. So I know that she's always helping someone. Dad... I'm never sure."

He nodded his understanding and started to eat. "So, you're putting your dad into a home. And you're hoping to find one that will put him in a straitjacket."

Kenzie snorted and almost inhaled her pad thai. She swore and laughed. "Yeah, that would get me on their good sides, right? I'm sure if I just said I had some questions about their programs and policies and wanted a tour, they'd at least take me around to some of the rooms or public areas. And maybe I would spot something... maybe not..."

"If it was really bad, if your patient was that traumatized by his stay there... it's probably more than one person. If he said he just didn't like this nurse or that orderly, I could believe it was just one person. But what you're talking about, for him to go downhill that much… I think it has to be more than just one or two people, don't you? If you keep your eyes open, and you're willing to believe what you see and not just write it off as an anomaly, as something innocent that you just misinterpreted…"

"You think I'll be able to see something."

Kenzie felt a little sick at the thought. Of course she wanted to go to Sunshine Care and identify if there really were abuse going on so that she could report it to the appropriate authority. Someone would take care of it and save the rest of the residents there from any further trauma.

But she really wanted to go there and be reassured that nothing was going on. That Kyle had made the wrong call. He hadn't seen anything abusive. He had misinterpreted his father's failing health and his reactions. That he hadn't gone through drug withdrawal after he had left Sunshine Care and his violent reactions to Kyle trying to escort him to the bathroom did not have anything to do with sexual abuse he had suffered there.

Or maybe even that Kyle had made it all up, trying to confuse things and convince them that he was a knight in shining armor, a man doing the best he could to help give his elderly father a happy and peaceful life. Not that he had abused or neglected Joseph Howard himself, had wanted his money or some other asset, or just didn't want to take care of a cranky old man anymore.

He wanted her to think that he was diligent and caring, not that he had tied his father down and waited for him to die.

23

Kenzie had talked things through with Zachary and believed she was ready for her foray into Sunshine Care to investigate just how bad their neglect and abuse was. Maybe she wouldn't see anything. She still hoped that she wouldn't see anything and could go back to work knowing that there were no abusers that deserved to be put behind bars working with the vulnerable elderly there.

She was so anxious approaching the nursing home that she nearly turned around and returned to work. Or home. To hide in her bed and pull the covers over her head and pretend that she didn't have any responsibilities. Her intestines were cramping, her heart was racing, her mouth was as dry as cotton and she hadn't even tried to talk to anyone yet. Her hands were shaking so badly that the staff at the nursing home were bound to think that she was the one who needed nursing care rather than her fictional parent.

She parked the car in a visitor slot and took several deep breaths, trying to calm her body down. She tried telling herself a story, hoping her brain would settle down and believe it.

"I'm not doing anything hard. I'm just going to walk in there and look around outside and in the lobby. See if there are residents smoking outside or sitting in the sunshine and make sure they look happy. Nothing hard. Just have a quick look around. Then I can turn around and come back to the car and go home."

Of course, she knew that she wouldn't, but she was willing to tell her body and brain whatever fiction was necessary to calm her autonomic nervous system down a bit.

She took one more deep breath, picked up her purse, and got out of the car. She locked the doors and headed toward the front doors of the Sunshine Care center.

It was a beautiful summer day, with lush greens and colorful flowers that seemed like they would last forever. The grounds were beautiful.

But there were no residents outside smoking or sitting in the sunshine just taking in the rays.

Kenzie supposed it might be risky to allow patients outside if most of them required medical care or were prone to wander. Maybe there was an enclosed courtyard where they could sit outside for fresh air.

She continued to coach herself, walking into the lobby. She looked around, expecting to see a few residents sitting in wheel-chairs enjoying time away from their rooms, sitting at the window, maybe waiting for a visitor. But there weren't any there, either. It was quiet. No PA announcements like in a hospital. No doctors and nurses walking briskly from one place to another. There was a receptionist with a computer at the front desk and no one else in sight. Kenzie swallowed and approached, her mouth still so dry she was sure that the woman would wonder what was the matter with her.

"Uh, hi," she smiled at the woman. "I wondered whether I could see—"

"I know you," the receptionist said in a slightly accusing tone. Kenzie was taken aback. She searched the woman's face, trying to figure out where she might know her from. She was perhaps in her late fifties, with deep creases around her mouth and her hair pulled back in a severe style. Not a bun, but something a little more modern and softer. She still looked like the librarians who constantly shushed Kenzie when she was a little girl. She had loved libraries and reading, but she'd had so many questions. She could never understand why you weren't allowed to talk to others at the library when it was so full of ideas and things to talk about. She probably *had* been too loud but, looking back on it now, Kenzie still thought that the librarians had been wrong to quiet her. It was a power trip. They just wanted to be able to tell kids to be quiet.

Kenzie looked at the nameplate on the receptionist's desk. Sylvie Johnson. She had no idea where she might have run into Sylvie Johnson before.

"I'm sorry, I don't recall…" she said, putting her hand out to shake, as her mother would have directed her. Be gracious and polite. If you don't remember someone, let them know, and then be pleased when they told you who they were.

"You're with the Medical Examiner's Office," Sylvie said in that same accusing tone.

"Uh…" Kenzie couldn't very well deny it. And she couldn't really keep up the fiction that she was there to find a place for her father. If her real identity was known, then she couldn't make things up that could be checked.

"You're here for the inspection. I didn't know they were sending someone from the Medical Examiner's Office. What kind of sense does that make? I suppose you were the one who reported it."

Kenzie swallowed. She raised her brows questioningly. Sylvie clearly had some narrative worked out already. As long as Kenzie didn't blow it by saying the wrong thing, maybe everything would still work out. She was there for an inspection? What kind of inspection would someone from the Medical Examiner's Office be doing there? Though Sylvie's words hinted that it *wasn't* something that the Medical Examiner's Office would normally be involved in.

"I'm not sure how much you were told…" she said tentatively.

If she could get Sylvie to parrot back what she knew, then

Kenzie could work with that information to develop her story. Though she wasn't exactly comfortable with playing into something that she knew was a fiction and they would probably figure out was wrong sometime in the future. Maybe sometime in the *near* future.

"I haven't been told a lot," Sylvie complained. "Someone would be coming to inspect the facilities. I'm supposed to call Dr. Carpenter when you get here, and he'll ensure that you have access to all the areas you need to see."

Kenzie nodded politely. Sylvie rolled her eyes and tapped a few numbers into her phone's keypad.

"Dr. Carpenter, that inspector is here to see you. Dr. Kirsch from the Medical Examiner's Office."

So much for not going there under the auspices of the Medical Examiner's Office. Kenzie had a sinking feeling that it was going to get back to Dr. Wiltshire, and he would not be happy about it when he heard what had happened. But what was she supposed to do? Say that she was with the Medical Examiner's Office but that she wanted to see the nursing home for personal reasons? That it wasn't anything related to a case and she wanted to see it anyway? She didn't know what inspection was going on or how Sylvie had recognized her as Dr. Kirsch from the Medical Examiner's Office, but now she was there and was going to have to go with it. She wasn't sure what she was going to tell Dr. Wiltshire but, hopefully, she would come up with something by the time they saw each other again.

It was only a minute before a doctor, tall and dark and slender, came down the hallway to the lobby. He nodded at Kenzie, readjusted his stethoscope, then reached out his hand to shake.

"Dr. Kirsch? I wasn't expecting the Medical Examiner's Office to get directly involved…"

Kenzie shrugged. "I was in the neighborhood."

It was lame, but at least it was true. They couldn't accuse her of lying about just happening to be there when they were expecting someone to come to inspect the facilities. She hadn't told them that was what she was there for. They were all just making their own assumptions.

"Well, not the best circumstances to meet you under, but I'm... pleased to meet you, I guess. Can I get you coffee, tea, a beverage?"

"I think we should just dive directly in," Kenzie advised. If someone else was going to be showing up for this same inspection, she wanted to be out of the way before that happened. Or at least to be most of the way through her tour by that time.

"Fair enough," Dr. Carpenter acknowledged. "Just follow me..."

24

Kenzie did so. He led her through a few hallways. Kenzie tried to keep track of where she was and take in everything she could as she went by patient rooms, large accessible bathrooms and showers, and nursing stations. There were no patients in the hallways. In a lot of the places she had visited—hospitals, Champlain House, and others—there were usually patients visiting, stretching their legs, getting some time out of their rooms. But everyone at Sunshine seemed to be confined to their rooms. Maybe Carpenter had taken her to the wing that housed the most severely afflicted patients first.

Most patient room doors were open, but a few were closed. Kenzie assumed that those patients either had visitors or were being examined or treated by staff. She was uncomfortable with the closed doors, having heard what she had from Kyle Howard.

"It's very quiet," she said to Carpenter, interrupting his tour guide spiel about the facility.

He looked at her for a minute as if he couldn't believe that she would be so rude as to interrupt him and was waiting for an apology. Kenzie looked back and didn't apologize. If there was abuse going on at Sunshine, then there was no reason for her to apologize. And if there weren't... then it was time for Carpenter to actually show her something instead of just walking her down the hall and expecting her to sign off on whatever inspection she was supposed to be doing based on her view of the green walls and shiny floor.

"It is quiet," he agreed. "This is a place for people to rest. How would you feel if you came here sick and could never get to sleep because people were always shouting, talking over the PA, or playing music? We want people to be able to get the rest and sleep that they need. To be able to think clearly without a bunch of outside stimulation distracting them."

"I was expecting there to be some common areas where patients could get together to play cards or watch TV. Don't they have any socialization or entertainment?"

"Patients can visit each other. They usually see each other in their rooms. A lot of them have a card table and a couple of folding chairs if they like to play games or do puzzles. There are TVs in most of the patient rooms. We prefer them to meet in their rooms rather than in communal areas. It is much easier to find patients if they're in their rooms, and they're less likely to spread viruses around if they meet in smaller groups rather than in crowds. It is hard to keep a large communal space virus-free, and many of our residents are very susceptible."

Kenzie had not seen any patients sitting at card tables as she had walked by the open doors of patient rooms. Maybe that was what they were doing in the rooms that were closed, but it was impossible to know. She didn't like Carpenter's explanation. Her suspicions were adding up.

Not that she had gone into it without any bias.

"What is your patient turnover like? Do you have a lot of people coming and going?"

"Well, I'm sure you understand that this is a care facility. The people being admitted have significant medical issues that need more care than an independent living facility can manage. So there are not a lot of move-ins and move-outs. But there are move-ins and… vacancies."

"People who pass," Kenzie said with an understanding nod.

And because the people in the home were under medical care, those bodies would not come to the Medical Examiner's Office unless the doctor supervising their care or someone in their family requested an autopsy. She wouldn't know if they had bruises, ligature marks, or signs of sexual abuse because she would never see them. As long as there wasn't anything that particularly alarmed a funeral home or loved one, the deceased could simply be buried or cremated without any investigation.

Because legislators had assumed doctors would always be honest and have their patients' best interests in mind.

"Do you have a lot of vacancies right now?"

He shook his head. "Two or three. About normal. It takes time to get rooms cleaned out and to get the next person in, but not too long. We try not to keep a waiting list—that is, we accommodate everyone we can and advise them to seek another facility if we don't have the space—but it is never long before the next admittance."

"You're in demand, then."

"Oh yes." Carpenter nodded, looking pleased with himself. "Very much so. We are one of the only affordable care facilities in the area. Imagine trying to get one of your parents the care they need, yet not being able to afford to give it to them."

"But it still costs thousands of dollars."

He stared at her. "Of course it does. Medical care costs money. We have overhead. Salaries. Maintenance. It isn't cheap to run a facility like this."

Even if they received government funding, which Kenzie was sure they did, there would still be a lot of costs to cover.

"I'd like to see some of the patient rooms. Talk to a few people, if I can."

"Talk to who?" He was immediately resistant.

"To patients. To see what the care level is like. Whether they have any complaints."

"No one has any complaints. I can show you our files. If

anyone has any complaints, we have a process for them to go through. And I can assure you, there have not been any recently."

"People might not always tell you," Kenzie pointed out. "They feel anxious about talking to you and only talk to their family members. Or just keep quiet, because they don't want to make waves. But that doesn't mean that there aren't actually things going on that need to be addressed."

"The Department did not say anything about you talking to patients."

Kenzie leveled a glare at him. He looked slightly cowed but did not back down.

"What kind of an inspection did you think this is?" Kenzie demanded.

"Well..." Carpenter seemed to wilt a bit at her hard line. "I just didn't think... I didn't think you would want to disturb the patients."

"Talking to patients is part of the process. I don't see how you could think we could proceed without talking to a few of them. And I would like to talk to some of your staff members as well."

"Yes... I'm sure we could make someone available." Carpenter's words were compliant and respectful, but his face twisted into a grimace. Not happy with either of these requests.

"And do you have an accident log? What other records do you keep to ensure that the standard of care is kept up?"

"We don't have a separate log. Any kind of accident would be written in individual patient files. But we don't have very many. Usually only if a patient is not compliant with the facility's rules. Some of our dementia patients, for instance." He gave a slight shrug with one shoulder. "They don't understand. We keep a close eye on them, but they sometimes take advantage of an opportunity if a door is left open or a staff member is distracted. It is impossible to keep anything from happening."

"Of course," Kenzie agreed. She hadn't expected the facility to be accident-free. And if there were physical abuse and neglect going on, they probably had more than their fair share of accidents to cover up unexplained bruises or other injuries. "I would like to see how you track those."

"I don't know…"

"I'm sure you know if there are any patients who have had accidents lately."

"As I said, there isn't a central log."

"And you don't deal with any of the patients directly? You don't get reports when there is an accident?"

"Well, yes, we follow all of the policies and procedures that we are required to, but…"

"Then you must know who has been injured lately, so I can follow up. Look at the file. Talk to the patient."

"They won't be able to talk to you."

"None of the patients?"

He looked trapped. Kenzie watched him, amused, as he tried to think his way out of the corner he had just talked himself into. She was no longer feeling so anxious and tongue-tied herself. She was actually enjoying digging down to find the truth, exhilarated that she had gotten as far as she had. But she was still anxious that the real inspector from the Department of whatever would show up any minute and spoil her success.

"Well… of course some of our patients would be able to talk to you, but you have to understand that these people are old and frail, and many of them don't remember what happened from one day to the next. If they can't remember, then they are prone to confabulation. I don't know if you know what that is?"

It had been a while since Kenzie had heard the word. But she remembered it well enough.

"It is when you are missing a memory, so your brain fills in the space, but the memory that you have is not necessarily what happened. And you may not know that it isn't a real memory, but just something that your brain came up with that fits the gap."

He nodded. "And at this age… there are a lot of gaps. It doesn't mean that they are consciously making things up or doing it for attention. Nothing like that. It just means… that you can't trust what they say."

Kenzie nodded. "So disregard it if it doesn't make sense." She remembered what Zachary had said about any resident's slip of the tongue being laughed off as a joke. Passing it off as confabulation worked just as well.

Carpenter nodded sagely. "Yes. And even if it does… you have to look at everything they say under a microscope. Is it *really* likely that's what happened? There's no point in confronting them because they don't know that they have made it up, but you can't assume that any memories are genuine."

"I'll keep that in mind."

Carpenter looked uncertain. He probably didn't know whether to be happy that Kenzie said she would keep it in mind or to be upset that she hadn't backed off on her request to talk to patients since they wouldn't necessarily be accurate in their accounts anyway. Apparently, he had been hoping that she would take his word, or what was recorded in the file, as gospel, and not bother to follow up with the unreliable patients.

"So," Kenzie said briskly. "Which patient should we talk to first?"

25

Kenzie knew that Carpenter would try to manipulate the inspection with his choice of what patients he allowed her to see. Of course he would try to portray the institution in the best possible light. He didn't want the place to get shut down, to lose its certification, or whatever other effects there might be if Kenzie reported that there was abuse going on at the facility. But she suspected it wasn't nearly that easy to get a nursing home shut down. For them to actually decide to do that, the abuse would have to be rampant. They would have to have multiple reports of abuse. It would have to be clear that it was something the management had ignored or endorsed. If Sunshine Care were shut down, they would have to find somewhere else to move each one of the patients, and there wasn't anywhere else in town that could take them. Especially not at the price they were paying. Things would have to be pretty bad for the government to decide to shut them down permanently. Kenzie couldn't see it happening.

"This is Martha," Carpenter introduced, taking Kenzie into one of the patient rooms with the door standing open. "Martha. Martha, are you awake? Can you wake up and talk to the doctor for a minute here?"

She lay still on the bed, mouth open, snoring lightly. Dr.

Carpenter approached the bed and shook her. "Martha? Martha, wake up."

It took a great deal of shaking for Martha to stir. Kenzie had been worried, ready to step in and start CPR. Though CPR at Martha's stage in life probably would not be welcome. Kenzie would be sure to break ribs, and they would be very painful. Martha probably had a DNR order. Probably everyone in the facility had a Do Not Resuscitate so that when their heart stopped, they would not be revived.

Martha opened her eyes and blinked. She licked her lips with a wet tongue and lay there smacking her lips for a few minutes like she was eating her breakfast.

"Hello, Martha," Kenzie greeted, positioning herself right in front of the woman so she was at eye level. "How are you doing?"

"She can't hear you," Carpenter said. "She's mostly deaf."

Kenzie raised her voice and tried again, speaking slowly, hoping that the woman would be able to read her lips and make out what she was saying.

"Martha? How are you?"

"That's nice, dear," Martha said, patting Kenzie's hand. "Nice you could come."

"Martha, my name is Kenzie Kirsch. I'm just checking in to see how you are feeling. I believe you had a fall last week?"

That was what Carpenter had told her, though he hadn't yet shown her the file backing his story up.

"What's that?" Martha asked.

"A fall. Did you fall down last week?"

"Yes, yes. That's right."

Kenzie wasn't sure she had understood a word Kenzie had said.

"What happened? Can you tell me about it?"

More lip smacking. Martha looked at Kenzie, smiling toothlessly. "What's that?"

"Did you fall last week? How did you fall?"

"Did I fall?" Martha repeated.

So she could hear something, at least! Kenzie nodded and

waited. Martha had a cast on her wrist, but she didn't look at it or show it to Kenzie to indicate that she had made a connection between what had happened to her and the broken wrist.

Kenzie nodded, encouraging Martha to tell her more.

"What's that?" Martha asked again. She turned her gaze to Dr. Carpenter.

"Who is this? Why is she here? Is she my daughter?"

"No, Martha," Carpenter said loudly. "She wants to know about your fall. About breaking your wrist."

He indicated the cast, and Martha held it up in front of her face, peering at it as if she had never seen it before.

"Is this what I did?"

"That's what happened, Martha," Dr. Carpenter agreed. "Do you remember falling?'"

"No." Martha turned her arm this way and that. "Did I fall down?"

"You must have really hurt yourself," Kenzie suggested.

Martha nodded when Kenzie spoke to her, acting like she understood and they were having a conversation, but her eyes were vague, and it was pretty clear that she had no idea what they were talking about.

"Does your daughter visit you often?" Kenzie asked, trying a different conversational approach.

"My daughter?" Martha tried to push herself up in the bed, but couldn't readjust her position. Kenzie didn't see any restraints, but she wondered whether there was a belt around Martha's waist under the blanket to prevent her from moving around in the bed. "Have you seen my daughter?"

"She visited you last week, Martha," Dr. Carpenter assured her in a loud voice.

But then, in a quieter aside, he spoke to Kenzie. "Her daughter died a few years ago. She doesn't remember."

Kenzie opened her mouth to object to him telling Martha that her daughter had been visiting the previous week. It was always better to tell the truth rather than to encourage further confabulation.

But was it really better that she be told, again, that her daughter had predeceased her and that she would never see her again? It seemed needlessly cruel to keep telling her that. Wasn't it better to tell Martha that her daughter was visiting her there weekly, that she was a loving and caring daughter, than that Martha was all alone and would never see her again? She looked at Carpenter. He was watching her expectantly, interested in seeing how she felt about this, whether she would continue the fiction or not.

"Did you tell your daughter how you fell?" Kenzie asked instead.

Martha looked at the cast on her arm. "I fell and hurt my hand."

"Yes. Do you remember how that happened?"

Martha shook her head. "Maybe someone pushed me?" she suggested.

Carpenter looked at Kenzie, shrugging as if to say, "What did I tell you?"

"Maybe we could talk to another patient," Kenzie conceded.

Carpenter patted Martha's shoulder, and they left the room.

"You must have some patients who are able to hold a conversation and remember what happened from one day to the next," Kenzie told him irritably.

He lifted his hands palms up in a helpless gesture. "I told you the kind of patients we are dealing with here. People don't come here just because they can't go up and down stairs anymore. They come here when they can't take care of themselves and their families cannot take care of them. They are too far gone to have much of a conversation with."

26

Kenzie looked around at the rooms branching off from the hallway. She knew that it couldn't be true. There would be a range of patients in the facility. Carpenter was trying to prevent her from talking to the people who could give her straight answers about what was going on in the nursing home. She walked over to one of the other rooms and entered. Carpenter came scurrying after her, objecting.

"You can't go just anywhere you please!"

"Oh? Is that what you'll tell my supervisor?"

"Patients have their right to privacy. The right not to be harassed by people like you, people they don't even know. Would you like to be in here and have random strangers coming in to look at you and ask you questions?"

Kenzie looked at the name over the patient's bed. "Hello, Ms. Stuart. How are you feeling this afternoon?"

"Oh, it's Monica," the woman said, waving the formality away. "Just Monica, dear." Her eyes were quick and alert. She looked Kenzie over and shook her head. "I don't remember seeing you before. Are you new here?"

Her eyes flashed over to Carpenter. She didn't greet him.

"I'm just visiting today," Kenzie explained. "I wanted to get to know a few of the residents here, find out what kind of a place it is."

"Well… I guess when you're here, you know you're at the end of the road, so it doesn't matter what it's like. You're here until the end."

"We still want to make sure that you're getting the care that you need. That they're at least making you comfortable and taking care of your needs for as long as you are here," Kenzie told her.

"I guess it's good enough."

"Monica gets everything she needs, don't you, Monica?" Carpenter encouraged.

She looked at him for a minute. Her eyes returned to Kenzie slowly. "Of course. I get everything I need."

"Maybe I could talk to Monica alone," Kenzie suggested.

"I don't think there's anything in the policies that says I have to leave you alone with a patient," Carpenter countered. "We need to protect our residents, you know. And protect you. You wouldn't want to be accused of doing anything to hurt her. Sometimes patients can get agitated. They think someone is stealing from them or wants to do something to hurt them. We can avoid any unfounded accusations by staying together."

Kenzie looked for a way around the argument. But of course, he was right. In the current political climate. The potential victim of an assault was taken at their word, and it was up to the accused person to prove that they hadn't done anything. And how was Kenzie or anyone else to prove a negative?

But Kenzie was sure that the two-person was not required every time a staff member entered a patient's room. It would have required twice the staffing, double the cost, and Sunshine Care would not be able to maintain its favorable pricing structure.

"You haven't had any concerns about the care here?" Kenzie asked Monica. "No complaints?"

Monica sighed. "What good would complaining do? I'm an old woman. I don't have anywhere else to go. In a few weeks or months, I'll be on to higher climes."

"The food is good?" Kenzie tried. "And they make sure that you get all of your meds when you are supposed to?"

"Sometimes, it is a long time between meals." Monica looked back at Kenzie and forced a bright smile. "But what do you expect when all there is to do all day is sit around waiting? Time is relative."

"I guess so," Kenzie agreed. "You don't have any books? What about games with the other residents? I hear that there are some card games going on…" She gave Monica a mischievous smile. "I suppose you're trying to keep me from finding out that you're skinning all of the other old ladies for their pension checks."

"Oh, I wouldn't do that," Monica laughed. Her expression sobered. "I wouldn't mind playing a game or two, but I'm the one who is more likely to be fleeced."

"Maybe there is some action in one of the rooms close by?" Kenzie suggested to Carpenter.

He shrugged. "I don't keep up on any ad hoc games the residents might put on. It's nothing to do with me. The patients can do what they like on that score."

"So they can get out of their beds and visit each other."

It was several seconds before Carpenter answered, his eyes fixed on Monica. "Of course the residents can get out of their beds and visit each other."

Kenzie was pretty sure that the look he shot at Monica was a warning that she was never to try. Monica smiled and didn't say anything back.

"We have our patients' best interests in mind," Carpenter reiterated. "This is a wonderful place to be. They're fortunate to have been able to get in rather than being on a waiting list somewhere. Parked in the hallway of the hospital."

Kenzie knew only too well that emergency cases were often kept in halls until a bed opened up. Sometimes for several days. She couldn't imagine that was very comfortable. Trying to sleep in a busy area while everyone did their best to ignore her. Saying nothing to her except to curse when they tripped over her.

"We couldn't ask for anywhere better," Monica said to Kenzie in a monotone.

The emphasis on not being able to ask rather than the possibility of there being somewhere better.

"Well, it was nice to meet you," Kenzie told Monica, giving her a nod. "I'd like to hear from you if you think of anything that you would like to share…" She looked at Carpenter and didn't feel right about giving Monica a business card. What would Monica think about having a visitor from the Medical Examiner's Office? It seemed sort of like having a visit from the grim reaper. And Kenzie didn't have a card from the Department that was supposed to be conducting the investigation, because she wasn't actually on that team. Not having a card for them would probably be a tip-off to Dr. Carpenter that there was something not quite right going on.

"It was nice visiting with you, too," Monica said politely. Kenzie led the way out of the room, eyeing Carpenter and wondering how much longer she would be able to pull off the charade. Sooner or later, the actual investigator was going to get there. Everyone was afraid to say anything in front of Carpenter, which meant she had nothing she could use.

Kenzie was about to suggest that they wrap up the tour. But as she turned around, trying to get her bearings, she heard something.

27

Kenzie cocked her head, trying to catch the thread of sound. It sounded like sobbing.

"Help me... please help me..."

She tried to figure out what direction it was coming from. There were no nurses around who seemed to be paying any attention to the crying. What few she had seen were always walking purposefully toward something. Avoiding having to accept any assignment from Dr. Carpenter as he made his way around the facility. Trying to appear to the inspector like they were hard at work and didn't have a spare moment.

"Where is that coming from?" she asked Carpenter, still trying to pinpoint it. She remembered what Kyle had said about their not taking care of someone who had fallen, just leaving him to lie on the floor crying.

It was possible that they had just gone to get a lift or piece of equipment to help get the patient back on his feet or into bed or had gone to get a partner to help to lift the man up. Just because there was no one there to help when he thought there should be, that didn't mean that they were ignoring his needs. Just that it took time to get there.

Or it could be that the man was on the floor crying because he had already been there for an hour or two and despaired of ever getting the help he needed.

And the man that Kenzie could hear crying? Was she going to ignore it just because she didn't have a contract with the nursing home? It wasn't her job to pick up people who had fallen—or to be at the hospital interviewing patients to find out if there were abuse. But she knew she couldn't just walk away and let someone lie there, potentially hurt.

Kenzie walked down the hallway, looking in the open doors. She didn't find anyone lying on the floor, but she eventually pinpointed the man who was sobbing and asking for help. He was lying in bed, not on the floor. Nothing seemed to be out of place. Nothing seemed to be wrong except that he was crying for help and no one but Kenzie and Dr. Carpenter seemed to be close enough to hear him and respond.

"Sir, what's wrong?" Kenzie walked in and got close enough to read the name on the placard over the bed. "Mr. Baker? Can I help you with something?"

He moaned. "Would you hand me that cup?" he begged. "I am so thirsty. I haven't had anything to eat or drink all day!"

Kenzie picked up the cup with the straw on it on the night table shelf next to the bed. She guided the straw toward the man's lips and held it there while he sipped. Despite his complaint that he hadn't had anything to eat or drink, he only had a swallow or two before resting his head back on his pillow again.

"Do you need some more?" Kenzie prompted. "That wasn't very much. If you're really thirsty…"

"The nurses here won't ever answer me. Every time I want something, they tell me to keep quiet and wait, and I'll get every-thing I need." Tears ran down his old, wrinkled cheeks. "But they don't give me everything I need. I beg and I beg, and they just laugh and say the sooner I die, the sooner they'll be able to get someone else in my room."

"Why would they want someone else in your room?" Kenzie asked.

Dr. Carpenter was standing right there, but his glowers didn't seem to have any effect on this patient.

"Because I ask for too much," the man explained, another tear rolling down his cheek. "They say I'm too demanding and they want someone who will be quiet and do what he's told."

Kenzie held the cup for him again as he licked his lips and looked toward her. He had another sip.

"I'm sorry to hear that," Kenzie soothed, though she really wasn't. She was excited to find at least *some* concrete evidence that patients were not being taken care of quite as well as they should have been. There *were* complaints, even if Dr. Carpenter wanted to cover them up.

"I'm sure it isn't as bad as all that," Carpenter said dismissively. "Our patients are all taken care of very well. It may be that he thinks he has been neglected for too long, but nurses cannot be running into the room every time he wants a sip of water. He looks fine to me."

Kenzie wasn't so sure. It had been some time since she'd had live patients, but Mr. Baker seemed thin and frail. His skin was papery and dry. She patted his hand, then took a moment to pinch and pull up a small section of skin on the back of his hand and watched to see how long it took to sink back down into its natural position. The skin stood there, peaked—tented, to use the technical term—and didn't settle back into place quickly.

"Mr. Baker is dehydrated. Maybe someone could come in more often to give him a drink if he is not going to be put on an IV. It can be dangerous for someone this old to be dehydrated. Things can happen very quickly."

"You don't need to tell me the dangers of dehydration," Dr. Carpenter said, a bit of a growl in his words. And he should have known better. He should have known when Mr. Baker first started to complain that there might be a problem. If Kenzie could see it, then shouldn't someone who worked with live seniors regularly see that the man was dehydrated and not feeling very well?

"I'll get a nurse to start an IV," Dr. Carpenter told her. "That will fix him right up."

"I don't want folks poking and prodding me," Mr. Baker protested. "I just want a drink. I just want someone to come when I call."

"Of course," Kenzie told him. "But you're so thirsty and not feeling well because you haven't been getting enough fluids. When they top you up with IV fluids, you'll feel much better."

"I don't like to be poked."

"I know. But you'll feel much better."

"He'll probably pull it back out," Carpenter told Kenzie. "Some of these people you can't keep an IV on. You have to wrap their arm so that they can't bend it and can't reach the IV to pull it out. It's not as easy as you think."

"They're people, not machines," Kenzie agreed. People didn't just behave the way they should, the way you expected them to. She had learned that much during her medical training. You had to reach them and explain things to them. And even then, sometimes old folks couldn't remember from the time you started the explanation to when you were finished what you were talking about. They would still be surprised and dismayed that you thought they needed to have an IV or whatever the procedure was that needed to be performed. Some patients would fight and argue with you the whole way, even if they knew that you would get your way in the end.

"Are you going to write it on his chart?" Kenzie asked when Dr. Carpenter headed for the door, clearly finished dealing with this patient.

"This isn't a hospital. I'll tell the nursing staff when I see them."

"You should write it down so that you don't forget—"

"You seem to think that you have some kind of authority over me," Carpenter snapped. "But you don't. You're here as a guest to observe, not to tell me what to do. I am in charge of this facility and will run it as I see fit."

"I just meant that you might forget before you have a chance to tell the nurses, since they are not here..."

"I am not going to forget."

"Okay. I'm sorry."

Dr. Carpenter looked at his large gold watch. "I think it is all of the time I can spare for this visit," he said. "I'm sure you've had a chance to see everything that you needed to?"

Kenzie hadn't seen as much as she had hoped. She had some indicators that something was going on at Sunshine Care, but she wasn't sure there would be enough for her to make a complaint or get anything done. There hadn't been anything that was outright proof of abuse or neglect despite Mr. Baker's tears and Monica's wary looks in Carpenter's direction.

"Before I leave, do you think I could..." Kenzie motioned toward the bathroom attached to Mr. Baker's room. "Use the facilities?"

"We don't have public restrooms here," Carpenter pointed out.

"Yes, I noticed that. That's why I wondered if I could duck in here for a minute..."

Carpenter rolled his eyes. "Fine, yes. Just be quick about it."

He didn't say, "Don't try anything," but he clearly would have liked to.

Kenzie let herself into the private bathroom and looked at Carpenter as she closed the door, wondering what he would do once she was out of sight.

She intentionally took a few minutes too long to return to Mr. Baker's room. Carpenter was standing in the hallway outside the door, talking on his phone. Kenzie smiled, glad to see that he was distracted from her and Mr. Baker.

"Say cheese for the camera," she told Mr. Baker softly.

In another minute, she was striding along the halls at Dr. Carpenter's side, being escorted back to the main lobby, where she would be expected to leave immediately.

28

Kenzie had been planning to go directly home after visiting the nursing home. She had told Dr. Wiltshire that she had something personal to take care of and would be back on Thursday morning. But she was only partway home when her phone rang. Checking the call display, she saw that it was Dr. Wiltshire. She answered immediately, ready to deal with a question about where she had left something or an emergency call-out.

"Doctor?"

"Kenzie... I hate to do this, but I wonder if you could come back to the office."

"Uh..." Kenzie waited for more information, hoping that if he needed her to find something for him, he would just say what it was, and she could tell him where to look. Or if there were an emergency procedure or a scene he wanted her to attend to, she would be happy to take care of it. "Sure, of course...?"

"Thank you. I'll explain when you get here."

He terminated the call. Kenzie flipped up her turn indicator and took the next turn.

What did he want to talk to her about? It was probably

nothing important. Just a question that he wanted to ask her or a file he needed to review. What else would it be?

But of course, she knew that it might be something else. That he had found out she had overstepped her boundaries and involved herself in some investigation that she should not have. He wouldn't call her back to the office for something unimportant.

Her stomach was roiling when she got to her desk. She wasn't sure whether to sit down and see what had come in while she was gone or to go directly to Dr. Wiltshire.

She knew that she should go to see him directly. She was just hoping for an excuse or distraction to do something else instead. Kenzie took a few breaths, hoping to calm herself down, but it wasn't working. Her body was still just as tense and tight as it had been, anticipating trouble. She continued to Dr. Wiltshire's office.

Kenzie knocked on Dr. Wiltshire's open door and walked in.

Wiltshire took off his rectangular-framed glasses and rubbed the bridge of his nose. "Have a seat, Kenzie."

She obeyed. She didn't like that he was looking so tired or annoyed. Did he just need to go home, but had to deal with something else that had come up instead? It might be one of their old cases, something that had come back with more evidence or additional questions from the police.

"What can I do for you, Doctor?"

"Well..." He rubbed both temples with a circular movement as he considered. "You can tell me exactly what you thought you were doing over at Sunshine Care."

"Oh." Kenzie leaned back in her chair and closed her eyes. How was she going to explain what had happened? She hardly knew herself how everything had resulted in her taking a tour of the facility as an expected guest inspector. "I... that's a tricky one."

"Really." He sounded very disappointed in her. Kenzie tried to figure out where to begin and how to frame it.

"Here's the thing... After Kyle Howard was in here, I couldn't stop thinking about Sunshine Care and what a bad time his father had had there. I was worried that if we didn't do something about it, that there would be other people in the same situation. Neglected or abused, stuck there with no one to help them. Not everyone will have a son as diligent as Kyle at getting them out of there when he realized there was a problem."

"Of course. I had my concerns as well."

Kenzie opened her mouth, trying to line up the next step. She didn't have any excuse for proceeding without talking to him. She and Dr. Wiltshire could have worked something out together. Or at least, if they had talked about it, Kenzie would have known better what she was getting into when she had gone home to Zachary and discussed strategies with him.

"That is why I filed a formal report with the Department of Disabilities, Aging and Independent Living." Dr. Wiltshire said. "As I am mandated to do within forty-eight hours of becoming aware of any elder abuse."

Kenzie swallowed and nodded. "Oh. I didn't realize that. You didn't say anything about it."

He nodded. "Clearly, we should have talked after that meeting. But I thought you needed to go home to Zachary and to get some rest. I didn't realize that you were going to…" He shook his head slowly, frowning. "I have no idea what you did. What you thought you were doing going to Sunshine Care."

"Well… I… I didn't intend for things to happen like they did. Initially, I just thought I would go there, have a quick look around, see if it is a place that we could recommend people to. Maybe talk to some residents having a smoke break outside. Talk to a nurse or two to get an idea of whether anything was going on there. Because I didn't have anything concrete, just the comments that Kyle made, and they could be totally wrong. He could be making it all up. Trying to make himself feel better by pretending it wasn't his fault. That someone else had done something worse and he was just trying to fix things."

"I see. And yet… you ended up doing quite a bit more than that, didn't you?"

"I guess I did," Kenzie admitted, the knot in her stomach very painful, and she was starting to feel nauseated.

"You went over there, holding yourself out as a representative of this office and of the Department there to inspect the facility, making an end run around the actual legitimate inspection that was in process."

"I didn't mean to do that. What I had planned was…" Kenzie stopped and considered. Was it really better to tell him about the plan she had worked out with Zachary? It all seemed very silly to her now—their great covert operation. "What I had planned to do was to go there as a potential client looking for somewhere to put my father. To ask for a tour or ask other questions that I had about their facility and the policies and procedures. Just to see if there were any red flags, anything that I could pass on to the police as evidence that there *was* neglect and abuse going on there."

"I see. Your father is ready for the nursing home, is he?" Dr. Wiltshire asked wryly. He knew who her father was and obviously thought it amusing that she would say that he was in need of care and supervision.

"No, I know that. It was just a line to see if I could get inside. Just for a peek into what was going on. To see if I could find anything that could be used as evidence, or at least a corroborating account."

"But that's not what happened. How did you end up on an official inspection tour?"

"That's on them, not me." Kenzie sighed and shook her head. "I walk up to the reception desk, and the woman there says, 'I know who you are' and calls the doctor. She announces me *by name and department* and says that I am there for the inspection. I didn't know what was going on or what else to do. They were offering me a tour, so why not take it?"

"Because you were doing so under false pretenses."

"But I wasn't; they're the ones who made a mistake. I never even told them my name. They made all of these assumptions, and they knew who I was."

"Because the Medical Examiner had made a report to the

Department about the possibility of abuse."

"But I didn't know that. And... *they* shouldn't have known that. How did they know that you had made a report and who I was when I got there? Aren't the names of the people who make reports kept confidential?"

"I don't know who screwed up. Someone at the Department clearly told Sunshine that they were under investigation and an inspector would be coming. And that it was something to do with the Medical Examiner's Office." Dr. Wiltshire admitted. "I suspect that after they found out about the report, they looked us up on the website, where there are pictures of both of us and other members of the team. So when you walked in, they recognized you. Knew who you were and what you were there for. Except that you weren't."

"I was only going to ask some general questions about a room for my dad and see if anything came up... the way that Kyle described things, I didn't think it would be too hard to spot someone who had fallen and wasn't being helped up, or staff that felt 'off.' I just thought that if I could look around a little, I could get something more concrete."

"You should have talked to me before going on this exploration. Especially under the umbrella of this office."

"I never intended for that to happen. I'm not sure I could have anticipated this would be the outcome..."

"Maybe not," Wiltshire agreed. "But for the purposes of this discussion, you *did* conduct an inspection under the guise of this office and the Department. Which makes it very difficult for the actual inspector who is supposed to be there to do his job. As far as the nursing home is concerned, they've already had to go out of their way to give one person a tour and don't want to do it again."

"I'm sorry. That was all unintentional."

"I see how it happened. But I'm not sure that is any excuse. You planned to go down there and snoop around and lie about who you were or why you were there in order to get something concrete. There are established protocols."

"Yeah. I'm sorry." Kenzie licked her lips. "Who called you? Was it someone at the Department, or..."

"Oh, no. I got a call directly from the nursing home the minute you stepped out their doors."

"I'm sorry. Was he really ticked off?"

"I think you could say that. He was not impressed with your visit and I think he had his suspicions that you were not the appropriate person to be there making the inspection. The actual inspector from the Department hadn't shown up yet for the actual inspection."

"What tipped him off?"

"You never presented an ID badge, letter of introduction, or inspection order. And I would guess that they've had an inspection there before and you were not doing the same thing as they had seen done in the past."

"I never planned to hold myself out as a representative of the Department, believe me."

"But you did. Even if you just accepted what they assumed, you still acted as if you were."

Kenzie nodded. "Yes. I guess I did."

"That is grounds for dismissal. You are a valuable member of this office, but something like that works against the reputation that we've tried so hard to develop here."

Kenzie swallowed and breathed through an open mouth, unable to get enough air. "Are you...?" She couldn't even bring herself to say the words.

"I am not firing you. As I say, you are very valuable to this department. But I can't have you going rogue on me, either. I need to be able to trust that you are going to do the work that I give you but not go off-track investigating something that you're not authorized to do. We have the public's trust. We need to hold ourselves to a high standard."

"Okay. Thank you. And... I'm really sorry."

"I'm glad to hear it. Now... what did you find out?"

29

Kenzie looked at Dr. Wiltshire to make sure that he was serious, and that was the end of the discussion of her being terminated. He didn't suggest any disciplinary action that might be taken against her for her failure to represent the Medical Examiner's Office in the best light. He gave her a firm nod and put his glasses back on.

Kenzie let out her breath. "Okay... well... not a lot that is conclusive, but I can understand why Kyle had his suspicions. There is definitely... a culture there. It didn't feel like a hospital, and it didn't have the same atmosphere as at Champlain House. I don't have much experience with senior communities or nursing homes, so those are my reference points. It felt more like... a warehouse for old people. Get them in, get as much of their money as you can, and just..." Kenzie frowned, trying to put it into words. "Do as little as possible until they die, and you can get the next person in their place."

"What were your impressions of the director? Dr. Carpenter?"

"I don't know. I didn't like him, but that's a personal judgment. I don't think he's that involved in the day-to-day care of the patients. He couldn't tell me any of the patient histories. I tried to get a log of accidents residents have had, and they don't keep one.

He said those things are just noted on their personal files, not in any central location. He didn't show me any of the patient files, but there wasn't anything on the chart of the one patient I talked to who had a fall with an injury. And he didn't note anything about the one gentleman's complaints about his calls being ignored or about the fact that he was dehydrated. He didn't mark any orders down on the chart and didn't call anyone to take care of it while I was there. Older people with dehydration can deteriorate very quickly. If I had discovered a patient in the hospital who was that dehydrated, I would have ensured that an IV was hooked up within a few minutes. Either do it myself or see that someone else was working on it before I left the room. I can't understand it."

"Unless, as you say, they are only warehousing people and don't care how ill they might be."

"They take a lot of money for deposit when patients first arrive there, and that's non-refundable, so it is more advantageous for them to keep bringing new people in than it is for them to preserve the health of the people who are already there. Best to keep moving people through the system so that you can get more new admits."

Dr. Wiltshire nodded, holding his hands palm-to-palm and tapping his lips gently. "It is a commercial enterprise."

"Very much so," Kenzie agreed. "And it feels like one. Not like… a resting place."

"And restraints? Did you find out what their policy is on restraints?"

"No. There were restraints on the beds of the rooms that I went into, even if they weren't in use. One woman—the one who had fallen and broken her wrist—I think she was strapped into her bed under the covers, but I couldn't see for sure. I wasn't about to go whipping her covers off…"

"No," Dr. Wiltshire agreed. "It doesn't sound like these people are being treated with much dignity, but we don't want to take what little they have."

"Yeah. I don't doubt that those who are most mobile are probably frequently restrained. There aren't any patients walking the halls or congregating in common areas. They are all in their rooms." Kenzie raised her brows at him and emphasized this. "*All* of them."

"That is unusual, in my experience with nursing homes. There are usually places where they can get together to watch TV, play games, do puzzles, or just talk with friends or visitors. They usually try to keep the patients as active as possible, encouraging them to get out of bed and do things. People stay healthier when they are more active."

Kenzie nodded her agreement. She was glad that Dr. Wiltshire agreed with her assessment of the conditions at the nursing home. It would have been difficult if she'd had to argue her points. It was hard enough admitting that she should not have been there and should have made it clear to them that she was not the inspector that they were expecting. She had been willing to push that boundary to get a better result. Maybe she would have seen the same things on a personal guided tour for the caretaker of a potential new resident; but she probably would not have been allowed to go into the patient rooms as she had.

Not that she had exactly waited for an invitation. Kenzie couldn't help smirking. She had gone there to gather intelligence, and she had gotten what she had been looking for, despite Dr. Carpenter's attempts to keep her from digging any deeper than he wanted her to.

"Is that about it?" Dr. Wiltshire asked.

"Well… there was just one more thing, but I'm not sure how you're going to feel about it."

It was, once again, later than Kenzie had expected before she got home. They should both be used to it, but she always criticized herself when she worked too long for too many nights in a row. There were some weeks when she was lucky to get home on time just one night. And she couldn't really blame it on Dr. Wiltshire. He often told her to go home and finish a job the next day. But she knew that the jobs would continue to pile up and if she were going to stay on top of things, she needed to finish as much as she could and not leave herself a big backlog of work.

Despite the fact that Wiltshire was nice and a good boss, he really didn't understand how much administrative work was involved in keeping the Medical Examiner's Office running smoothly, or was in denial about how far she would get behind if she did work just the usual hours.

Or maybe it was her fault because she didn't want to stay in just an administrative position, but wanted to be able to participate in postmortems and the nuts and bolts of being a medical examiner, and someday to be able to run an office of her own. If she wanted to have time to participate in the autopsies, she needed to put in some extra time to clear the administrative work out of the way first.

She was in a bit of a bad mood when she got home and opened the door between the garage and the kitchen.

Zachary was in the kitchen when she pushed the door open, not in the living room like he usually was, so she was startled to find him right in her way when she stepped in.

"Oh!" Kenzie pressed her hand to her chest. "What are you doing in here? I wasn't expecting that."

Zachary chuckled. "Sorry. I didn't mean to scare you. I was just putting out some drinks for us."

Kenzie looked at the soft drink cans and pitcher of water on the table in confusion. "Well… that's nice."

Zachary took in her confusion. "Tyrrell. For supper."

"Oh, no! I forgot. And I'm late." Kenzie swore. "You should have called to remind me when you saw I was running late."

He raised his brows and shook his head. "I should interrupt you when you already have too much to do? No, that doesn't sound like a good idea."

He was probably right, when she thought about it. He was

likely to get his head bitten off. Calling her when she was working late to tell her she needed to get home to deal with company and make them supper was a good way to end up in the doghouse for a week.

And they didn't even have a doghouse.

"Man, I'm sorry I forgot about it. Is he here already? Could we reschedule?"

In answer, Kenzie heard the toilet flush.

"He's here," she answered herself. "Okay. I was going to make some pasta and garlic bread, but we don't have to do that. Or we can eat late so I have a bit more time to pull everything together. What do you want to do?"

He flapped his hands at her, shooing her away. "I want you to go have a shower and relax and get out of your work clothes. You're tired. I'm dealing with supper."

"What are you going to do?" Kenzie couldn't help the snap in her reply. Zachary was going to take care of supper? The man could barely boil water or bake a frozen pizza without losing track of what he was supposed to be doing. Kenzie always took care of the meal preparation. Or at least the planning and coordination. He helped her on occasion, but Kenzie was the one giving directions to make sure that he didn't forget to turn on the oven or to take the pizza out of its wrapper, that the table was fully set, rather than Zachary just placing a couple of plates on the table and calling it done, and all of the other little things that had to be coordinated to make dinner work, even when it was just the two of them.

The times that he had been in charge of dinner, they ended up with takeout or with ice cream for dinner. Which wasn't too bad at the end of a very long and stressful day, but they couldn't live like that. The rest of the time, they had to have a somewhat grown-up, responsible diet.

"Go shower," Zachary insisted. "Or if you don't want to shower, then at least change. Or sit down and relax. You need time to unwind. I don't want you to be tense all evening."

Kenzie was more than a little flummoxed. She was the one who was supposed to be taking care of him and telling him what he needed to do to stay on top of his mental health. She looked at him closely, searching for any sign that he wanted her to insist that she was taking over and take the responsibility out of his hands. But he looked back at her steadily and didn't back down.

"Fine," Kenzie conceded. "I could definitely use a bit of a break."

30

Kenzie took Zachary at his word and left him to take care of the dinner arrangements. He was a grown man. He could certainly figure out a way to feed himself and his brother. Even if it was just frozen dinners and soft drinks. What was wrong with that? There was no reason they had to act like anything was different just because Tyrrell was there. He had seen them at their worst. He knew that things didn't always go smoothly and that Kenzie was not the perfect hostess that Lisa would have wanted her to be.

So she had a shower and changed into something more comfortable, though not her pajamas, since they did have company, and, when she emerged from the bedroom later, there were definitely signs that someone was cooking. There was a hearty Italian spice fragrance permeating the house. And she hadn't heard the smoke alarm go off.

Not yet.

She joined the men in the kitchen and greeted Tyrrell properly this time, saying hello and giving him a quick hug. "I'm sorry, it's been a long day."

Tyrrell looked surprised. "You don't have anything to apologize for. The Goldman men have provided."

Kenzie grinned at his macho tone. "You have, have you? So what is on the menu for tonight? Mountain lion that you chased down, killed with your bare hands, and roasted over a fire you started by banging two rocks together?"

"Close," Tyrrell told her. He stepped to the side so she could see the crowded kitchen counters. "There was a lasagna in the freezer. We brutally tore up some lettuce for a salad. Actually, we didn't; it was pre-chopped. And we have provided a selection of the highest-end salad dressings."

Kenzie smiled and shook her head at the mess on the counter. They hadn't done too badly, all things considered. Kenzie would have made garlic bread as well, which Zachary and Tyrrell both acted as if was manna from heaven. So maybe that wasn't a good idea; they wouldn't have had any room left for the lasagna or salad.

"That looks great. I'll set the table."

Kenzie moved around them while she got out the dishes and cutlery and arranged everything for them.

"Use a potholder!" she told Zachary when she saw him taking the lasagna out with a dishtowel pressed into service. But it was too late at that point and she could only hold her breath while he placed the pan on the top of the stove, hoping that he wouldn't burn himself.

Zachary gave a flourish with the dishtowel. "All done. *And* you can use it to dry dishes."

Kenzie sat down and let the two men handle the rest of the arrangements. Zachary served pieces of the lasagna from the pan while it sat on the stove rather than making a space for it on the table. Kenzie didn't want to tempt the fates that Zachary could avoid burning himself again. She added salad to her plate and topped it with salad dressing. She tried to relax her shoulders and all of her muscles that had started to tense up again.

"This is really great, you guys. Thanks for doing this. I meant to get home in time to get everything done, but my plans fell apart."

"He's my brother. I should be the one that does all the work when I invite him over," Zachary pointed out.

"Yes, but we don't usually make the guest do the cooking."

"He wanted to. Right, T?"

"That's right," Tyrrell agreed. He started digging into his lasagna without dishing up any salad. "Got to polish up my domestic skills, you know. Girls like that kind of thing."

"They do," Kenzie agreed. "And they like guys who can clean up, too."

Zachary took a look around the kitchen. "I'll do that." He rose and started picking things up from the nearest counter.

"Later," Kenzie told him, immediately regretting the comment. "After supper. Don't worry about it right now. I want to enjoy the meal with you."

Zachary stood looking at the mess, an empty box in his hand. He was clearly having difficulty stopping himself once he started. He heard Kenzie say that she wanted him to eat with her, but was already stuck on the track of cleaning up. Kenzie stood and took the box from his hand, putting it back on the counter. "It's okay. We'll do it together later."

"I can do it. I shouldn't have left everything out like that. We never leave a mess like that during dinner."

"It's fine. It was a joke. Just leave it and let's enjoy our meal. You guys did a good job. It's delicious."

She gave him a little tug toward the table, and Zachary broke through his inertia. He turned back to the table and sat down in his chair. He gave a slight headshake.

"*I'll* do it after dinner. You don't need to."

Kenzie didn't bother trying to argue about it. She just sat down at the table and resumed eating. Zachary would probably forget all about it by the time they finished eating anyway, and she could clean things up the way she wanted them done.

"So, what happened at work today?" Tyrrell asked politely. "All of your plans going off the skids."

Kenzie considered how much to tell him. Zachary would get

more of the story later after Tyrrell went home. "Well, I was going to get off early. I had arranged to run a personal errand and then I was going to come home right after that, and I would have had as much time as I needed to prepare everything. But after my errand, before I could get home, I got a call from my boss asking me to come back to the office. So…" Kenzie shrugged. "That's what I did, and then we had a meeting and discussion." Zachary was looking at her with concern. After all, he knew what personal errand she had been planning on and would want to know if there had been trouble with Dr. Wiltshire. She probably wouldn't tell him that he'd said she could be dismissed for what she had done. Kenzie avoided meeting Zachary's eyes, keeping the conversation light. "And then after the meeting, I had to stay to get some other stuff done. By that time I had forgotten about you coming, and I just wanted to get everything ready for when I got back to work in the morning."

"Was it an emergency?" Tyrrell asked. "Why would he call you back like that when you had arranged to take the time off? That's sort of a rotten thing to do."

"No, no. I understood why he needed me back. I don't blame him for calling me. But it did make for a long day. I just really appreciate you guys looking after the meal. It's a real treat to have someone cook for me."

They each made varying comments about being glad to do it and how real men cooked dinner now and then. Kenzie smiled as she had another bite of the lasagna, which was remarkably tasty. Maybe not up to Pat Parker's standards, but good for a frozen dinner. And it wasn't burned or frozen in the middle.

"How are things going for you?" she asked Tyrrell. "With work…?"

Tyrrell had been underemployed for a number of months, since he had come out of his last rehab. He had been able to find casual labor and short-term stints, but nothing that would support him or allow him to support his children, who were living with his ex-wife. Having a history of leaving previous employment to go on several-week or months-long drinking binges was not exactly good for the resume. Even prospective employers who were sympathetic and believed that he was currently sober did not want to take the chance of hiring an employee who was unreliable and potentially a danger to himself or others if he happened to show up on a construction site or some other job drunk one day, or just leave them in the lurch without so much as a word.

"About the same," Tyrrell said, not looking happy about it. "I have a few new leads to follow up on, but it's the same old, same old. People don't want to hire a drunk. Even a dry drunk. It's going to be a long time before I have enough of a track record that people won't be worried I'm going to let them down and go back to drinking. And even if I promised them that was never going to happen... I can't exactly control that. I can't promise I'll never fall off the wagon again, not after the number of times I've done it. They're right to be worried about it."

Even though there were programs that would hire recovering addicts or ex-cons, Tyrrell had been through several of them before, and people were unwilling to take him on again.

"You've been doing great. Don't let them get you down," Kenzie encouraged. "You'll find something better and, in the meantime, don't let all the negative voices shut you down."

"Good advice," Tyrrell agreed lightly.

Though Kenzie had a feeling, he was mentally adding that she didn't have a clue how difficult that was. She looked at Zachary, hoping that he would contribute something to the conversation that would boost Tyrrell's spirits. Maybe she shouldn't have asked him about his work, knowing that the answer was likely to be negative. But he had asked her about hers, and Kenzie had automatically followed up by asking him about his.

"Heather said that she had some contacts," Zachary said. "She was going to follow up and see if they could do anything."

"Yeah, that's where these new leads I have to follow up on came from. Her and Grant. They're good friends."

Zachary employed their older sister Heather part-time, but he couldn't afford to hire Tyrrell too, or he probably would. If there were things related to the investigations business that Tyrrell would have been interested in. He was a sociologist, so it was possible that he would be interested in the more complex criminal enterprises. But Zachary's bread and butter tended to be smaller jobs. He couldn't rely on the big jobs always rolling in at the right time and being enough to keep him going, so he worked on a lot of routine traces, insurance files, and other corporate investigations. Not as many adultery cases anymore, which he was very happy about. They had always been emotionally taxing.

Kenzie couldn't exactly hire Tyrrell at the Medical Examiner's Office. There were some lower-skilled jobs that they hired for. Moving bodies around and prepping them for postmortem didn't involve a lot of medical skills, just strong muscles and some training in how to move them properly. There were small companies that did crime scene clean-up, but Kenzie suspected Tyrrell would not have the strong stomach needed for that job. It would drive most people to drink.

Maybe she could search out some potential employers using the Kirsch family foundation's company database. She might find some programs or employers who would be good for Tyrrell to query.

"I'll keep my eyes open," she told Tyrrell, not wanting to get his hopes up by promising anything she didn't have.

He nodded, but he probably got that line a lot from people who never got back to him with anything. He didn't bother trying to show any enthusiasm about it.

Sunshine Care might be looking to fill some positions soon...

Kenzie pushed this thought away. Even though it might be true, she wouldn't really have an inside track on that, and Tyrrell wouldn't want to be involved with a company with such a bad reputation. If they even had any positions that he would be interested in. She was sure he wasn't interested in changing bedpans or swabbing floors for the next ten or twenty years until something else opened up to him.

They switched to other, less personal topics of conversation and lingered over the lasagna. The hot shower and good food were having the desired effect, and Kenzie felt much more relaxed and mellow than she had been when she'd gotten home.

It was a good thing that Zachary hadn't suggested that they go out to eat or that Kenzie could whip something up for them, even if it were just sandwiches. She would have remained in a foul mood if she hadn't been pampered a little.

"Do you want to watch a movie or play a game?" Zachary suggested as they finished off their meals. "Or do you want some time to yourself?"

"What do you want? Do you want just to do guy things together? Or all of us?"

Zachary shrugged and didn't give any indication what his preference was. Tyrrell didn't offer anything either.

"Well…" Kenzie thought about her day and what she would do if she had time to herself. Chances were, she would just log in to her work email and get all wound up again about Joseph Howard's case and the potential abuse at Sunshine Care. "I wouldn't mind doing something together. I don't think I want to go off on my own. So what do you want to do?"

31

Things had been pretty quiet at the morgue, but it was early in the morning. There was still the potential for plenty of excitement. Dr. Wiltshire was not yet in. Kenzie was nearly finished going through the latest emails to make sure that she had a good handle on what would need to be done during the day. She was glad she had taken the time to clear the decks the night before, even though it had made her late getting home when they had been planning to have Tyrrell over for dinner. It was good that she hadn't remembered that at the time, or she would have been flustered and in a hurry to get out. That was when mistakes were most likely to be made.

And it had all turned out well. Zachary and Tyrrell were perfectly capable of getting dinner ready. Lisa might sigh in exasperation over Kenzie making a guest help prepare his own dinner, but that hadn't been Kenzie's choice. And Tyrrell wasn't a guest; he was family. He had lived there for a few weeks before Kenzie had gotten him into the rehab facility. Once someone had lived there, he belonged. He had been in the kitchen. He had prepared his own meals there. What was the point of acting like he was a visiting dignitary?

All in all, the evening had worked out nicely, and she had been much more relaxed going to bed after having her job threatened than she would have predicted.

The phone rang and Kenzie picked it up. "Medical Examiner's Office."

"MacKenzie."

Kenzie looked at the call display. "Dad. What are you doing calling me on this line?"

"Well," he sounded amused, "you weren't picking up your cell phone."

"Yeah… I have my cell phone set to do not disturb because I am working."

"Can I interrupt you for five minutes, just to see how my daughter is doing?"

Kenzie suspected an ulterior motive, but she didn't yet know what it was. "Your daughter is doing fine. Is that all, then?"

He chuckled. "Who raised you to be such a smart mouth?"

Kenzie had to laugh at herself too. "Well, I might have been raised by two strong adults who believe in speaking their minds and taught me not to be a shrinking violet."

"Might have," he admitted.

"Oh, speaking of my two parents…" Kenzie remembered her last conversation with Lisa. "Didn't you tell me that Mother had asked you to get me to sign those papers right away last week?"

"I probably did. I don't recall. They're not still waiting, are they? I really think you need to take your responsibilities with the foundation seriously."

"They're done. I did get them back to Mother. But she said that she didn't ask you to call me about them; you just took it upon yourself."

"I don't recall the conversation," he said without concern. "It might have just been a throwaway comment like, 'I hope MacKenzie can get these back to me right away.' I honestly don't remember. Does it matter?"

"I just… don't like you getting between Mother and me. We have a complicated enough relationship without you putting yourself in the middle. If I have to navigate around you and interpret what you're saying and whether it was actually something Lisa asked you to do or whether you just made your own call on it, I'm going to end up cross-threaded with her. It's better if I can deal with her directly, and you stay out of it."

"I didn't mean to complicate things."

"Well, it does. If I'm getting one message from her and another from you... I don't want that. Unless you're each conveying your own opinions. Just don't... interpret her for me. Let us deal with each other."

"I agree. But... the foundation isn't just Lisa's business. I have something of an interest in it as well." His tone was dry. Because, of course, it was his foundation. His family's legacy, not Lisa's. She might run it, but he had the final say.

"Yes," Kenzie said reluctantly. "Of course it is. But you didn't say that you wanted me to sign them because you had an interest in them and wanted to push things through. You said that Lisa wanted me to."

"I don't recall exactly what my words were. Do you?"

There was silence for a moment while Kenzie thought about it. She couldn't swear that he had said the request had come from Lisa. That had been her impression, but maybe that was only because she thought of the foundation as being Lisa's business, and Walter just being adjacent to it. Calling her because he'd happened to stay over at Lisa's and knew she was concerned about getting the paperwork turned around quickly.

"No," she admitted. "Maybe I jumped to conclusions. Sorry."

"Not a problem. Thank you for looking after them, whatever the reason. I appreciate you taking more of an interest in the foundation recently."

"Oh! While we're talking about the foundation, I had a question for you."

"Of course."

"Zachary's brother, Tyrrell, he's looking for work. He has casual work right now, casual and temporary work, but he needs something stable. Something he can support himself on and hopefully afford to pay child support as well."

"Yes?"

Walter had never had to worry about child support when he and Lisa had divorced. For one thing, Kenzie and her sister had both been over eighteen at the time. And for another, Walter had never had to worry about having enough money to support his family. Even if he hadn't made a good living from lobbying, he had enough family money that he could have chosen never to work and would still have had enough.

"It's hard for him. He doesn't have a lot of experience and has a history of leaving jobs without warning. He's a recovering alcoholic and it's hard finding anyone that will risk it."

"That's certainly understandable."

"I know. I agree. But I'm trying to think of what I can do for him. I wondered if there are any companies or programs in the foundation database that might offer work for someone in that kind of situation, or to provide some extra funding so that someone who is underemployed can still support his children."

"It might be worth having a look. You could do a few searches. Get Hillary to help you. I'm sure you could call a few places."

"Okay. I guess I'll take a look."

"What's Tyrrell's background?"

"Well, similar to Zachary's. They both went into foster care, but Tyrrell was younger and didn't get moved around as Zachary did. But he still ended up being an alcoholic. Lots of Adverse Childhood Experiences to contend with. That predisposes him even if he hadn't had a parent who also had addiction issues."

There was a silence from Walter.

"Actually, I meant what is his educational and work background. What is he looking for?"

"He's looking for whatever he can get, to be honest. He has a degree in..." Kenzie frowned, trying to remember. She had talked to Zachary about it, had helped to update Tyrrell's resume. "In Behavioral Science, I believe."

"Really."

"Well, yes! A lot of very well-educated people end up addicted. One doesn't rule the other out."

"No. I wasn't thinking of that," Walter protested, but Kenzie wasn't sure she believed him. "What I was thinking was, we have been talking about hiring someone else to help with the office. It would start with lower-level clerking, maintaining the database, tracking grant payments, and so on. But it could evolve into something more, interacting with some of the programs we want to fund. Evaluating their social impact so we get the most bang for our buck. Your mother and I agree that we should make a larger contribution toward mental health. It's just as important as physical health, and there is a nexus between them. Keeping patients and caregivers mentally strong and resilient improves the health of those who have mental illness and are often neglected in the physical arena. You can't really separate physical and mental health. We should focus on more than just kidney disease and organ transplantation. That's Amanda's legacy. But we have become more aware of the issues with Zachary's struggles, and I think that in honor of your place in the family and the foundation, we need to include mental health issues in our targeting."

Kenzie had remained silent during Walter's speech, too stunned to say anything at first. When he wound down and waited to hear what she had to say, Kenzie was still trying to unwrap it all.

"Are you saying that the foundation might be interested in offering Tyrrell a job?"

"That's one of the things I'm saying."

Kenzie had heard the rest, but she wasn't sure if she believed what Walter had recited to her. The foundation wanted to fund more causes concerning mental illness because of her involvement with Zachary? What were the chances that was true?

Was he just trying to get on her good side before making an ask?

"You would take on a recovering alcoholic with a poor employment history?"

"Most alcoholics will have, won't they?"

"Well… some people manage to hide it a little better than Tyrrell, to stay gainfully employed even though they are drunks. But yeah, a lot of alcoholics have a pretty bad work record."

"It would be pretty hypocritical for us to say that we want to help people with these issues, but to refuse to consider employing those who have successfully made it through rehab and are starting over."

"Right. Yes. I guess so."

"Why don't you talk to Hillary about it? See what help she needs. Talk to her about Tyrrell and whether he would be a good fit. I'm not going to hire Tyrrell without knowing if she would work well with him. But let's get the ball rolling and see."

"Okay." Kenzie blinked several times, trying to clear her mind. She had never considered the possibility of the foundation directly employing Tyrrell. "Thanks, I'll do that."

"Good," Walter approved. "And… read your emails. We have been trying to keep you in the loop on what we are working on and future directions. It's not helpful if you never read them."

"Umm… yeah." Kenzie had to admit that she had been neglecting the increasingly frequent missives from the foundation addresses. She just wrote them off as being routine and not anything that affected her. "Sorry about that. I'll pay more attention."

D r. Wiltshire arrived just as Kenzie was hanging up the phone after her call with Walter. He raised his brows as he approached her desk. "Are you all right, Kenzie?"

"Oh, yes. Just fine. I was just talking to my dad."

Dr. Wiltshire's face remained appropriately blank. If he understood any of the ongoing friction between Kenzie and her father, he made no sign of it. "Everything okay with him?"

"Yes. It was just an interesting conversation. I'll have to think about it. It *could* be something good."

He chuckled. "I wouldn't have guessed that from your face."

"No. He and I don't always see eye-to-eye, so I don't know whether... how things might work out. We'll see." Kenzie gave herself a shake. She grabbed a stack of message slips. "Those are for you. Nothing that looks too urgent. Have you... heard anything back from the Department?"

"Not yet. They have several days to make their inspection and fill out their reports. So we have to wait and see what comes of it. With what you saw and your feelings about the place, I hope they will be able to make some recommendations. Maybe get the troublemakers out of there."

"Yeah, me too." Kenzie wasn't going to bet the farm that it

would happen. She knew of other investigations that had gone south. While the government seemed to be very quick to take children out of their homes at any allegation of abuse, the same standard didn't seem to apply when investigating facilities. Professionals, it seemed, were less suspect than untrained parents. Or, in the case of Joseph Howard, untrained adult children. They wouldn't make any rush to judgment on whether Sunshine Care had a problem.

But Kenzie was working on that. With any luck, she would have something to show the Department. Something that would make a difference.

"Do you think they will do anything?"

"There's no predicting right now. It's just a waiting game."

Kenzie sighed. "I suppose."

Dr. Wiltshire hesitated. She expected him just to nod and go to his office, but he lingered a little longer. "I have been in this business for a lot longer than you have…"

Kenzie nodded. He was the voice of experience. The one who could tell her that she was being too headstrong and needed to find a way to moderate herself. Not to jump into the middle of a situation and think that she could change things and make everything right. That wasn't the way the world worked.

He leaned against her desk. "I have seen some seniors come through here with shocking injuries." He swallowed and cocked his head slightly. "They are almost always reported as accidents or self-harm. But when you turn over an eighty-year-old man and find a boot print on his back, you know it wasn't just an accident."

"That's awful." Kenzie had seen her share of horrible things, but that was one she would find disturbing no matter how much she saw. It wasn't a good thing to become calloused to the things that people did to each other. Especially to the vulnerable.

"It's good that people are becoming more aware of the abuse the elderly are subjected to. It's good that we're talking about it. But I think we have a long way to go before we can be satisfied that we are treating them humanely."

"No matter how hard we try, there is still child abuse," Kenzie agreed.

"Yes. And there always will be child abuse and elder abuse. But we do the best that we can to draw awareness to it, to reduce it as much as possible, and to shine a light on it when a patient comes through here who has been the victim of abuse of whatever kind."

"But there are channels to go through and procedures to follow," Kenzie finished, anticipating his caution.

"Yes. And that isn't always easy to do. Sometimes we want to jump into the middle of things or to use this office to make a statement. But that isn't always the best solution. It's best to work within the law."

Kenzie nodded. "Yeah. That makes sense. I know. We don't want to mess anything up so that the police or the Department can't use the evidence we find. We can't be political or show a bias. We have to show that we have been impartial in everything we do."

"Not easy," Dr. Wiltshire said. "But necessary. If we want the police to be able to do their job, we need to do ours."

"I'm sorry about yesterday. I should have talked to you about it. Worked something out that was more... proper. I didn't mean to mess things up for this office."

"I'm not getting after you. We have talked about that, and it is done. I just want you to know that even though we have to sit back and wait, I understand how difficult that is."

Kenzie appreciated his sympathy. He'd been in the business a lot longer than she had been, but he was just as outraged as she was over what had allegedly happened to Joseph Howard. He had just learned the weight of responsibility that was on his shoulders and to follow the established rules. Like reporting the possibility of elder abuse through the correct channels instead of rushing in to investigate it himself. A discipline that Kenzie would have to learn.

33

The rest of the day passed without incident. They could work on the cases they had scheduled without being interrupted by some other emergency or pressure to look at a different case. Kenzie was clearing off her desk and locking her computer right around the time she should be closing up shop. She would get home, and she and Zachary would have a quiet evening together. Maybe on the weekend they could go for a hike or meet some friends. Or meet some friends and take them on a hike. Fresh air and social interaction would be good for her.

Kenzie was pretty relaxed going home. Other than just about losing her job doing something stupid, things were going pretty well in her life. It was good to be in a stable relationship and to see Zachary doing well on his current med protocol. He was the happiest she had ever seen him, and she thought that both of them deserved that happiness after all that he had been through and all of the work they had put into learning tools and strategies that would improve their communication skills and build a stronger relationship. After the initial bumps in their relationship, she had not been sure they were made for each other or would ever be able to reach that point.

It wasn't perfect, of course. Nothing ever was. But things were good.

She parked her baby in the garage and entered the house through the kitchen. Zachary wasn't on the couch waiting for her. He would probably be surprised to see her home so early. After the schedule she had been keeping lately, it was no wonder he wasn't watching for her arrival. She walked down the hall to her home office—*their* home office— and found him packing a bag.

Kenzie's immediate reaction was that he was leaving her. He'd had some kind of breakdown and decided they couldn't be together anymore. Or he and Tyrrell had decided to go off on some venture together and Zachary was going back to his old apartment, which Tyrrell was currently living in. Or maybe he'd been having an affair, and that was why he had seemed so happy lately. *That* would be a real kick in the pants.

"Zachary?"

He startled and turned to look at her. "Oh, Kenzie. You're home!" He looked around and picked up his phone, checking the time on the face before sliding it into his pocket. "You're early. I didn't just lose track of time."

"Yes," Kenzie forced a laugh. "I can't fault you for being surprised. It isn't like it happens very often. And for the record, this is *on time* not early."

Zachary looked down at the black bag in his hand, then up at her. His expression was puzzled. "I was just packing some things," he said, as if he could tell she was upset but wasn't sure what she had to be upset about. "For the surveillance job tonight."

"Oh." Kenzie let out her breath with a sigh of relief. "Oh, you have a job!"

"Yes." A crease formed between his brows and he shook his head. "I told you that, didn't I?"

"Not that I remember. I would have at least written it down on my calendar so that I would know where you were. You're leaving now...?"

"Pretty soon. I'm glad I got to see you before going out. I really didn't tell you?"

"Do you remember telling me?"

"No… but I don't remember *not* telling you. I thought I had. I was sure I had. I'm sorry."

"It's okay. When you have a job, you have a job. I'm not normally home at this time anyway. How late do you expect this to go? Is it a couple of hours or all night?"

"More likely to be all night."

"Okay… I wish you *had* told me. Maybe I would have set up something with a friend."

"You still could." He looked concerned. "You could call one of your friends and see if she could do something… or a few of them. Get together for drinks or a movie. Or whatever else you like to do together."

It wasn't like Kenzie had spent a lot of time with girl friends since Zachary had moved in with her. A few times, when it had been someone's birthday or when she knew Zachary was going to be away. Even though Zachary had been in the hospital for weeks before and after Christmas, she hadn't done anything extra. It was pretty hard to do anything with friends when all of her spare time was spent visiting with Zachary at the hospital and then going back home and trying to get enough sleep to be able to focus the next day at work. The focus thing wasn't just because of lack of sleep, but more to do with the fact that her mind was on him and her concerns with his welfare almost all of the time. But being well-rested was the best way she knew to combat it.

That and a lot of coffee.

Kenzie smiled and nodded her agreement at Zachary's suggestion. "Maybe I will," she agreed so that he wouldn't worry about her all night. But she doubted that she would call anyone. She'd had her heart set on a quiet evening at home, and she didn't feel like calling around to friends at the last minute to see if any of them could spend time with her. She didn't want to convey that the only time she wanted to do things with them was when Zachary was away.

"You should spend more time with friends," Zachary said. "I feel like you don't get out a lot and that's my fault."

"And you? You should go out with the guys now and then too. Tyrrell, Mario Bowman…" She tried to think of who else to add to the list, but there weren't many people that Zachary felt comfortable hanging out with. Moody and often depressed, it was not easy for him to make long-lasting friendships. People wanted a relationship that would give something back and not always be one-sided. Not just Zachary being depressed and sucking the life out of them. Kenzie suspected that all his time in foster care had damaged his ability or willingness to make friends. When he knew he was just going to move again in a few weeks or months, what was the point in getting to know someone new? Why get to like someone and build a friendship, only to be pulled away and dropped into a new home because the one he was in was not able to tolerate his behavior?

"We at least go to see Mr. Peterson and Pat," Zachary reminded her. "We haven't seen much of your family or friends lately."

"Well… yeah. We should set something up. Go out to dinner or a play or something." She waved her hand as if wiping this off of a whiteboard. "But not tonight. Tonight, you have work and I have some things I've been hoping to get to."

"Are you sure?"

Kenzie nodded. "Sure, I'm sure. You finish getting your stuff ready to go."

He pulled out his phone and looked at the time again. "I have time for a quick bite. We can still have supper together."

"Yeah? That would be great."

34

K enzie was later getting to bed than she should be on a "school night." But she didn't like going to sleep alone and knowing that Zachary was out on surveillance, possibly doing something dangerous. She wanted him beside her in bed. Even if they sometimes kept each other awake tossing and turning, she didn't feel like things were normal if he wasn't there with her. Her heart beat too fast. She considered whether she should take a sleeping pill. She didn't want to lie awake, alert to every sound the house made.

But she didn't want to take a pill if she didn't need to, either. Zachary might only be a few hours, and she wanted to wake up when he got back. Just to greet him and cuddle for a few minutes before going back to sleep.

It was funny that she would prefer to wake up and kiss him and go back to sleep than to sleep through. Kind of sweet too.

Eventually, she decided to try it without a sleeping pill. If she couldn't settle down and get to sleep in good time, she would get up and take a pill. She would probably still be able to wake up when Zachary got home anyway. The pills weren't that strong.

She read for a few minutes in bed, waiting for her eyes to get droopy, then shut off the light and lay down. She put her hand on the spot where Zachary normally slept and waited for sleep to take her. Long, slow breaths and thinking about him being there in a few hours. Long, slow breaths, and in a few minutes, she would be asleep.

Something awoke Kenzie abruptly. She jumped awake, and lay there with her muscles tensed, waiting for a sound. For a moment, she didn't remember that Zachary wasn't there beside her. She felt for him, wanting to reassure herself that he was still there, and then found that he wasn't. Had he gotten up to use the bathroom, and the noise had just startled Kenzie? Had he heard something and gotten up to check on it? She listened to the creaks of the house for a minute, alert, before remembering that he was out on a surveillance job. That was why he wasn't beside her.

He had probably returned and, as quiet as he had tried to be, had woken her up. He would tiptoe into the bedroom in a moment and climb into bed with her. As long as he wasn't too wound up. If he was hyped up after his surveillance job instead of tired out, he might take a few minutes doing something else before he decided to go to bed. But what would have hyped him up? Normally, surveillance jobs were dead boring, and he would just have been watching a house for signs of activity for several hours.

But something could have happened. A suspect fleeing. Following an adulterer back home. A break-in. It all depended on what he had been there to watch for.

"Zachary?" she called. "I'm awake. Come on in."

He would tell her about it, and then Kenzie would go to sleep. Maybe talking about it would calm him enough so he could go to sleep too. If not, she would at least fall back asleep knowing that he was home safe and sound and would go to bed when he could.

There was no answer.

"Zachary?"

There was the faintest sound of footsteps coming down the

hallway. Stealthy, as if he wasn't sure he had heard her and still had to be quiet so that he wouldn't wake her.

"How did it go?" Kenzie called. "Was it boring?"

The bedroom door moved slowly. She waited for Zachary to come in and tell her about it. It would take his eyes a minute to adjust to the dark. He would pause in the doorway, then walk in when he was sure he wouldn't trip over something on his way. Kenzie was always careful not to leave anything on the floor where he might trip over it. Still, she guessed that he had been in enough unfamiliar bedrooms growing up in foster care, tripping over items carelessly left out by other foster children, that it had become an ingrained habit, even when he no longer had to be so careful.

"Zachary…"

He crept into the room. Kenzie watched his form as he moved across the room. Not to his side of the bed, empty and waiting for him, but around the end and up the far side to where Kenzie lay. What was up? He knew by now that she was awake. But maybe he just wanted to sit by her for a moment to visit and then would go back out again. He didn't want to lie down yet, just to say hi and let her go back to sleep.

The shadow stopped in front of Kenzie and was still. He just breathed, looking at her.

"Zachary?" Kenzie asked uncertainly. Was he upset about something? Having a meltdown? Or a stroke? She reached for the bedside lamp.

He grabbed her arm before she could reach it. Held her tightly. His fingers were as hard as iron. He must be in the middle of some kind of episode. He never grabbed her like that.

"It's not Zachary," a voice whispered, calling Kenzie by an imprecation Zachary would never have used. "It's your worst nightmare."

Kenzie tried to pull away. She wanted to grab her phone—dial 9-1-1—scream and let someone know that something was happening to her. But she couldn't scream and he wouldn't let her go. He didn't want her to turn on the light or to grab her phone.

He was in control. Kenzie lashed out with her other hand and tried to untangle her feet from the blanket to kick him.

Who was in her house? How had he gotten past the burglar alarm?

As if in response to her thought, the burglar alarm started to wail. There was a delay, of course, after someone entered the house. Time for them to disarm the burglar alarm by entering a code. But he hadn't had the code, because it wasn't Zachary.

He didn't tense and pull away, scared by the noise. He continued to hold her tight in his iron grip.

"You think you're so smart? You think you can come in there pretending to be someone you're not, to try to smear our reputations and that there are no consequences? Do you have any idea what kind of damage you could do? Good people. We are good people, and you are smearing us, making accusations of things we would never do. How can you behave like that? How can you do something like that?"

"I don't know..." Kenzie couldn't speak, couldn't get the words out in any order that made sense. "Who? I never... I don't know..."

"You're so high and mighty? You call yourself a doctor? You're not a doctor. Doctors take care of *sick* people. Not *dead* people! You are nothing but a charlatan. You're a made-up doctor, and you don't deserve to be called one. You should be disbarred. Or whatever they do to doctors who break the rules and aren't really doctors. You should be fired for this crap..."

She swallowed and tried to work up the saliva to answer him. But what was she supposed to say? Was she supposed to argue with him? Reassure him? Scream for help? She couldn't think of anything that would help the situation.

"Please! Who... who are you? What are you doing in my house?" Her voice was weak and breathy. It didn't sound like her at all. Her father would be disappointed. He had always been proud of her when she had argued back and stood up for herself. He had made sure that she had been taught self-defense. Unlike the many powerful men who wanted pretty little princesses, he had wanted his daughter to be a strong woman—outspoken, confident, tough. And here she was, lying in her bed, whispering to the man who had broken into her house.

Where were the police? How long would it take the police or security company to get to the house? She had triggered the alarm accidentally before. They called for a keyword to confirm that it was a mistake. But her phone was on Do Not Disturb mode and lay on the bedside table, dark and out of reach.

They would send someone to the house. They would knock on the door. Maybe the burglar had left the door hanging open and they would immediately know that there was an intruder. They'd see that it wasn't a false alarm and would act accordingly.

But when?

The shadowy figure seemed unconcerned about the loud alarm wailing in the night. He didn't try to run or act like he was in a hurry. Maybe he knew security companies. Knew how long it would take for them to get there to verify that there really was an emergency.

"You keep to yourself and mind your own business. You don't do anything like that again. Just stay out of my business."

"I don't know who you are."

He let go of her arm. Kenzie was relieved. Then he struck out, hitting her in the face. Kenzie cried out in surprise and pain. Her eyes were flooded with tears and she curled her body into a ball to protect herself.

"Please! Please!"

The man didn't speak another word. There was no further blow. The seconds ticked by. Minutes. The alarm continued to blare. Kenzie opened her eyes and ventured a look at the space that the shadow had occupied. The figure was gone. He had slipped out of the room while she'd been cowering. Kenzie sat up slowly, swallowing and trying to figure out what to do next. She had to remind herself to breathe and sat there for a few seconds, just taking air in and pushing it out. She was lucky to be able to do that.

What if things had happened differently? What if he'd brought a gun? What if he had killed her?

Her cell phone was no longer dark and silent. The screen was lit up and it was vibrating noisily on the side table. The name of the security company was on the screen.

They had bypassed the Do Not Disturb mode by calling several times in rapid succession, signaling to the software that it was an emergency. Kenzie looked around to make sure that she was alone and grabbed it off of the side table. She swiped to answer the call and held it close to her ear, clutching it like a life preserver.

35

Who is this?" the caller demanded.

"Kenzie Kirsch." She couldn't remember the verbal password. Her brain was whirling, and she didn't have any idea what she was supposed to say.

"Dr. Kirsch? Are you okay?"

"Yes."

"Your burglar alarm has been tripped."

"Yes." She gulped. "I'm here. I'm at home."

"Is it a false alarm?"

"No."

"One of our men is in front of your house. Are you alone?"

"Yes… I think so. I think he's gone."

"The next person in the door will be a security guard. Don't be scared. He will secure the scene and make sure that the intruder is gone. What part of the house are you in?"

"My bedroom. In bed."

"He's entering the house now."

The alarm quieted. Kenzie could hear the guard's footsteps. Heavy, booted feet, not the quiet movements of the burglar.

"I'm in here," she called out to him.

"Be there in a minute, ma'am. Stay calm."

Kenzie did. It was reassuring to know that he was there. That he was checking every nook and cranny where an intruder might be hiding, like her father checking under the bed and in the closet for monsters when she was scared to go to sleep as a child.

She hadn't really been scared to go to sleep. She had been amused by his willingness to check for monsters that didn't exist. It had been part of a game. She wasn't afraid of the dark or of monsters. She just liked knowing that her father's love for her extended far enough to take the time looking for imaginary creatures to calm her for the night.

The booted feet came down the hallway. "Ma'am?" the security guard was in the doorway. "Dr. Kirsch?"

"Yes."

"Just stay where you are. I'm going to take a minute to clear this room and then go on to the others. Wait until I come back."

"Okay."

He was just a shadow moving around the room, but she wasn't afraid of him. She was starting to review the invasion in her mind, trying to sort out who it had been and why he had come. She was lucky that he hadn't brought a gun and shot her. It would have been too late before the security force or the police arrived. But maybe they would be able to identify him from the security camera at the door he had entered through. She'd felt safe with the burglar alarm. And it had done its job. But if the intruder had wanted to harm her more than he had, he could have.

The security guard checked the bedroom, the closet, and the en suite bathroom and then thumped back out into the hallway. After the entire house was cleared, he returned to the bedroom.

"Would you like me to turn on the light now, ma'am?"

"Yes, please."

He pulled goggles away from his eyes before he flipped the switch, bathing the room in light. There were sirens outside. Kenzie wasn't sure how long it had been since the time that the burglar alarm first started to blare. Three minutes? Ten? It couldn't have been long, yet it seemed like it had taken them forever. The security company had been faster, which Kenzie supposed was why she was paying for their service.

"How are you doing?" The guard was a young man, maybe mid-twenties. He looked her over. "Do you want me to get an ambulance, ma'am?"

"Call me Kenzie." Kenzie touched her nose and cheekbone. Puffy. Starting to swell up, but feeling the bones, she was sure they were not broken. "No... I'm okay."

"Are you sure? We should have the paramedics at least give you a quick check."

"I'm a doctor. It's fine."

"The police are here." He touched the earbud in one ear. "They will want to come in to have a look around and to talk to you about what happened. Are you okay with that?"

"Yes."

"They'll want to come in here to check the scene. Do you want to talk to them in here or somewhere else? In the living room or outside?"

Kenzie looked down at herself, thinking about modesty for the first time. She did not generally sleep in the nude, so she was wearing pajamas and, while not the heavy flannel ones she wore in the winter, they were acceptable.

"I think... the living room," she decided. She didn't want to be in the bedroom while they examined it. She didn't want to think of it as a crime scene and to see them examining the bed or anything else in there. She would already have to deal with the memories of one intruder in her bedroom. She didn't want to be there when the police violated the sanctity of the room too. But she didn't want to be subject to the scrutiny of her neighbors by meeting the police outside. The living room seemed like the best bet. Or maybe the kitchen, if she wanted a cup of tea or glass of water to steady her nerves.

The security guard nodded and waited for her, confirming this information over his mike. Kenzie got slowly out of bed and stood still for a moment, making sure that she was steady. She had been hit in the face. She didn't want to realize too late that she was dizzy on standing and end up flat on her face.

But everything in the room stayed where it was supposed to, including the floor, and she passed the guard, letting him follow her out to the living room. Kenzie sat down on the couch and grabbed one of the throw blankets to wrap around her legs and feet. She looked around the living room. Nothing appeared to have been touched.

The police came in through the front door, radios noisy as they called back and forth to whoever was in charge.

"We'll take a look around," one of them said, "then come back to talk."

"Down the hall, first door on the left," the security guard informed them.

"She okay?" One of the cops nodded toward Kenzie as if she couldn't answer for herself.

"I'm fine," Kenzie told him irritably. The security guard looked toward her and said nothing. He'd clearly figured out that she would rather speak for herself than have him answer questions for her. The cops had a look around, not just in her bedroom, but through the rest of the house. It had already been cleared, so Kenzie wasn't worried about the intruder popping out from a closet somewhere and just waited patiently on the couch for the cops to talk to her.

"Okay," one of the cops, a big burly guy, positioned himself in one of the easy chairs and faced Kenzie. "Why don't you tell me what happened here tonight? Just take your time and describe it from the beginning."

Kenzie took a deep breath and tried to describe what had happened in careful chronological sequence. But she found herself getting confused occasionally, unable to put something into words or getting the order switched around, suddenly finding that she needed to tell the cop, whose nameplate said O'Neil, something that she had left out that he needed to know. But he was patient and sat there nodding and making an occasional note in his little field notepad. He didn't ask questions, just letting her talk.

"Do you know who this guy is?" he asked, when she was finished.

"No. I can only assume… that it is related to one of the deaths the Medical Examiner's Office is working on. I'm assuming it's something to do with Sunshine Care. I was there a couple of days ago looking into patient conditions. That's the only thing I can think of."

"You think you might have met him there?"

"No. I only really met one of the male staff there. Dr. Carpenter. And the body shape and voice are all wrong. I can't see him doing something like this anyway. I don't think he is the kind. But this guy… must still have heard about me visiting there. I assume they had to tell staff something about the investigation into the care center."

"And you think somebody didn't like that."

"Yeah."

"I see. But you don't have any names or faces…"

Kenzie shook her head. "No… I don't really know anyone there. But they might have known who I was. The receptionist knew me when I arrived. Probably had looked up my picture on the Medical Examiner's Office web page. Anyone else could have done the same."

They were supposed to have taken Kenzie's picture down from the website but, like everything else to do with law enforcement, there was a huge bureaucracy to cut her way through and a backlog of work that might have been months or years.

"And how would he have found your address?"

"I don't know. There are databases you can subscribe to. Even places that you can go online and just give them your credit card number, and it will spit out all of the last known addresses and phone numbers for anyone."

He nodded at this. Kenzie assumed that, being a law enforcement officer, he had access to a number of these databases and knew all about how you would get someone's address or phone number even if it were unlisted. That was something that Zachary was very good at. It was scary to watch him work and to realize how little privacy a person had in the modern world.

"Did he make any threats?"

Kenzie tried to sort it all out. She had talked to the police before, and she knew he would continue to ask her questions over and over again in different ways, hoping to shake loose one more piece of information that might make the difference in solving the case. Memory was a strange thing. Kenzie would probably remember things over the next few days that she didn't even realize she had seen or heard.

36

There were raised voices outside. Not yelling, just an increase in volume and the number of voices talking at the same time. Kenzie turned her head to look out the window and saw Zachary approaching the house. Talking to the police and trying to work his way in, despite the fact that it was a crime scene the police would want to keep clear.

"That's my partner," she told O'Neil, "Tell them to let him in."

She stood up, prepared to go to the door or outside to meet him and reassure him that she was okay. He wasn't yelling and having a meltdown, but he was bound to be pretty anxious about what had happened that had resulted in so many emergency vehicles being parked in front of the house.

O'Neil relayed this information over his radio and, in a moment, Zachary broke free from the little knot of cops and made his way to the door. He was past the entryway and into the living room in an instant, spotting Kenzie and immediately going to her to give her a tight hug. He withdrew slightly and looked intently at her face.

"Tell me what happened," he ordered, feeling for the couch without taking his eyes off of her. They both collapsed into the couch, and Zachary held Kenzie's hands, waiting for the story.

Kenzie found it easier to talk to him about it. She didn't have to back up as many times as she had when telling her story to O'Neil. It flowed more naturally, and Zachary already knew the background about Sunshine Care, so she didn't have to fill him in on that part.

To begin with, he was holding her hands too tightly, but he relaxed his grip as she continued to describe what had happened and he realized that she was okay. When she talked about the intruder holding on to her arm, Zachary pulled her arm out and twisted it slightly as he examined it. Kenzie could see that the burglar had left bruises.

"Was he wearing gloves?" Zachary asked.

"Uh... no."

"Might be able to get transfer DNA off of your skin. Fingerprint too, maybe."

As if Kenzie didn't know the technologies available. Getting either DNA transfer or fingerprints from skin was challenging, but not impossible. Even if they could get both, it wouldn't help unless he was already in the system. If he weren't, then Vermont law enforcement were prohibited from even making a familial match on a public DNA database. The technology that had allowed the police in California to find the Golden State Killer was not available to them.

"I suppose if the police want to try." She looked at the police officer. "Do you know how to take fingerprints from skin? We need to try to pick up the prints first, then to swab after."

He looked at her skeptically. "I've heard of them doing it on TV, didn't know it was possible in real life."

"We do it at the morgue sometimes," Kenzie said. "Don't see why the same technique wouldn't work on live humans."

"Well, that's good," Zachary put in, rubbing her back in a soothing circle. "I wouldn't want them to have to kill you first."

Kenzie chuckled. "No," she agreed. "I can show you how to do it," Kenzie told O'Neil. "I've got everything I need in my death kit. I've got one in the car."

He raised his brows. "You keep a 'death kit' in your car?"

"Well, in case I have to attend at a scene. People get murdered at night, you know. It's a lot easier to just get in your car and go than to have to drive all the way to the morgue to get your equipment and then drive out to the scene. Just like a 'go bag' in any other on-call job."

He shook his head slowly. "I would never have even thought of it."

"Well, most professions *don't* require a death kit."

"Only one or two," Zachary contributed.

O'Neil was looking at the two of them as if they were bonkers. Probably most home invasion victims didn't joke around about death kits. But Kenzie felt a lot better being silly about it and enjoying Zachary's wry sense of humor. It was much better than sitting around wondering if they would be able to find the guy who had broken in.

"How did he get in?" Zachary asked O'Neil, apparently thinking along the same track. "I went through the door so fast I didn't even notice whether it was forced or picked."

At least he knew her well enough to know that she hadn't left the door unlocked or the burglar alarm off.

"Forced," O'Neil advised. "Crowbar between the door and the frame, popped it right open."

"Did they check for fingerprints? Around the doorframe? It's not as likely as if it was picked, but sometimes people put a hand on the doorframe to brace."

"That will be up to the detectives. I'm just taking Dr. Kirsch's statement."

"We need to make sure they do," Zachary told Kenzie. "Need to be sure they are following up on all possible leads."

"Okay, well, you can talk to them. You're not going anywhere, are you?"

"No." Zachary smiled, looking relieved. "I'm not going anywhere."

"Why weren't you here?" O'Neil questioned.

"I was out on a job. I'm a private investigator. Had a surveillance job tonight."

"And that finished right at the same time as this attack? That's an interesting coincidence."

"No. I got an alert about the burglar alarm being tripped. So I left the job and came home."

"Took your time getting here."

"I don't have lights and siren. People tend to get upset if I just blow through all of the intersections," Zachary pointed out.

"It was *not* Zachary," Kenzie told O'Neil, glaring at him. "I would have recognized if it was him. And why would he do something like that, anyway? Why would *he* want me to stop the investigation into the Sunshine Care home?"

"Is that what this was about?" Zachary asked. "That nursing home?"

"I think it must be. He didn't say specifically, but I assumed that was what he was talking about."

"He thought that if he threatened you, it would stop the investigation by the Department of the Aging whatever? How would breaking into your house and threatening you stop that investigation?"

"People don't behave logically," Kenzie told Zachary, something that he had often pointed out to her. "They behave emotionally. He thinks that if he yells and stomps his feet enough, he'll be able to get his own way. But that's not the way that it works."

"That rarely works with the government," O'Neil contributed, his mouth quirking up slightly.

"Rarely," Kenzie agreed.

37

Kenzie didn't get much sleep. After the initial investigation was finished and the responding officers were gone, she and Zachary went to bed and talked and cuddled.

Zachary appeared to be calm, especially while the police officers were still there. But Kenzie had seen that his eyes were constantly moving around, looking for any danger, hypervigilant. The danger was past, but he wasn't reassured. He wasn't going to be able to relax enough to go to sleep. He would be keyed up for hours. As they lay, Kenzie with her head in the hollow of Zachary's shoulder, she traced a circle on his chest, over and over again, trying to keep herself alert and Zachary calm.

"Do you need an anxiety pill?" she asked. "Maybe you should take something so that you can settle down and sleep."

He shook his head. "I don't want to."

"You don't want to take a pill?" Kenzie knew that he didn't like to take them unless it was really necessary, but it seemed like this was a situation in which he might agree that it was necessary if he were going to be able to go to sleep.

"I don't want to settle down and sleep."

Kenzie raised her head slightly to look at him, but she couldn't see his facial expression in the darkness.

"You don't want to sleep?"

He shook his head. "No. I want to make sure everything is okay."

"It is. It's fine. The police cleared everything. The guy is gone. The door is secure for now, and the security guy will replace it tomorrow."

"No. He could come back. I have to be sure."

"He's not going to come back."

Zachary didn't argue the point. Kenzie knew there was no point in trying to talk him into it. He would continue to think whatever it was that was stuck in his brain. He could get like that, obsessed with one idea or thought and unable to let it go. She didn't know whether it was just part of his ADHD or was a sign that he was slightly into OCD territory. The two had many over-lapping symptoms. Throw in PTSD and some other learning disabilities on top of it, and life got really interesting.

"You could still sleep for a bit," Kenzie coaxed. "You'd wake up if he came back. Trust me."

"No. I want to be clearheaded."

"You'll have more problems if you don't sleep. It makes your depression and other stuff worse. You need a good solid sleep each night to stay healthy."

"I know," Zachary said in a firm, no-argument tone. "I was prepared for a night of surveillance, so I had extra sleep last night and an afternoon nap. I'll take a sleeping pill before bed tomorrow and be caught back up again."

"You're not caught up if you go without sleep tonight."

"Go to sleep," he advised. "I'm full of caffeine and ADHD meds. There's no way I'm sleeping tonight."

"You took ADHD meds at night?"

"To keep me focused and awake on surveillance."

"That's not recommended—"

"Most ADHDers are not private investigators, so it wouldn't be."

"You could mess up your whole circadian rhythm—"

"I'm going to bed tomorrow night at the regular time. With anxiety and sleep meds onboard and the ADHD meds out of my system for twenty-four hours. There won't be a problem."

He had been operating as a private investigator for years and had been on surveillance more times than she could count, so she knew that he had the experience to make this call. It rubbed her the wrong way as a medical professional, but she couldn't exactly explain why. He wasn't abusing the ADHD meds. She knew he was more likely not to take them when he needed them than he was to take them when he didn't. But of course, she had always been taught as a doctor that you took ADHD meds during the morning and then avoided them later in the day to allow for sleep. No double-dosing and staying up all day and all night studying as a med student.

But if Zachary had been a shift worker, it would be perfectly appropriate for him to take his ADHD meds before the beginning of a night shift instead of in the morning when he needed to unwind to go to sleep. Tonight, he had been on night shift. Or had been planning to be, before Kenzie's burglar alarm had called him home.

"Sorry about the alarm," she told him. "Making you come back here before your job was done."

"Some things are more important. I can try again in another night or two."

"But you won't be able to bill for both nights, will you?"

"I'll charge for the time I spend on the job."

"Even though you couldn't stay as long as you needed to?"

"Yes."

Good for him. Kenzie was glad he was careful of his billings and didn't let clients walk all over him. He was a professional and investigating took time and effort. As long as she had known him, he had been careful to only hire on with paying clients, not friends who expected a favor or deeply discounted prices. Except, maybe, that time that his ex-wife Bridget had asked him to take on a case. Kenzie had a feeling he had not charged for that one.

"And it really didn't mess things up that much?"

"No. It will be fine. Some nights, nothing happens. Sometimes, something does. You can't predict what day or time will be productive."

"What kind of case is it?"

He rubbed her head. "Go to sleep."

"I don't know if I can."

"Try," he advised.

Kenzie drifted off for a while without ever hearing the answer to her question.

When Kenzie got up in the morning, Zachary wasn't in bed. She wandered out to the living room, yawning and rubbing her eyes, but he wasn't set up there. She couldn't smell any coffee. Had he fallen asleep in the office or spare room when his ADHD meds had eventually worn off? She went down to the end of the hall and checked out the home office, but he wasn't there. She tried the door to the spare room, expecting to find him sprawled on the guest bed asleep, but he was not. Kenzie rotated in a circle. The bathroom door was not shut. She had not missed checking any rooms.

Anxiety started up in her belly. She knew it was silly to be worried about Zachary and where he might have gone. He might have gone out for a walk, getting some fresh air and taking pictures of the birds and trees that Vermont was famous for. That would be a good, healthy choice. Or he might have gone the other direction and decided to go out and get them coffee and donuts, which she wouldn't fault him for. There was any number of reasons that he might have gone out. Especially since it was later in the morning than it usually was when Kenzie got up. Normally she would have been at work. But she had left a message for Dr. Wilt-shire the night before explaining what had happened and that she was going to take the day off to recover.

Kenzie looked around once more, as if she might have just missed Zachary behind the refrigerator door, in the garage, or with his head stuck in a closet somewhere. But he was nowhere to be seen. She retreated to her room, got back into bed, and picked up her phone. She tapped his contact picture and waited for him to pick up.

"Kenzie. You're up."

"I'm up, and you're not here."

"Sorry, I thought I would get home before you woke up. I won't be long; I'm on my way back."

"I thought maybe you went out for coffee and donuts."

There was a slight pause, and then Zachary agreed. "Of course. What kind did you want?"

"Whatever. Something low fat and healthy."

He laughed. "I'll be sure to get you a diet donut. Zero calories."

"Perfect. See you soon!"

She was laughing when she hung up the phone. If he was on his way back but needed to stop for donuts, she had enough time for a quick shower. What better way to start the day than with a brisk shower, coffee, and donuts?

38

She was in the shower for a little longer than she had intended and, when she got out, Zachary was home, and the house was filled with the smell of fresh coffee and (not) zero-calorie donuts. Kenzie toweled off and ran her fingers through her damp hair, then pulled on a robe and joined him. When they kissed, Zachary already had coffee on his breath. Kenzie grabbed hers before sitting down.

"How are you doing?" Zachary asked. "You didn't get enough sleep."

"No. I'll have a nap this afternoon. What about you, though? You didn't get any."

He shrugged. "That's okay. It was planned. I'll be fine until tonight."

"You know you shouldn't do that very often."

"Do I?" he countered.

Kenzie had to admit that he did not. He was almost always home nights. Maybe he didn't sleep as many hours as she did, but he usually slept every night. Except for that period before Christmas when he had gone three or four days without sleep, and that had been really bad. That was probably why she was so worried about his missing one night of sleep when he kept assuring her that he had planned for it and would be fine.

What if he didn't sleep the next day and the next as well? It could be the beginning of a run.

But it was his choice, not hers, and he looked good, not like he was running on fumes. They sat down and shared their coffee and donuts, enjoying an unusually lazy breakfast.

"So, where were you this morning?" Kenzie asked. "You're not usually out this early. Were you back to check on the guy you were surveilling?"

"No, I stopped by the nursing home."

"The nursing home." Kenzie looked at him blankly, not understanding. Did he mean Sunshine Care? And if so, what had he been doing there? He didn't know that she had nearly been fired. He couldn't just go to Sunshine and say that he knew her or was following up on her inspection. "Why would you be there?"

He indicated his phone. "Downloading video."

"Oh." Kenzie's heart raced. "I thought we were going to leave it for a week to make sure that we got plenty of footage."

"The camera is still in place. I just downloaded remotely from the parking lot." He shook his head at her. "I didn't have to go inside," he assured her. "I just had to pull over for a couple of minutes where the signal was the strongest."

"Why did you change your mind?"

But of course, she knew why he had changed his mind. Because of Kenzie's visitor of the night before. He had apparently come from Sunshine Care, which meant things were getting bad over there. It meant that too many people knew about Kenzie and her investigation, and things could go south very quickly. In the unlikely event that someone found the spy camera Kenzie had left in Mr. Blake's room, they would know exactly who was responsible. With everyone there under suspicion, anyone could strike back against Kenzie, and it was best to figure out who the culprits were as quickly as possible, rather than obtaining all the footage they could.

"I'm hoping that we caught your friend," Zachary said. "If not… maybe the police can leverage it to identify him and put him away."

"It won't be the police; it is the Department investigating it. Under the direction of the Attorney General."

"The police are investigating the break-in. If we have evidence that ties in to the break-in, then we'll need to turn it in to the police."

"And get a police investigation going alongside the Department of Disabilities investigation?"

Zachary shrugged. "They run multi-jurisdictional investigations all the time. Why not?"

Kenzie took a bite of her donut. "Why not?" she conceded. "I guess there's nothing to stop them."

"The sooner we can get some arrests, the better."

Kenzie nodded. She didn't want to say too much about the night before and get emotional. She wanted to think about the home invasion and its impact on her life as little as possible. To limit the amount that it did impact her. If she didn't think about it, she could just go on as if it had not happened.

"Are you okay?" Zachary asked, watching her.

"Sure. I'm fine."

"You've got a pretty good shiner this morning."

"That should earn me at least one day at home, shouldn't it?"

"Definitely. Send Dr. Wiltshire a picture. Maybe he'll give you next week off too."

"I'd go stir crazy if I couldn't get into the office for a week."

"Zombie."

"I'm not a zombie," Kenzie grinned, looking for a way around saying that she would just miss her work if she were away for that long. It wasn't the bodies, necessarily, just something to keep her busy and make her feel like she was making a difference. "I just *happen* to work at an office with a few extra bodies lying around."

Zachary chuckled. "Zombie."

39

K enzie had wondered how long it would be before the
detective assigned to her case would show up to ask her
some more questions and hear her account with his
own ears. Or if anyone would come. There hadn't been any
damage to her house other than the door and doorframe, and
nothing had been stolen. She hadn't been threatened with a
weapon. She had only received a bruise during the incident. It was
possible that they would write it off as something not worth investigating. They probably had more important and interesting cases
to work on, and Kenzie's home invasion was not related to any
other criminal proceedings.

Except that it was; they just didn't know about it yet.

Detective Donald showed up mid-afternoon without a
warning call to let them know he was on his way. He just showed
up on the doorstep, ringing the doorbell, and was busy examining
the damage to the door when Zachary opened it. Zachary looked
at Donald, waiting for him to introduce himself.

"Detective Donald," he introduced himself curtly. "Criminal
Investigations. I'm looking for Kenzie Kirsch?"

Zachary stepped back to allow him in. Donald looked at the
damage on the door for a moment longer, then looked around the

front entryway, his eyes traveling to the electronic security panel before landing on Kenzie, standing slightly back from Zachary.

"Miss Kirsch, I assume."

"Doctor," Zachary corrected.

Donald's eyes flicked over to him, then back to Kenzie. "Dr. Kirsch. I'm sorry. Detective Donald. How about you walk me through what happened from the minute the intruder broke in through the door."

Kenzie shrugged. "I really don't know. I wasn't out here. I was asleep in bed."

He took a few steps toward the hall, waiting for her to show him. Kenzie rolled her eyes, grumbling to herself, and motioned for him to follow. She took him in and pointed to the bed. "So... I was here, sleeping. I woke up when he broke in, I guess. I thought that someone was here. Figured it was just Zachary getting home."

"You were out?" Donald asked Zachary. "Pretty late at night, wasn't it?"

Zachary nodded. "Yes. I was out on surveillance. Didn't expect to get home until the morning."

"You're on the job?"

"Private investigator."

"Oh." Donald's eyes immediately fell away from Zachary, indicating his disinterest. He looked back at Kenzie. "So you thought it was Zachary, but obviously it was not. When did you figure that out?"

"Not until he was right here. He was quiet, and..." Kenzie walked over to sit on the bed and tried to picture everything she had seen in her mind's eye. "I guess he was close enough to Zachary's size and shape that I didn't figure it out until he was right here." She pointed to where he had stopped beside the bed. "He didn't get into bed, he came around to this side and I couldn't figure out why. And then he started to talk, and I knew it wasn't him, but he was right there."

"Did you try to call the police? Give him a warning? Do you have any weapons in the house?"

"No. I reached to turn on the light, and he grabbed me and started talking. I didn't get a chance to pick up the phone until after he had left. Everything must have happened in just a minute or two. The security company said they were here within five minutes of the alarm going off, and the police were here within seven. It seemed a lot longer than that… and it seemed like just a few seconds."

Donald nodded. "And what did he say? He threatened you?"

"Didn't you read the statement that the officers took last night?"

"Of course, but I would like to see what you remember today. If anything has changed. Sometimes people remember new things. Sometimes they may realize that the timeline was different or understand something that was said that they didn't at the time."

"Well… he threatened me, yes, said that I needed to stop investigating. I assume he meant this death that I was writing the postmortem report for. He was previously at a nursing home, and I have been asking some questions there. I understood that the man was from the nursing home. Worked there. And that what I was doing was putting his job in jeopardy."

"Well, that narrows the field a little. You didn't tell this to O'Neil last night?"

"I did. But I don't have any proof that was what he was talking about. He was vague and roundabout."

"We don't need proof. If you think that he is an employee at the nursing home, a male employee of roughly your husband's size and build, who sounded like a young man… that narrows the suspect pool pretty significantly. That's something we can work with."

"Speaking of the nursing home…" Zachary started.

Donald turned to look at him. "You weren't here when it happened, so you're not a part of this conversation."

"You should listen to him," Kenzie told him.

He looked at her, then back at Zachary. "You weren't here."

"No. But when Kenzie was thinking of going to the nursing

home to ask some questions and see what was going on, I had some suggestions for her. Things that you might be interested in. Evidence."

"Evidence?" Donald's interest sharpened. "Physical evidence?"

"I gave Kenzie a micro camera to take with her, which could be mounted and record covertly, and the recording retrieved remotely."

"And you used this camera?" Donald looked at Kenzie and then at Zachary. "You do know that we have laws about recording people without their consent, don't you? This is not something that we can use in court."

"Vermont actually has very few recording laws," Zachary countered.

"In which case, we fall back on the federal laws, which say that someone being recorded has to give consent."

"If you post a sign that says they are under video surveillance, then they are presumed to consent to the recording."

"And you put a big sign up next to your little spy camera?" Donald asked sarcastically. He looked from Zachary to Kenzie.

"I didn't need to. There was already a sign in the room. The rooms are monitored by closed circuit camera so that patients can be monitored and staff supervised," Kenzie explained.

"But that isn't for your recording."

"It informs them they are being recorded. It doesn't say by whom. If an employee knows that his employer is monitoring him by video, then he should know not to do anything illegal on camera, right?"

Donald blinked at her a few times. He obviously knew that this was going somewhere. They had something on camera that they were willing to share. But he needed to accept that it could be used as part of his investigation. He looked from Kenzie to Zachary, evaluating them.

"Just what is on this video?"

"Evidence of neglect and abuses at Sunshine Care. Which I believe is what my attacker was talking about."

"You are sure that he works there."

"Pretty sure, yeah," Kenzie agreed. As she had told him, she didn't have definitive proof that he did work there but, five minutes ago, he had been satisfied that if she thought he worked at Sunshine, he probably did. She couldn't think of what else the man could have been warning her off about. That was the only investigation that was controversial. The other postmortems that she had done had all been straightforward, with no suggestion of homicide or other crimes against the victims.

"Okay," Donald finally agreed. "I'd like to see this recording."

40

Kenzie and Zachary had not been able to watch all of the video. That would take some time. But they had scrubbed through it quickly and tried to mark each time someone came into Mr. Blake's room. Interactions with the staff were generally over within thirty seconds, so it was pretty easy to watch that bit and then forward to the next one. Kenzie wasn't confident that they had found all of the entrances and exits of the staff. Some of them were so quick that it was easy to miss when looking at more than twenty-four hours' worth of recordings. They would go through it more slowly later. Or Donald or someone in forensics would. Since Kenzie wasn't actually a police investigator.

Zachary sat his laptop on the mobile desk in the living room, with Kenzie sitting beside him and Donald on one of the chairs. They didn't all have to crowd around the laptop screen, because Zachary set it up to broadcast to the TV, which was large enough for everyone in the living room to view comfortably. Zachary started at the beginning, with a shot of Kenzie looking up at the camera after it was activated. She turned around and spoke to Mr. Blake.

"Say cheese for the camera."

"So Mr. Blake knew that he was being recorded and gave

P.D. WORKMAN

consent too," Zachary pointed out. "Kenzie told him he was on camera."

Donald grunted. Kenzie knew that he would have difficulty explaining that to his boss and eventually the DA if it were to be used as evidence in court. Was Mr. Blake coherent enough to understand and give consent? Did the sign in the room advising that everything was being monitored and recorded constitute notice and consent from any of the staff who walked into the room? That would be up to the lawyers and judge to sort out, but Kenzie thought they had a pretty solid position.

Kenzie turned her back to the camera and walked out of the patient's room into the hallway. Where Kenzie knew she had met Dr. Carpenter and been hustled back to the reception area and told to be on her way. The door to Mr. Blake's room was left open.

"This is Sunshine Care," Kenzie announced. "Two days ago in the afternoon. Dr. Carpenter, the director of the home and I had just talked to Mr. Blake and, on examination, found him to be dehydrated. Dr. Carpenter said that he would give the staff orders to put Mr. Blake on an IV to replenish his fluids and make him more comfortable. He didn't write down the orders or a note while I was there."

Donald nodded. Kenzie pointed to the time in the corner of the screen. Amazing that a tiny camera like that could not only take such a clear picture, but also was able to sync time with the satellites that orbited the earth to ensure it was always correctly configured. Zachary scrubbed through the next couple of hours of video so that Donald could see the time passing rather than just jumping from one part of the video to another. He could see that no one had come into the room to see to Mr. Blake.

When the video resumed playing at normal speed, a nurse came to the doorway, poked her head in to look at Mr. Blake, and then she turned her head to talk to someone in the hallway and continued on her way outside the room. No interaction with Mr. Blake. No recording of his pulse or other vitals. No IV. No one to help him with his cup of water.

Zachary resumed scrubbing the video, and they both watched carefully until they reached the next scene they wanted to view.

"It's six o'clock," Kenzie noted the time in the corner of the recording. "And there is the dinner cart."

They all watched the tray-laden cart as it was pushed past the room. It did not stop to deliver a dinner to Mr. Blake. Zachary let it continue to play at standard speed. They all watched the empty doorway and the time advancing.

Donald shifted restlessly. He looked at Zachary and Kenzie. Then back at the screen again. The time continued to advance, and everyone waited. Of course, whoever was pushing the dinner cart might be taking it down to the far end of the hall and beginning to distribute dinners there. It might be five or ten minutes before they got back to Mr. Blake's room. Maybe even more.

Donald looked at Zachary, waiting impatiently. "Point taken," he growled. "How long before they took him his dinner?"

Zachary sped up the playback, not scrubbing to the next interaction, but letting Donald watch the video at 4x speed, and then 8x. The window in the patient's room darkened as the sun set. Kenzie looked at the time indicator. Nine o'clock. Donald looked at them again.

"Where is his dinner?"

Kenzie shook her head and shrugged.

"Did they think he was on IV, so he didn't need dinner?" Donald suggested.

"I don't know what they thought. But normally, you would still feed someone who was on IV. And of course... he wasn't on IV."

They looked at Mr. Blake lying in the bed. No IV stand beside him, no tube to his arm.

"Dehydration can be very dangerous," Kenzie said. "Especially to the elderly. In a few hours, they could fall into a coma and die."

"Please tell me that you don't have video of this guy dying because nobody bothered to hook him up to an IV."

Kenzie shook her head. "He's still hanging in there."

Zachary forwarded to a night nurse walking into the room and actually going to Mr. Blake's bedside to check on him. They watched her take his wrist to check his pulse, and pick up the cup on the bedside table and hold the straw to Mr. Blake's lips so that he could have a drink. She walked out of the view of the camera, probably to the restroom, and returned with the cup, which she once again set on the bedside table. One drink, maybe half a cup of water, since Kenzie had pointed out that he was dehydrated and Dr. Carpenter had said that he would order an IV.

It was a good thing that Mr. Blake was resting in a temperature-controlled environment. If he had been hot or walking around, he would have lost even more fluid and they might just be watching his murder on the video.

The nurse left again. Zachary jumped through each of the bed checks during the night, the night staff usually entering for a moment and giving Mr. Blake another sip from the cup, but sometimes just looking in through the doorway and moving on to the next room.

"There are no night meds," Kenzie said. "No monitoring other than checking his pulse. Luckily, he had one. No IV was ever inserted. Either Dr. Carpenter forgot to give the orders, or the staff didn't follow through."

The window was beginning to get light again. A male nurse entered the room. This was, Kenzie realized, the first male nurse who had appeared on the video since they had started it. She analyzed him, looking for anything familiar in his appearance. His size and shape, the way he moved, anything that might tip her off, whether this was the man who had broken into her house. Donald was looking at her.

Kenzie shook her head. "I don't think so," she said, answering his unspoken question. "He's too big, I think. I would have noticed that he was quite a bit taller and broader than Zachary."

"Are you sure?"

"Not one hundred percent. I had just been jolted out of sleep. Everything happened pretty quickly. I might have missed things.

But I think I would have noticed earlier that he wasn't Zachary. He just doesn't look the same."

This was the first nurse who had any more interaction with Mr. Blake than just checking his pulse and giving him another sip of water. He moved efficiently around the bed, changing Mr. Blake's clothes and diaper, sponging him down, and shifting his position onto his side instead of his back.

"That's the first time anyone has moved him. Someone who is lying in bed all day needs to be moved every two hours to avoid bedsores. I couldn't see any on the video, but they can develop very quickly and get infected."

"So you see this video as evidence that he was being neglected."

"Yes," Kenzie said. "He definitely was. Failing to put him on IV when he was dehydrated, not giving him any dinner or evening meds, not moving him for…" Kenzie tried to calculate it, "sixteen, seventeen hours."

"Does he get breakfast?"

Zachary advanced the video to the meal cart being taken around again. This time, a nurse placed a meal tray on the rolling table in Mr. Blake's room and pushed it in front of him. She offered him a drink from the cup with the meal, and then left again without a word.

"No morning meds," Kenzie observed. "If the patients in this facility are that frail, I would expect almost all of them to be on some kind of medication. I don't know about Mr. Blake specifically, but he hasn't received anything yet."

Mr. Blake's shaky hand went to the breakfast tray to pick up a slice of toast. He nibbled it until it was gone, Zachary playing the video at 4x speed. Then Blake's hands fell back to his side and he lay still until another staff member returned to pick up the tray. No one tried to feed him what remained on his plate.

"Eighteen hours," Kenzie said, looking at the clock. "And he's been changed and turned once and has had one piece of toast, some water, and whatever was in the cup. No IV and no meds."

Donald nodded his head, looking grim. Maybe they wouldn't be able to figure out who it was that had broken into the house and warned and attacked Kenzie, but for sure, there were going to be some repercussions for not feeding this one old man. How many others were suffering as he was? How much of their business plan was getting as many new patients with their money as possible, then neglecting them until they died, opening up rooms for more?

Kyle Howard was lucky he had gotten his father out when he had. Even though Joseph Howard ended up dying at home, at least he had been somewhere that someone cared about him. From what she could tell, Kyle had done his best to look after his father, even if he had been absent while he worked. Joseph Howard had still gotten more attention at home with the health care worker coming in twice a day than Mr. Blake was getting at Sunshine Care.

41

They continued to watch the surveillance video, jumping from one point to another as nurses stopped in the doorway to look in at Mr. Blake. A few of them entered to give him a drink or another meal. There was no lunch, as far as Kenzie could see, but he did get supper on the second day. She watched the man who brought the meal in and put it down on the rolling tray.

"It could be *him*," Kenzie suggested.

Zachary and Donald both turned and looked at her blankly.

"Oh," Donald said, waking up and apparently remembering why he was there. "You think that could be the man who broke in?"

"It could be. He seems... familiar. He's the right size and build. The first one we've seen on the recording who is. So it's possible, though I would never be able to swear to it."

"Worth getting as much information as we can about him," Donald said. "See what's in his background, if there have been any complaints about him. If he is known to be violent in any other setting. Sometimes one thing will lead to another..."

He made a note of the timestamp. "Can you get me a still of that?" he asked Zachary. "I'll have to send a copy to our AV guys, of course and, if I ask them, it will probably be three days before I actually get it. If you could message it to me…"

"No problem," Zachary agreed. He stepped through the video until he got what he figured was the best, most identifiable view, and then captured it and sent it to the number Donald gave him. Kenzie felt good, knowing he was going to do something about it. He would act on what was going on at Sunshine Care and follow up to find out if that was the man who had attacked him. It was progress on two fronts. Then everything at the Medical Examiner's Officer would settle down and go back to normal.

"Well, this was helpful," Donald admitted. "Is the rest pretty much the same?"

Zachary let the video run for a moment, playing through the scene of the man who might have been Kenzie's attacker giving Mr. Blake his meal, helping him to eat a few spoonfuls, and wiping his face with a napkin. It was the most interaction anyone had had with Blake yet, and Kenzie felt guilty for suggesting that he might be a criminal. There could be several men at Sunshine Care who had the same build. It wasn't proof of anything. There was some talk after Mr. Blake ate as much of the meal as he could. A tiny amount. His stomach was probably shriveled to the size of a walnut because of how he had been starved.

Mr. Blake asked after his son, whether he was coming to visit. Kenzie paid attention to the nurse's answers, trying to detect whether it was the same man as had threatened her the night before. It could be, but there was nothing to clinch it. No special phrase or accent like there would be if it were a TV show. Of course, he didn't know when Mr. Blake's son would visit next, if he ever would. He gave Blake another sip of his drink and said it was time to get him to bed. Kenzie had picked the best spot she could to place the camera, but it still wasn't ideal, and they could not see what was going on when the nurse had his back to the camera and was blocking the view of Mr. Blake.

They stared at the screen as the nurse blocked the view of what was happening. It couldn't be intentional, of course; he'd had no idea that Kenzie's camera was where it was. But Kenzie couldn't help but wonder if he were trying to cover something up. She remembered Kyle's concerns about sexual abuse. He hadn't known anything for sure. His father might have just been embarrassed at his son taking him to the bathroom. He might have felt humiliated about having to be helped to the toilet or having an accident. It might be nothing to do with any assault. But would a nurse or other staff member have been in a position to take advantage of him? The video showed that it was definitely a possibility. Even with a camera in the room, they couldn't tell for sure what was going on as the nurse spoke softly to Mr. Blake and changed him for bed.

When the nurse left the room, Zachary jumped forward to the next scene. Mr. Blake was crying, and an overweight female nurse was standing in the doorway, berating him loudly for having pressed his call button.

"He has a call button?" Donald asked. "Why hasn't he pressed it before now?"

Kenzie stared at the screen. "Well, uh…" she gestured to it. Wasn't it obvious? Why would he press it if he knew how she would react?

"My leg hurts," Mr. Blake complained, an old man sob in his voice. "Please, I need help. My leg hurts. Make it stop."

She continued to shout at him, telling him to go to sleep and not to bother the staff with his complaints.

"Please help me…"

Her shouts drowned out his pleading. She walked the rest of the way into his room and slapped him across the face, telling him to stop. Donald was out of his seat, fists clenched, ready to take on the image on the TV. He caught himself and gave a little laugh, shaking his head at his own reaction.

"I can't believe I…"

"I believe it," Kenzie said. "Remember, this is not the first time that Zachary and I have seen the video. Believe me; I wanted just as badly to jump through that screen and stop her. It's horrible. I have a knot in my stomach that's bigger than my stomach…"

Mr. Blake wept, but didn't voice any further complaint or ask for help. The nurse threw a few more choice curses in his direction before leaving. She did not hit him again. Even so, Kenzie was unable to relax when she disappeared from the scene, listening to Mr. Blake crying in pain. There were a couple more shots of nurses looking in the door at Mr. Blake, but they apparently did not see the need to enter and deal with whatever was wrong, and Mr. Blake did not press his call button again.

Donald sat down and leaned back. "Is that it?"

"I retrieved this video early this morning," Zachary said. "I don't know what happened after that. The device is still recording, I'll be able to retrieve more, but I was out of there before seven this morning."

"I'm going to go over there," Donald said. He shook his head, probably remembering that there was already an ongoing investigation. But he wasn't going to wait any longer. Regardless of how many people were being hurt at Sunshine Care, however many staff members there were who were negligent or abusive, he needed to see that Mr. Blake was okay. He needed to confront them about what they had seen on the video.

"What are you going to tell them about the video?" Zachary asked.

"I… have no idea."

"Maybe…" Zachary considered. "You can say that his son was trying to reach him and could not get through. He wanted a welfare check made, as he's out of the country."

Donald stared at him for a moment, then smiled slightly. "You'd think that this was how you made a living, or something."

"I'm pretty good at coming up with believable stories," Zachary admitted. "Blame it on a childhood full of getting into trouble."

Donald chuckled at that. He probably thought that Zachary was joking but, knowing what she did of his childhood, Kenzie knew that it was probably entirely true. He had spent a lot of time in trouble, and had probably spent almost as much time trying to come up with a story that would get him out of the penalty box again. Blame it on someone else. Come up with a reason that would excuse his lapse. He was very good at figuring out what people wanted to hear.

"Okay," Donald agreed. "I'm doing a welfare check on behalf of his son, who is out of town. We know he has a son because he was asking when he was going to come to visit." Donald looked at his watch. Kenzie was sure he was calculating how long it had been since that slap. Since that poor man had been writhing in pain, trying to stop crying, because he knew that no one was going to help him. "I will follow up with you to get that recording."

Zachary nodded. "I'll get it to you. Save it to the cloud so that you can download it."

Donald stood up. "I'll let you know what happens."

42

Kenzie doubted that Donald would call them back to tell them how his trip to Sunshine Care had gone. He would run into roadblocks in every direction. Even if he could get Mr. Blake the care he needed, the last thing he would be worried about was getting back to Kenzie and Zachary to let them know how things had gone. Cops didn't report to civilians on ongoing investigations.

They had watched the video again after Donald left. The most important scenes, followed by the less important ones, and then started watching the entire video at 4x speed. Kenzie didn't know how Zachary could do it. Her eyes and head were fatigued and there was no way she could continue to do it all day. But this was one of the things that Zachary was good at. Hyperfocusing on video evidence until he finally was able to see everything there was to see.

"You don't need to watch everything," Zachary told Kenzie when he realized she was too tired. "I'll mark everything, and you can look at the flagged bits later." He leaned back in his chair. "It only takes six hours to review twenty-four hours' worth of video at 4x."

"*Only* six hours." Kenzie shook her head. "I don't see how you can stare at the screen for that long. No wonder your eyes get dry."

He grinned. "I can look at screens all day."

"Whoever would have guessed that you could make a living at marathon TV watching."

She had to remind herself that this wasn't a paying job for Zachary. It was something he was helping her with. He should have been working on his own files rather than spending so much time on one of hers. But she wasn't about to tell him to leave it alone. He had been invaluable to her so far.

She was cleaning the kitchen when Detective Donald called her back. She looked at her phone but didn't recognize the number. She answered it anyway, knowing that it might be something to do with the break-in. The security company, insurance, the guy who was coming to fix the door, or one of the law enforcement officers on the case. It seemed like a dozen people were involved in cleaning up the aftermath of the burglary.

"Kenzie Kirsch."

"Dr. Kirsch. It's Detective Donald."

"Oh, hi!" Kenzie sat down at the table to take a break from her cleaning and hear what he had to say. "How is everything?"

"I just thought I'd circle back and let you know what we found out about Mr. Blake. This is all confidential, of course, but as you and Mr. Goldman were involved in bringing the situation to our attention…"

"Is he okay?" Kenzie was really worried that with the amount he was being neglected and abused—as proven by the video recording—that they would be too late to help him. The dehydration alone was enough to kill him.

"He's been transferred to the hospital, and they say he is holding his own."

"Oh, good. I'm glad you got there in time to help him."

"As am I. He looked pretty bad when I got there. His leg—you remember he was complaining about pain in his leg on the video

217

—was all black and blue, like it was bruised. But the hospital said it wasn't from being hit. It was a blood clot."

"Oh, the poor man." Kenzie closed her eyes. She had seen patients with blood clots and knew how painful it was. "How long had it been left?" She tried to calculate how much time had elapsed between his pressing his call button and Donald getting there to check on him. And how long it would have taken the hospital to see what was wrong and get the clot dissolved in order to restore circulation.

"They said they don't know if he'll keep the leg or not. They'll have to wait and see."

A large clot cutting off the circulation of blood to Mr. Blake's leg for an extended period would result in the death of the cells that were no longer oxygenated, which could lead to gangrene and amputation.

"That poor old man. I can't believe that the nurse just slapped him and wouldn't even look at his leg to see what was wrong. She was just angry at being interrupted from whatever game she was playing on her phone or staff member she was flirting with. That's terrible."

"We are now coordinating with the Department of Disabilities, Aging and Independent Living's investigation. They have been… alerted to the fact that there is a video showing both neglect and abuse. They are gathering what they can of the surveillance video recorded by the home itself. There will be… many, many hours of tape to be reviewed."

"Actual tape?" Kenzie asked, "Or is it digital?"

"I don't know what kind of system they have. It doesn't look like it is a very modern set-up. I'm not sure that all of the cameras are working. But there is still a lot of information to be recovered."

"Well, at least you can view it at a higher speed. That's what Zachary's doing right now."

"He's watching it again?"

"Yes." Kenzie laughed. "It's what he does."

"I guess it pays off. So that's the information about Mr. Blake.

I have yet to figure out who the nurse who slapped him was. Everyone is remaining pretty close-mouthed about who was on duty last night and, of course, everyone on the night shift is now home sleeping, so they are unavailable. But we'll sort that out. And then the man who broke into your house…"

"I'm not *sure* it's the man that I pointed out on tape," Kenzie reminded him. "It's just a possibility."

"Well, I would say it is more than a possibility at this point. The guy has run."

"He's run?"

"Not answering his phone. I sent officers by his home, and he's cleared out. Left the furniture and stuff he didn't need behind, packed a bag, and ran. Everything of value has been removed, other than the TV. No computer, tablet, cash, jewelry, nothing like that. All of his paperwork and mail. He clearly knew that the investigation was going to find something."

"He seemed nice on the video. One of the only nurses who actually spent any time with Mr. Blake."

"Yes," Donald conceded. "It's too bad he had to be one of the bad guys. It would have been better if he and the others who are doing a good job could have just stayed and worked with new management to turn the place around. There will be big changes and, as you said, it looked like he was one of the good ones. I'm not sure why he ran, other than… breaking into your house and threatening you. If he hadn't done that, I don't think we would have anything against him. But…" Donald trailed off. Then his voice returned more strongly. "But it is early in the investigation, and you never know what else he might have done while he's been there. If you're the kind of person who will break into a woman's house and hit her in the face because she's trying to do the right thing, then chances are, you've stepped over another line some-where along the way."

Kenzie gave a short laugh. "Yes, I would guess so. I doubt that's the first time he's ever bent the law a little."

43

Kenzie updated Zachary on the news from Detective Donald. He was relieved that Mr. Blake had been taken to the hospital where he would be treated rather than abused. Of course, there was never any guarantee that there wouldn't be negligent or abusive workers at the hospital either. Kenzie and Zachary had learned this lesson too well in the recent past. But there would be a lot of eyes on Mr. Blake. A lot of people from different agencies making sure that he was treated well and given the best shot possible at recovery. If he had one stray bruise on him during his stay there...

Zachary had finished watching the video recording and walked Kenzie through the newest points he had flagged. It didn't take long, since they were all incidents that had been too brief for them to notice the first time they had scrubbed through the video at a higher speed. Kenzie was not happy that there were so many examples of abuse and neglect of just one patient in a day and a half. Of course they would be treating any other patient exactly the same way they treated Mr. Blake. They wouldn't just have all picked him as their target. Maybe some patients who were more mobile or had closer family members who would listen to their complaints had been spared the full treatment Mr. Blake had gotten, but Kenzie had to doubt that the abuse had been limited to him.

She caught Zachary looking at the time on his phone several times as the day drew on and they had their supper. Kenzie had her suspicions about what that meant.

"You're not going out tonight, right?"

Zachary looked at her, startled. "What?"

"Don't act like you didn't hear what I said. I just want to make sure that you're staying home tonight. You're not going out, right? You'll catch up on that surveillance job in a few days, not tonight."

"I could probably do it tonight, and get it done and out of the way."

"No. You didn't get any sleep last night. It wouldn't be a good idea to miss again tonight. Besides," she nudged his foot under the table. "I need someone here to protect me tonight."

Zachary smiled. "You're tough. You don't need to be protected."

"Even someone tough still needs to be protected some of the time. You know that."

He raised his brows and nodded.

"I don't want to be home alone tonight," Kenzie said more seriously. "I want someone with me to hold me and make sure that everything goes okay, and that I can be calm and go to sleep. I don't want to get freaked out because I'm alone in the house."

"Yes." Zachary bought into this immediately, nodding and putting his hand over hers on the table. "I'll stay home. The surveillance can wait for another time."

"Good. I don't know how long it will be before I feel comfortable being alone at night. It might take a little bit."

"However long you need," he assured her.

Kenzie wanted to tell him that he might as well give up on nighttime surveillance altogether, because she wasn't sure if she would ever be comfortable being left at home alone at night again. Anything could happen while he was gone. She didn't want to impose a time limit for recovery on herself. It would take more than a night. It might take more than a week or a month. She needed to know that he would be there for her no matter how long it took.

"It didn't seem like it had affected you that much," Zachary said slowly. "You seemed… very strong. Like you took it all in stride. I didn't realize."

"I'm good at covering things up. That doesn't mean that I don't feel them."

"I didn't mean that."

"Just because I act fine and joke around and make light of it, that doesn't mean that I don't feel it as strongly as anyone else. Just that… I'm trying to keep my sanity and not be dragged down by it. Things can happen that really affect you, but you don't let anyone know what they are. Until later."

He gazed at her for a long moment without saying anything. Then he nodded and broke eye contact. "Of course. I just didn't realize that you did that too."

"I don't think it's just you and me. I think everyone does, to an extent. So… this is me telling you that I don't want to focus on the break-in or have a big deep conversation about it, but it still affected me and I'm going to need some time to get past it."

"Okay. If you want to talk about it… I'm here. And if you don't… I'm here too. Maybe you want to set up an appointment with Dr. B to talk about it. She's very good at anxiety and trauma-related stuff."

"I know she is. I've seen her work with you, and she's always been good with our couple's therapy. I just don't know if I want her to be my personal therapist. I'd rather have someone… with more separation. Someone who is not working with you too."

That way, she could be sure that no confidences would be broken in either direction. The therapist wouldn't need to remember what had been said in couple's counseling and what had been said in private sessions with Zachary or with Kenzie, accidentally slipping one day and giving away a secret that one of them held. She was more concerned about her own confidences, of course, but she also didn't want anyone who might betray Zachary's confidences. He needed to be in control of what he shared and what he didn't. She didn't kid herself that he told her all of his thoughts and feelings or that he had told her everything she needed to know about his past. It would be a lot of years before they had unwrapped all of that, if ever.

Kenzie's phone rang. She looked down at it. They had a no-phones-at-dinner rule, but they were finished eating, so it was probably okay if she got up from the table to take it. She looked at Zachary to see how he felt.

"Go ahead. I'll clean up."

He would *start* to clean up. But he would probably get distracted halfway through and she would have to do the rest. But that was okay with Kenzie today. She would finish up whatever he forgot about. Provided he at least started on it.

Kenzie stepped away from the table, nodding her thanks and raising the phone to her ear to answer it.

"Kenzie Kirsch."

"Dr. Kirsch." The voice was muffled and seemed far away. Kenzie wasn't sure whether it was a bad connection or something going on in the background on the other end.

"Hello? I can barely hear you."

"Dr. Kirsch." It was a little more clear, as if she had moved closer to the phone, but it was still not the best connection. Definitely a woman, though, so not Detective Donald. "I need to talk to you."

"Yes, go ahead. I'm listening."

"I want to talk face to face."

"Who is this?"

The caller didn't answer.

"I'm not meeting some stranger alone," Kenzie advised. She had made that mistake once and she would never do it again.

"We need to meet."

"I don't see why. You can tell me what you want over the

phone or send me a message. We don't need to meet face to face. Who is this?"

"I'm… someone with information that you want."

"You must have a name. Anonymous sources aren't much good to me. How am I supposed to verify anything? If you have information, you should go to the police. They'll be able to help you."

"No, not the police. You're different. You're a doctor."

Kenzie heard the words the caller didn't say. *You understand.* What would Kenzie understand better as a doctor? She knew that she should leave the investigation to Detective Donald and the Department of Disabilities, Aging and Independent Living, but if there was information that was coming to her from someone afraid to talk to the authorities, didn't she have a responsibility to find out what that information was? To get whatever she could? They could all vet it once she knew what it was but, without knowing anything, she couldn't tell whether it would be of any use to them and how to best handle it.

The caller could be a complete crank. She might not know anything about any of Kenzie's cases, but had just happened to see her name in the news or on a report somewhere. Cranks were like that sometimes. They fastened onto a random person and decided she was the only one who could help.

"What kind of information do you have?" she asked reluctantly. "What is it you're calling me about? I'm really not interested in changing my cell phone service provider," she teased. As if this woman might just be a telemarketer with a fresh approach. But her joke seemed to confuse the caller.

"What? No. I'm not trying to sell you something!"

"No? What kind of information do you have? And why do we need to meet face to face?"

"I'm not asking for money for my information. I just think that you should know what's going on. Someone should know. And… I'm not going to be around for long."

"Where are you going?"

"Everyone is in a panic. People are quitting or threatening to quit. They said that we need to read our contracts, because we are required to give proper notice and all of that, but people are just abandoning ship like drowning rats. I can't stay in a place like this."

"Are you at Sunshine Care? Is that what you're talking about?"

"I… I can't tell you where I am. But yes, it's about Sunshine."

"There is a joint police and Department of Disabilities, Aging and Independent Living investigation going on. The Department of Disabilities includes doctors and medical professionals if you want to talk to someone with a background in medicine or patient care. You should call them. They'll meet with you and help you figure out what to do."

"I don't want to talk to them. Do you know how often we've had those stupid people through this facility? How many times they've just turned a blind eye to everything, said that they don't have enough proof, or said that the home has to start doing this or that but never followed up? People are still getting hurt. The same thing is going to happen again. They'll look at what's happening in the home, and then they'll just shrug their shoulders and walk away."

The knot in Kenzie's stomach tightened. She thought of Mr. Blake begging for help. Of his pressing the call button even though he knew that the staff would be upset with him, crying and pleading for them to help him as the flesh in his leg began to die. Of how he had been slapped for asking for help. How many other people like Mr. Blake was she willing to let be hurt?

"I'm just one person. There's not that much I can do. I'll just have to pass the information on to the police."

"But they'll listen to you because of who you are. You're the Medical Examiner. They have to listen to what you say."

"I'm an assistant in the Medical Examiner's Office," Kenzie corrected. "And nobody has to listen to me. They don't want me interfering in the investigation. They want me to keep the Medical Examiner's Office out of it."

"How can you? People will just keep dying."

And they wouldn't come across Kenzie's table, because as they died under Dr. Carpenter's care, and the care of the other doctors employed by Sunshine Care, they would not be suspicious deaths. He would certify that they had been ill and had died of natural causes and release them directly to the funeral homes. There would be no ripples felt at the Medical Examiner's Office. That was how it was meant to work.

"I don't know what I can do to help you," Kenzie apologized. "I think you're going to need to go to the police or the Department and explain what you know."

"Don't you want to know about the man who broke into your house?"

Kenzie felt a chill. How had this woman heard about that? From the police? From the man who had done it? Kenzie couldn't imagine it would be common knowledge at the nursing home. It wasn't like the man who had attacked her would be telling everyone about it. Detective Donald would not have made a general announcement about it.

"Do you know something about him?"

"We can talk about that when we meet."

Kenzie sighed. "I am not going to meet with you. Do you want... what about a video call? Then we could be face to face, but no one would be in any danger."

Kenzie didn't want to suggest that she would be in danger if she met with this informant, but that didn't change the fact that she would be. She couldn't control who might show up at the meeting place. She could be murdered or kidnapped. She wasn't going to take that risk. Not this time. Even if she was curious about how the caller knew about the attack, and if she really knew the identity of the man who had done it. Or how to find him, since Donald had said he had run. Did her caller know where he had run to? Maybe he was with her. Maybe they were partners—all the more reason to be extra cautious. The burglar might have other ideas about ways to get back at Kenzie for the disruption she had caused at Sunshine Care.

"I don't know..." the woman considered this. Kenzie was proud of herself for coming up with the idea. The woman could have her face-to-face meeting without Kenzie being in additional danger. And, of course, she would pass any information she got on to Detective Donald so that he could investigate it further. She wouldn't be directly involved in anything. Everybody would be happy.

"It's easy enough to do," Kenzie persisted. "I don't know why you feel like you need to see me face to face, but you could. And I wouldn't have to put myself at risk."

"What do you think I would do to you?" the caller scoffed.

"I've seen bad things happen," Kenzie said, deciding she didn't need to know any details. "There is no guarantee that you are working alone, and I don't want to take any chances that you've got half a dozen men willing to do whatever you tell them to."

"You think I work for some kind of gang?" She laughed. "That I'm some kind of gang boss, telling people what to do? Order them to what, kidnap you?" She laughed again.

"I have no way of knowing. I don't know who you are. You won't even give me your first name. You could be anyone. You could be a man using a voice changer."

The woman apparently did not have a comeback for this. Kenzie wondered in the ensuing silence if she had unwittingly hit on the truth. That it wasn't even a woman who was calling her. That it was a man masquerading, hoping to draw her out. Maybe the man who had attacked her. That would explain how she knew about the attack, which was not public knowledge.

"Fine," the caller finally agreed. "I suppose we can do a video call. But I would rather meet you face to face."

Kenzie was sure she would. "That's not going to happen."

"I said okay. So how do I reach you?"

"You can set up the call and then just text me the link to connect."

"To what number?"

"To this number," Kenzie said, frowning.

"I thought I called a landline. At the Medical Examiner's Office."

Which was forwarded to Kenzie's cell so that she wouldn't miss any important calls.

"Well then, send it through the *Contact Us* form on the Medical Examiner's Office website."

"And you'll get it?"

"Yes. Are you going to give me your name?"

"You can call me... Deep Throat."

Kenzie rolled her eyes. "You've got to be kidding me." Maybe that was the answer to why she thought she had to meet with Kenzie face to face. It was the drama, the way she had seen meeting with informants play out on TV. Spy stories, dramatic portrayals of Watergate. She thought it was all a game.

"Why?" the woman questioned, apparently hurt. "What's wrong with that?"

"I'm not calling you Deep Throat. I'll call you... Jane. You're a nurse? I'll call you Nurse Jane."

"I don't really like the name—"

"You had your opportunity to pick a name and you didn't. So you're Nurse Jane."

"Fine." Jane's voice was sullen. "I don't care. What difference does that make?"

"Use the name Jane in the *Contact Us* form so I know it's you. Send me the link to the meeting you set up and what time you want to meet. Then... we'll talk."

There was no reason the woman couldn't give Kenzie whatever information she had on the phone right then. There wasn't any need for them to meet face to face or over video call. Information was information. But just in case Jane did have information that Kenzie wanted, she would accommodate the woman and find out what it was.

44

Kenzie had expected Jane to send her a message regarding the proposed meeting within seconds of getting off the phone. She refreshed her email several times looking for the Contact Us form message, but didn't get one. Maybe it was all a hoax, and they had been planning something for her. Kenzie was not prepared to deal with another murder or kidnapping. Kenzie sent herself a message through the form to ensure that it was not broken. She could call Jane back at the number she had called from, but she didn't want Jane to have her cell phone number.

Maybe she had changed her mind.

Whatever it was, Kenzie was happy not to meet with Jane. It was better that she didn't get involved in the investigation any more.

Dr. Wiltshire would agree. Detective Donald would agree, and Zachary would probably agree as well, despite his own penchant for digging deeper.

So, Kenzie would continue with her evening and not worry about Jane Doe's call.

She returned to the kitchen to finish clearing up after supper. As expected, Zachary hadn't managed to clean up the kitchen completely, but he hadn't done a bad job of it. There were a few pieces of cutlery on the table, a bottle of salad dressing, and his small spiral notebook, which he had apparently started jotting something down in before following some stray thought and pursuing it down a rabbit trail on his computer. Kenzie put the cutlery in the dishwasher, the salad dressing in the fridge, and wiped down the counters and table before starting the dishwasher. She picked up Zachary's notebook and walked up to his mobile desk in the living room, where he was hard at work, his eyes intent on the screen.

"You left this in the kitchen." Kenzie put it down beside his mouse hand.

While he often blocked her out when he was hyperfocused on something, undeterred by any attempt to get his attention, her movement in putting his notebook down did pull him out of his focused state, and his eyes moved over to the notebook to figure out what it was and why she had just put it down there. He picked it up, and his hand went automatically to his pocket to tuck it away, while his brows drew down.

"What? Where did that come from?"

"It was in the kitchen. On the table."

"Oh, was it?" He laughed and shook his head. "Thanks." He leaned back and stretched. "You're off the phone. Was it a work call?"

"Well… no, not really. I'm not sure what to call it. It wasn't a personal call either. It was someone who wanted to meet with me about Sunshine Care."

Zachary's dark brows drew down. "I don't think that's a good idea."

"Neither do I. I suggested that we video call instead, if she really has to see my face. I don't understand why she's so insistent that it has to be face to face, but I'm not going off to meet a stranger." Kenzie almost opened her mouth to say that she'd made that mistake once before, but then ground her teeth together to keep from saying anything when she remembered that he still didn't know about what had happened. He had been in the hospital at the time, and Kenzie hadn't found a way to bring it up casually since then. She wanted a way to say it that wouldn't cause him to go off the deep end or to worry about her.

"That's good," Zachary agreed. "Anything could happen. You don't know if she's really who she says she is. Or if she's working with someone else."

"That's exactly what I said."

"Good." He looked at her. "So you're not meeting?"

"We might have a video call. But so far, she hasn't gotten back to me with any details, so no. Maybe a video call. But definitely not in person."

"Good," he repeated. "Did you want to do something now?" He motioned to the TV. "Watch a show or play a game? Read a book?"

"I wouldn't mind just vegging in front of the TV. I know it's not good for our bodies just to lie around, but I'm so tired today. I don't know why, since I've barely done anything, but I'm just completely wiped out."

"It's emotional. And you're short on sleep from last night too. It isn't exactly like you've had a restful day. Not dealing with cops and watching surveillance video."

"I guess not. I don't feel like I've done anything, but somehow the day is gone and I'm spent."

"Let's see if there is something good on, then." Zachary picked up the TV remote and turned the TV on.

Kenzie's phone rang again. She shook her head and picked it up to look at the screen, sure it would be Jane again, irritated that Kenzie hadn't answered her email inquiry or worried about something else that had happened at Sunshine Care. But it wasn't Jane's number; it was Hillary, the woman who kept things running smoothly at the Kirsch family foundation.

"Hello?"

"Kenzie. Sorry to call you so late, but I didn't want to catch you at work, and I'm not sure what time you're usually home."

"Yeah, it varies by quite a bit. But you managed to get me at home today. What's up?"

"I have emailed you a few documents you need to review, sign, and return to me. It's not so urgent that I have to call you at home to get you to deal with them immediately. That's just one of the things on my list. When you can get to them, I'd appreciate it. Tomorrow would be fine."

Kenzie would probably deal with it that night. Despite Hillary's attempt at not riding her about getting those documents turned around immediately, she would be waiting for them and would not be happy if Kenzie took a day or two to get around to them.

"Okay. I'll take care of that."

"Also, I was talking to Walter, and he said that you were going to send me some information about a candidate for some of the admin work that I need a hand with?"

"Oh, that's right. I hadn't gotten around to that yet. We were talking about Zachary's brother."

Zachary's head turned toward Kenzie, cocked slightly, listening to the conversation.

"He's underemployed at the moment and I would really like to get him into something more suitable and where there is some room for advancement. It was Walter who said that there might be a place for him at the foundation. Just doing some office lackey work for you to begin with, but maybe moving into a position where he can help to screen companies that are looking for grants and help to target the programs with the most social impact."

Zachary raised his brows at this. Kenzie frowned. Had she not mentioned anything about it to Zachary? Probably not. Other things had forced Walter's suggestion out of her mind, and she didn't want to get Zachary's or Tyrrell's hopes up before she was sure there was a good chance of it working out.

"Oh, of course," Hillary said warmly. "I'd be happy to talk to him and see if there's a good fit. What is his background?"

"He's a college graduate, got a degree in Behavioral Science.

But he has problems with addiction issues of his own, so he hasn't been able to hold down a job for long. He's in recovery right now. Went through a twelve-week treatment program and did really well. He's back on his feet, and I'd love to see him doing something other than boring postholes or flipping burgers."

"Sounds like there are possibilities there," Hillary agreed. "Send me his information—resume, contact details—and I'll have a look over it and give him a call."

"Thanks, Hillary. I'll do that. Sorry I hadn't gotten around to it yet. I should have written it down after talking to Walter."

"I'll look at that information when you send it, then. Now I have a few more things on my list of things to deal with for Walter."

Kenzie heard a note of exasperation in her voice and chuckled. "Good luck to you, then. Thanks."

She hung up. Zachary was looking at her with open interest.

"Sorry I hadn't given you a heads-up," Kenzie said. "I wanted to make sure that he had a good chance of getting it before I mentioned it to anyone."

"Tyrrell working at your family foundation?"

"Yeah. I was asking my father about what programs there might be that could help him out, and he was the one who suggested that maybe Tyrell would be a good match for working with the foundation."

Zachary looked pleased with this, but more cautious than Kenzie would have expected. "That would be..." He trailed off. "I was going to say that would be great, but I'm not so sure that it is. I'd love to have him into a better job, but I worry about it being with your family."

"You don't think it's a good match?"

"I just know that he'll probably screw it up at some point, and I don't want to be on bad terms with you or your parents because he leaves the foundation in the lurch. Mixing family and work can be a bad decision."

"Or it can be a good one, like you asking Heather to work with you."

"Yes." Zachary nodded. "She's been great. But she's a lot more stable than Tyrrell. She doesn't have an addiction. Or a history of failed jobs."

"She basically had no work history when you took her on. And no training in what you wanted her to do."

He considered this and looked a little surprised. "Well... yes, I guess that's true. I'm not saying I don't think it's a good idea for Tyrrell to work with the foundation. Just that I don't think it's a good idea... if they think that he's going to be able to be... reliable. When chances are, he won't be. He'll work there for a few months and then go off the rails again."

"We don't know for sure that's going to happen. He may be able to hold it together this time. With our support and a good job... he might find his place."

Zachary nodded. "Yes... but his history isn't good."

"You heard me tell Hillary that. I want everyone to know right from the start what we're dealing with. But if no one gives him a chance, there's no way to find out if it will work."

"You haven't told Tyrrell yet?"

"No. Do you think I should tell him before I send his resume over?"

Zachary chewed on his lip, then shook his head. "No. Let's take it another step before we do that."

Kenzie nodded. That had been her instinct as well. She didn't want to get Tyrrell's hopes up. But if Hillary liked what she saw and was willing to interview Tyrrell... at that point, she would have to tell him, wouldn't she?

45

Kenzie didn't remember until the next morning that she needed to sign the foundation documents and send them back to Hillary. And when she checked her email, she found that Jane had finally gotten around to sending her a message through the Medical Examiner's Office website with the details of the video conference she had set up.

And, of course, she had picked a time that Kenzie would be busy at work. She couldn't exactly drop everything to take the call.

Kenzie looked around herself and realized that she could, in fact, take the call whenever she wanted to. It was a Saturday, and although she had chosen to come in to tackle the jobs that she had missed the previous day, she didn't actually have a list of things that she had to do, so she could take a break for the call with Jane whenever she pleased. She was not officially on shift.

She still didn't like the time of the meeting being dictated, rather than Jane asking her what time would work well for her and making sure that she would be available. But Jane saw herself as the one doing Kenzie a favor and thought she should be able to dictate the terms.

As far as Kenzie was concerned, she was the one doing something for Jane. She should have just insisted that the woman talk to the police. That was the right course to take. Instead, Kenzie had somehow let herself be pulled into something that she knew she should not be.

Kenzie signed the documents Hillary had sent her, scanned them, and returned them. Then she worked diligently through the other jobs that she should have done on Friday when she had decided to stay home and take care of her own physical and mental health. There was physical and electronic filing to do, and Kenzie had to check for new sign-ins to make sure that all the bodies were there and all the paperwork was filled out correctly. Dr. Wiltshire's desk had been left in a mess.

Nothing out of the ordinary.

Dr. Wiltshire wasn't around, so Kenzie had the run of the place. When the time that Jane had set for the video meeting arrived, she commandeered the boardroom and used the video equipment in there instead of just her phone. She would be able to see Jane on the big screen and would be able to move without worrying about leaning outside the camera range or having the camera pointed directly up her nose.

Five minutes before the meeting was scheduled to start, she clicked on the link and let the app run through the connection procedure and setting up the camera and microphone. Kenzie looked at the screen and waited for the second square to pop up, indicating that Jane was connecting.

The appointed start time passed and Kenzie shifted around anxiously. Had something happened to her informant? Or was it a power play, showing Kenzie that she had the upper hand?

Or maybe she was just chronically late, and Kenzie was reading too much into it.

Or a technology glitch.

Kenzie checked the message she had received through the website again to ensure that she had the right time and connection link. She might have copied something over wrong. But everything seemed to be correct.

It was nearly ten past when a bubble popped up that said that Jane was connecting. Kenzie noted with wry amusement that the call connected with Jane's account name clearly labeled. Lea Skinner. In a few seconds, Lea Skinner disappeared and was replaced by Jane.

She had thought that she would recognize Jane when she saw her. That she would be one of the people that Kenzie had talked to the day she visited the nursing home. Maybe it would even be the man who had attacked her. He probably wouldn't show her his face, but would hide behind a virtual mask or avatar. But she had known all along that it might be someone using a voice changer app or device.

"Hi," Kenzie said. She looked at the corner of the screen where the time was displayed. "I was getting ready to hang up. Thought you weren't coming."

"Sorry, I ended up not being able to get out when I thought I would." Jane looked around as if she were afraid someone might be watching her. From what Kenzie could tell, Jane was sitting in the driver's seat of her car. Not driving, luckily. But with the windows rolled up, the car was a good place for Jane to ensure that no one would overhear her. Not like a room where someone might be listening at the door or a restaurant or mall where someone might be hovering nearby or even reading lips from a distance. She was isolated. Protected.

"Well, let's get this show on the road, then," Kenzie said briskly. Jane might be in the driver's seat, but Kenzie was the one who was in control of the situation now. Jane was meeting Kenzie on her ground and, if she really had information that she wanted to give to Kenzie, now was the time. If Jane messed around, Kenzie could just terminate the call. Jane couldn't force her to take another. And Kenzie could go directly to the police with what she knew. Jane didn't have any leverage other than the suggestion that she might have information that Kenzie would be interested in. And she might not even have any information they didn't already have. Kenzie and the police were already sure that there was abuse going on at Sunshine. They didn't need anyone else to tell them that.

"You're really her," Jane said, looking her over. "Kenzie Kirsch. I looked you up, and you're really her."

"Yes," Kenzie agreed. She didn't need anyone telling her who she was.

"And you're the one who started all of this? The investigation into Sunshine Care?"

"Partly me, yes. Based on what we discovered in a postmortem and the testimony of the decedent's son. Our office filed a report on suspicion of elder abuse. And the Department started their investigation. I… happened to visit Sunshine in person at the same time as the investigation was being launched."

That was all true, though it masked the fact that Kenzie had not actually been at Sunshine as part of the investigation.

"There have been reports filed before," Jane said. "What makes this one any different?"

"You tell me. Have the others turned anything up?"

"No. The investigators have been in and out and have never followed through on anything. They might tell the administration that something needs to be changed, but they never do. Nothing changes. Only maybe it gets worse. Every time, they figure out they can get away with more and more, and no one really cares."

Kenzie hated thinking about Mr. Blake and the other residents, seeing people come to investigate conditions at the home and then just to turn around and leave again without changing anything. Every time, sinking deeper and deeper into despair. Knowing that no one was ever going to rescue them from the torture they were going through. How long had Mr. Blake been there? A few weeks? Months? How long had they been starving and abusing him?

"Well, things are going to change this time," Kenzie said with assurance. "Arrests will be made. No one will be able to gloss over it this time."

"I hope not."

"But you said you weren't going to stay there. You're going to run away. Why are you going to run if you know what's going on there and haven't been a part of it? Why don't you stay and help to rebuild afterward? Help the patients to heal and recover."

"I can't stay there. And as far as everything changing... I don't think you can do that. I don't think you can make them change how that place is run. And I don't want to be a part of it anymore."

"Then why are you afraid to go to the police? Just tell them everything you know. They can't retaliate if you're leaving anyway."

"They can't?" Jane repeated. She stared through the camera at Kenzie. "They came to your house, didn't they? You don't work there, and they still retaliated against you."

"Well..." Kenzie couldn't very well deny that. "But I'm told that the guy who did that has already run. He's not going to come after me if he's already left town."

"Who says he's left town?"

"The police think he has. He packed a bag and left."

"That doesn't mean he's left town. He could just be somewhere else here. In a hotel or couch surfing at a friend's house. There's nothing to say that he's gone out of town."

Kenzie made a mental note to ask Donald whether the guy had credit card charges out of town or anything that pointed to where he was staying.

"You think he's still here?"

"I don't know. But he's not the only one to be afraid of."

"How many people are involved in this? It seemed from the vid—it seemed like there would have to be a lot of people involved in the abuse or covering it up. With the amount that was going on, I don't see how it could be hidden."

"I don't know." Jane shook her head and again looked around her surreptitiously to make sure that no one was watching or listening to her. "One person starts doing something... not bothering to do what he's told... making fun of the patients... and he attracts other people to him that are the same way. Maybe they start to get their friends hired. They put pressure on anyone who calls them out. Makes them back down. They keep getting away with it, even though these inspections keep popping up. And that just makes them bolder... I can't stay there. It's toxic. I don't want to be bullied. I hate how they treat the patients, but if I say anything, even being diligent in my work, they think I'm going to rat on them and try to make trouble. I hate them."

Kenzie nodded. "Who is it? Can you tell me some of their names?"

"Names? I can't give you names." She shook her head anxiously. "No. I just... I'm sorry, but if I name names..."

"Then why are you here? Why are we both here? If you aren't going to give me any information we can act on, then why bother? Just run away."

"I'm not running away," Jane protested, her voice sullen as a teenager's. Did she feel like she was being judged unfairly? She had just finished saying that she was going to leave the nursing home and not name any names. It was ridiculous to say she wasn't running away.

"What are you doing, then? You're leaving. You're not helping anyone. You just wanted to make sure that I was aware that there was abuse going on? Great, but I already knew that. Why do you think I was over there in the first place?"

"But you're *someone*. You can do something about it."

Kenzie shook her head. "I'm not anyone. I'm an Assistant Medical Examiner. I don't have any say in what happens in the investigation. I shouldn't have even been at the nursing home. I got in trouble for that. You might think that I can effect change, but..." Kenzie shrugged. She should probably dial it back. If Jane didn't think Kenzie could do anything with the information she was given, what was the point in giving it to her?

"No," Jane insisted, shaking her head. "You're the Medical Examiner. That's big. And your dad is that big lobbyist, and your mom does all kinds of stuff with charities. I know their names. They're on all kinds of A-lists."

"How do you know who my parents are?"

"It's not hard to find out. I can find things out. You can influence this investigation. You can have your dad *make* them do something about Sunshine Care. He can call on his friends. Pull in favors. People like you have *pull*."

Kenzie shook her head. The woman had no idea what life was like for Kenzie. She didn't go around calling on her parents for favors. She did her best to be independent of them. To make sure that no one could accuse her of calling in favors.

"You need to stop these people," Jane said desperately. "You can't let them keep hurting people."

"I need names. How can I stop them if I don't know who they are? Is Dr. Carpenter involved? What doctors and nurses know what is going on or are a part of it? How do you expect anyone to know that?"

"They're pulling the video. I hear that they have a hundred video feeds to analyze, and that it goes all the way back to Christmas."

The thought of that much video was dizzying. How could anyone analyze that much video? It would take years to watch it and catalog each misdeed. Who had the time for a project like that? Even with all of their detectives on it, Kenzie couldn't see how such a massive project could be accomplished. There were still other crimes to investigate. Everything wouldn't stop while they looked into Sunshine Care.

"Do you know how long that would take?"

Jane shook her head. "It doesn't matter. It's all there, right? I don't need to tell you anything because it's all on the video."

"We need to know who the people in the video are. We need to know what's going on when their body blocks the camera from recording what is happening. And it would take months… *years* to analyze that much video."

"They can get the FBI to help. They can get computers to watch it. Then you'll know everything that happened."

"No. Only everything that happened in front of the cameras.

I'm sure plenty happened outside of the range of the cameras too. And people knew where the cameras were. They wouldn't do anything overt in the view of the camera."

"You can stop them. Request more resources." Jane's eyes were bright. "Get your father to make them put more money into it. Into getting people to review the tapes. They have to watch them and stop them from ever hurting anyone again."

"Does Dr. Carpenter know?" Kenzie demanded. The man had certainly been circumspect during the inspection. He was either dense or hiding something. "Tell me that."

"I don't know. He never talks about it. He never talks to me. But does he *know* about it? He must."

"How often does he go into the patients' rooms? When does he interact directly with the patients so they could tell him about it?"

"He must, though. He's the one that's in charge. He must hear things."

"Maybe." Kenzie agreed. "Or maybe he doesn't want to hear things and makes sure that the communications go through someone else. So that he can always deny that he knew anything."

"He knows, he must."

Kenzie sighed. "Is that all, then? You just wanted to see me face to face so you could tell me to stop all the bad guys. Even though you don't know who they are. Even though you won't do anything to help."

"That's not how it is. I can't. They know who I am and, if I talk to the police, they'll know it was me and come after me."

"Then why did you come to me?"

Jane looked at her for a long time without saying anything. Her face twisted into expressions of frustration, anger, and grief as she tried to work through what to say to Kenzie. How to get Kenzie to *make them stop.*

"I just... had to do *something.*"

46

I have one question before you go," Kenzie said.

Jane wiped at her eyes. Kenzie couldn't see any tears, but she believed that Jane was feeling emotionally spent about everything that had happened and the energy and will it had taken to talk to Kenzie about it, even if she hadn't provided anything particularly helpful.

If they had been meeting face to face, then maybe Kenzie would have given her a hug or a warm touch on the arm to comfort her. As it was, she felt very far away from Jane.

"What did you want to ask?" Jane queried with a sniffle. She looked as if she were expecting Kenzie to launch more accusations at her. Maybe to accuse her of being one of the abusers instead of just someone who had stayed quiet, allowing the abuse to continue.

"The son of a man that I talked to, whose father came through the morgue a little while after he had been at Sunshine Care, said that he thought that there might have been sexual abuse."

Jane looked at her with wide eyes. "Sexual abuse of who?" she asked. "The nurses?"

Kenzie hadn't even thought along those lines. If there was abuse of the patients and a culture of violence toward those who might spread the dark secrets of Sunshine Care, then it wasn't a stretch that there might have been violence, sexual or otherwise, aimed at the nurses and other staff as well.

"I didn't mean the nurses," she clarified. "I meant the patients."

"The patients?" Jane shook her head. "They're elderly! In their eighties and nineties, most of them. And very frail. No one would be having sex with them."

"Sexual abuse isn't about whether they are attractive or not," Kenzie said. "It's about power and self-gratification. It has very little to do with the victims. Could there have been anything like that going on?"

"No. Certainly not." She shook her head, definite. "I would have known if something like that was going on."

"Would you? It would probably be going on behind closed doors. Cloaked as patient care. You never thought that anyone took longer to clean or change a patient than you thought it should take? You never walked into a patient's room and startled another staff member? Someone who looked guilty or like they were hiding something?"

Jane's eyes closed halfway. Kenzie wasn't sure whether she was thinking about or imagining the scenarios that Kenzie suggested or if she was trying to hide her own thoughts and memories. Her face was a mask, giving away nothing.

Because it was too horrific to think about? Or because she knew that it had been going on and didn't want Kenzie to read that in her face?

"Did you ever see anything?" Kenzie pressed.

"No. I never saw anything like that. Nothing that ever made me think that someone was doing that. I think..." She shook her head, frowning.

"What?"

"That son probably just overheard staff members talking. Sometimes they say things that are inappropriate. That someone might interpret the wrong way."

"Oh?" This was not the scenario that Kyle had described, but

Kenzie wanted to hear more about what Jane had connected with the possibility of abuse.

"Because people talk sometimes, you know, say inappropriate things. Things about patients or the jobs we do. In a place like Sunshine, where you spend so much time taking care of... things that people can't do for themselves... there's just a lot of pressure, and... I think that people say things to distance themselves from the patients. To pretend that we aren't all going to be there one day, where we can't take care of ourselves or our bodily functions."

Kenzie tried to put the pieces together with her own experience at medical school to try to put it into words that made sense. "You mean... saying things about patients' intimate parts. Sexualizing or desexualizing them. Making raunchy jokes. Using... explicit language. That kind of thing."

Jane nodded. "Yes. It's just part of... changing diapers for adults. Dealing with patients who don't know what is improper to do in front of other people because of dementia. Or old people who are flirty or make lewd suggestions. It's just... How do you deal with all of that professionally? People say things. But that doesn't mean that there is any abuse going on. Just... talk. Humor to lighten the stresses of the job."

"Maybe it isn't all talk. You don't think it is possible that staff members could be sexually abusing patients? Taking liberties when they change a patient or take them to the toilet. Gratifying themselves. There are a lot of closed doors when you walk along the halls."

"That's just for patient privacy. There are cameras in all of those rooms. No one could get away with abusing the patients that way."

"You already know that they are getting away with abusing patients in other ways. Hurting them. Neglecting them. Not giving them needed fluids or medications. Starving them. Slapping them when they are too demanding."

"Are you talking about that man they took to the hospital yesterday? Poor Mr. Blake?"

"He was crying in pain, calling for help. He had a blood clot in his leg, which I'm sure you realize is very painful. But instead of helping him, the nurse who answered his call slapped him and shouted at him."

Jane looked down. "That poor man."

"If that kind of thing can happen under the view of the surveillance cameras and not be addressed immediately, then that tells me that it would be easy for sexual abuse to be going on out of camera range or with the view partially obscured without anyone noticing or caring. Since the nurses are often involved in personal care, no one would think anything of activities that involve undressing or touching those areas of the body."

Jane shook her head, not saying anything.

"And the culture you have described, where not only is abuse rampant, but also ribald talk about the patients is normal and accepted… I can't imagine that there's *not* some level of sexual abuse going on."

Jane closed her eyes the rest of the way and shook her head. "No. Just talk. Nothing physical."

But even with Jane denying it, Kenzie felt like she had her answer. Poor Joseph Howard. And poor Mr. Blake. And the same went for all of the patients at Sunshine Care. And at other facilities. It was so easy to take advantage of the vulnerable.

"Well…" Kenzie straightened up, signaling that she was ready to end the call. She suspected that Jane wished she had just hung up five minutes earlier. Before they had to get into the distasteful topic of sexual abuse. "I'm afraid that's all the time I have for this call. Was there anything else?"

"No." Jane shook her head. She was definitely second-guessing her decision to go to Kenzie. Kenzie didn't know whether it was just that feeling of having told someone too much and regretting it or whether Jane hadn't gotten something out of the conversation that she had hoped to. She seemed to think that Kenzie had some way of remedying the situation at Sunshine Care, when Kenzie had even less impact in that area than Jane did. Jane was there; she knew what was going on. Kenzie was an outsider with only a few glimpses of what was going on inside and no way to change anything.

"Okay. You know how to reach me if something else comes up. But I would suggest going to the police instead. They're the ones who can do something about it. Telling me these things—or not telling me anything—doesn't do anybody any good."

Jane nodded her agreement, her mouth a straight line. She disappeared from the screen, apparently having thumbed the end call button with the thumb of her hand holding the phone, without making any other motion.

Kenzie sat looking at the end screen of the video call for a minute, running through the conversation in her mind and wondering if she had gained anything at all, or if she had just managed to make someone else upset with her. She'd have the entire workforce at Sunshine Care gunning for her before too long. She tapped a few buttons on her phone and called Detective Donald.

47

She reached his voicemail. Kenzie supposed that he wasn't really on duty on a Saturday. Unlike a detective on TV who only had a couple of days to a week to solve a crime and had to work at all times, day and night, he was in it for the long haul and needed to protect his own time for himself or his family. While he probably worked long hours each day, he might work a week on and a week off, or on four days and then off for three days. Something that allowed him some sanity and time to recuperate. Other detectives on other teams would work other shifts. She would just have to wait until Donald was back on. She left him a brief message and hung up.

Before she completed her walk from the boardroom table to her desk, her phone was ringing. Kenzie looked at it as she sat down and saw that Donald was already returning her call.

Kenzie swiped the call. "Hi."

"Dr. Kirsch. You had something further?"

"I don't actually think that it's very helpful to you, but I had a video call with one of the staff at Sunshine Care. I tried several times to get her to deal with the police, but she wouldn't, so eventually, I just took her call."

"I see. And you didn't find anything that you thought helpful?"

"Not really. I can give you a copy of the call, though."

"A copy?" Kenzie could practically hear his eyebrows climbing higher as he asked for more detail.

"She wanted to meet face to face, but I wouldn't do it. I told her that I would meet her on a video call if she wanted to see me face to face, but I wasn't going to meet her somewhere."

"That's probably wise. You wouldn't want to walk into some kind of ambush."

Kenzie's gut clenched and her heart raced. She was still not over it. Still unable to tolerate words like "ambush" or "kidnapping" without reacting physically. She took a deep breath and tried to continue without letting her voice waver.

"Exactly."

"But don't those video call facilities have an electronic voice that tells everyone they are being recorded?" Donald asked. He'd clearly been in a few recorded meetings himself.

"Yes. If you record them using the video call app."

"I see. But you didn't record it using the app."

"No."

"More hidden spy cameras?"

"Not exactly, no. I used the camera and mike in our boardroom down here. They have good video conference facilities, the sound and camera hardwired into the computer that runs the video call. I just... propped my phone up on the conference room table in front of me so that it captured the big screen and used its built-in microphone. It won't be a high-quality recording, but I played back a minute of it, and the audio and video are both clear."

"Aren't you sneaky? That PI boyfriend of yours has been teaching you some tricks."

Kenzie had to admit that living with Zachary had definitely made her more aware of things like bugs and covert surveillance. Before living with him, she had never thought much about how much of what she did might be observed or recorded by an outsider. Or of the situations in which she might want to surveil somebody else. He had enlightened her. Probably as much as she had taught him about postmortems and many of the unusual things that might show up in an autopsy.

"Living with him might have exposed me to a few things," she admitted with a smile.

"Well, in this case, that is good for me. But you still need to be careful of covertly recording people. The spy cam at the nursing home was more than a little bit over the line."

"They knew they were being recorded," Kenzie repeated. "They just didn't know *all* of the people they were being recorded by."

Donald grunted.

"You need to get me the recording, then. What is the easiest way for you to get it to me? Cloud sharing? A USB drive? If you're in the building, I can have someone come downstairs to fetch it. Or you could take it up. I'm not at the office, but someone will be at the desk."

"So much for our days off. I'll send you a cloud link so you can access it if you ever have a moment."

"No rest for the wicked," Donald said. "We are actually getting ready to make a series of arrests in relation to Sunshine Care. We'll hit the nursing home first to net the people working today and prevent anyone from calling out to warn others. Then we'll move on to those who are home."

Kenzie's heart sped in anticipation. Something *was* being done. Despite Jane's certainty that the joint investigation was not going to make a lick of difference, they were moving forward to do something about it. And faster than Kenzie had anticipated. She knew that building a case like this, where so many different people were involved in what amounted to a criminal enterprise, it could take months or years before they had the evidence they needed to make the arrests to shut it down. Arresting just a person or two on the bottom rungs would not shut down the enterprise. They needed to make sweeping arrests, following the criminal conspiracy up the line.

"How many arrests?"

He probably wouldn't tell her. It was confidential, a police action being put into play as they spoke. He wouldn't want a civilian like Kenzie to know about it. Someone who could make a phone call and mess everything up for them.

"A significant number," Donald said. "I'm sure you will hear about it later."

If it would be big enough to make the news, as Donald was implying, then there must be a lot of them. Would Dr. Carpenter be one of them? Kenzie's attacker, if he was still in town rather than on the run as they had initially thought? And what about Jane? How complicit was she in what had happened at Sunshine Care? Was she really just an innocent bystander, bullied into silence, as she had suggested? Or had she been more involved than she admitted? Kenzie was inclined to think that she was a bit more guilty than she would have Kenzie believe. Maybe not enough to warrant criminal charges, but perhaps a few misdemeanors? Or possibly offered a deal if she would turn on the worst of the perpetrators to ensure they were convicted?

"I'll be looking forward to it. Thanks so much for making sure that the arrests go ahead. I was afraid that... it would all just fall through the cracks. There wouldn't be enough evidence for you to take any action."

"There is always the danger of that. But I can't take the credit. A lot of people have been coordinating information in this investigation. Not just the police department and the Department. It's been quite the circus getting everybody lined up and the information assembled. A lot of people working long hours to make sure that all of the I's are dotted and T's are crossed."

"All in the past few days?"

"No," Donald confirmed what Kenzie had suspected. "There has been interest in Sunshine Care from various quarters. Several inspections in the past have not turned up a lot of information but have added to what we know. Your findings and the spy cam video have helped to move things along a bit faster, but they would have hit the tipping point soon either way."

"That's good." Kenzie didn't like the idea of everyone relying on her for everything. It was good that there was plenty of corroborating evidence from other quarters, that the case would have gone ahead even if she hadn't noticed the mark on Joseph Howard's neck, hadn't followed up with his son, and hadn't found out about the neglect and abuse he had suffered at Sunshine Care. It would all have come to light sooner or later, even without her. There was some comfort in that.

She could go home confident that many of the perpetrators at Sunshine Care would be sleeping in cells that night.

48

Zachary was not alone when Kenzie returned to the house.

Kenzie looked at Tyrrell and tried to remember whether Zachary had mentioned that he was coming over. She was sure she hadn't forgotten a planned dinner party this time. Tyrrell might have just dropped by for a chat, or Zachary might have called him for something else. They might have decided to get together to hang out for a while, Zachary knowing that Kenzie would be gone for at least a few hours. She was glad they were spending more time together, supporting one another. So much of what they had been through was not something they could share with anyone else. Other people could not understand all that had gone on in their childhood home or how they had been affected by the disaster that had ended in their being separated. Other people could not understand the difficulty of growing up in foster care, dealing with addiction and mental illness, and trying to put back together a family that had been ripped apart decades before.

Even though they had not shared the same experiences after being separated, there was still enough of a shared basis that they connected in a way that they would probably never connect to anyone else other than maybe the other siblings.

Tyrrell smiled. "Hey, Kenzie."

"How are you doing?"

"Good. I got a call from Hillary today."

"Oh!" Kenzie smiled. "I guess she liked your resume, then."

"I really appreciate you passing my name on. Especially since... it's a family thing. I don't want to mess up any relationship with your family. I don't want to screw things up."

"Let's just take it one day at a time," Kenzie said. "Don't put extra pressure on yourself."

He nodded slowly. "I'll try not to."

"Did she want you to come in for an interview?" Kenzie asked tentatively. Of course Tyrrell wouldn't be there to thank her if Hillary had turned him down as a candidate.

"Actually, she wanted me to go to Burlington to see what I would be doing to see if it is something I want to do. So I *think* that's further along than an interview. I think I've got the job if I want it."

"Sounds like it. That's great!" Kenzie realized, though, that there was another problem. The foundation offices were in Burlington, and Tyrrell's apartment was in Roxboro. It was too far to commute. "What... um... what about it being in Burlington? I hadn't thought about it before because I mostly deal with them by email. And if I need to go to the office to do something, I combine it with a trip to see my mother, so it's never *really* out of my way."

"She said I could work remotely for most of it. There might be some stuff that they want me to be at the office for, but usually, I can work by email or connecting with their server—and mailing physical packages back and forth when there are paper forms to be entered into the database or things like that. And maybe sometimes they'll want me to take a meeting here so that Hillary doesn't have to make the trip herself. Later, when I'm more up to speed on the foundation and its vision and policies and everything. Not right away."

"Oh, good. That saves a lot of travel time! And maybe if you get bored or don't like being alone, you can bring your laptop over here if Zachary is doing computer work too. Hang out and pretend you're office mates."

Tyrrell looked at Zachary, raising his brows questioningly. Zachary nodded. "Sure. That could work out sometimes. Just give me a call to make sure it works. That I'm not out in the field."

"That's what he says when he goes shopping," Kenzie teased.

They both laughed.

"That's really good," Kenzie reiterated. "I hope that it's something you like."

"I'm willing to do anything right now," Tyrrell said. "But from what Hillary said, it sounded like it could grow into something I can use my degree for, which I had kind of given up on. A while just doing data entry and filing and grunt work while I learn the ropes, and then if that works out and we're all still interested… moving up the ladder."

"I think this calls for a celebratory drink," Zachary said.

Kenzie and Tyrrell both looked at him. Zachary went to the fridge and pulled out several cans of soda. "No need to look at me like that. I haven't completely lost my mind."

"I just thought… you'd slipped a cog," Tyrrell said, picking up a can of ginger ale.

Even when Tyrrell was not there, Zachary rarely drank. Sometimes a beer or a glass of wine at dinner. Very occasionally, something in the evening with Kenzie. But the timing had to be right. He could not take alcohol with some of his medications, so he had to be sure that he would not need to take one of his anxiety pills or sleeping aids that night and that he hadn't taken anything in the preceding hours that was contraindicated. It was a delicate balance, so usually, he just didn't drink. But now and then, it was pleasant to have something together.

Just not when Tyrrell was there. And they didn't keep any alcohol in the house since he had gotten out of his last program so that there were no temptations when he came over to visit.

Zachary chuckled and popped open a cola for himself. Kenzie shook her head at them both. She took Zachary's can from his hand and poured an inch into her glass. She didn't actually want any, but a celebratory drink was a celebratory drink.

"To the foundation," she said, raising her glass.

The others echoed the toast and clinked glasses.

49

It was Sunday morning, which meant that Kenzie was not going to work. She tried to keep at least one day a week clear so that she and Zachary could have some quality time together and she could sleep in and recover from the week. Some Sundays, they traveled south to visit with Lorne and Pat, but they had visited the week before, so Kenzie hadn't felt the need to set anything up.

Despite Sunday being a sleep-in day, she hadn't actually been able to sleep past sunrise, so she had decided to run her errands first thing in the morning before the stores were busy. She would be able to get things done twice as fast if she could beat the crowds. Zachary, of course, was already up. It was rare that he slept past sunrise himself. Often he was up several hours before she was. She didn't know how he could survive on so little sleep, but somehow he did, and she tried not to worry about it.

"Do you want to come along?" she asked him.

Zachary didn't look up from his computer.

"Zachary."

He still didn't move. Kenzie moved toward him and stood directly in front of him. When he didn't respond, she put her hand in front of the screen.

Zachary flinched back. "What? Oh, sorry. Did you say something?"

"I didn't mean to startle you."

Sometimes getting his attention when he was hyperfocused on something was almost impossible. Touching his shoulder or hand was just as likely to startle him, but repeating his name or increasing the volume rarely had any effect whatsoever.

Zachary waved off the apology. "I was just into something. I wasn't listening. What did you ask?"

"I just wanted to know if you wanted to come with me. To do some shopping and run errands. But if you're that focused on what you're doing, I should probably just leave you to it."

He shrugged. "Yeah... I'm kind of into the flow."

"Say no more. Did you need anything else added to the shopping list?"

"Umm... no. I can't think of anything."

He rarely could. And he didn't think to write things down as they occurred to him. So instead, Kenzie had to face the "Did you remember to get...?" questions when she returned and unpacked the groceries, which was annoying when she had just spent all that time planning out and doing her shopping with no input from him.

"If there's anything you want, I want to hear about it now, not when I get back..."

"No, I don't think so. I haven't noticed anything."

"Snacks, batteries, something you want for lunches?"

She should be asking herself about lunches, since she was the one who was always too busy to make herself a lunch and then didn't like what she could get out of the vending machine at the office. She knew she should buy something that she would enjoy eating for lunches, but she was never sure what she wanted. She just knew it wasn't stale sandwiches and chips from the machine.

"Nope," Zachary shook his head. "Can't think of anything."

His eyes were back on the computer screen. "Did you see the—"

"Think about it for a minute," Kenzie insisted. "Don't just tell me that you don't need anything when there are things that you need me to pick up."

He pointed at his computer screen, opening his mouth to tell her about something that he had read, then stopped when he saw her stern expression.

"Uh… okay. Let me think about it for a minute." Zachary stood up. He wiped his palms on his pants, then went to the kitchen and started looking through the kitchen cupboards and the fridge to see if there was anything he was missing that he would want replaced. Eventually, he had checked all of the pantry shelves and fridge drawers and shook his head. "No. I don't see anything. Maybe some soup."

Kenzie didn't know if she had ever seen him eat soup. "What kind of soup?"

"I don't know. Canned soup. Something you can just heat up in the microwave."

"What flavor? Tomato soup? Cream of mushroom? Meatball?"

"Meatball soup?" Zachary echoed.

Kenzie spread her hands apart. "There are all kinds of soup. What kind were you thinking?"

"What we used to get sometimes when we were kids… I don't know what it was called or what was in it…"

"What you used to get when you were kids." That wasn't very enlightening. "What did it taste like?"

He shrugged. "Soup."

"What color was it?" He had already said he didn't know what was in it, so there was no point in asking that again. But she would think he could at least tell her whether it had beans or noodles in it.

"Sort of yellowy and clear. There were… little bits. Hmm. Stars?"

Kenzie blew out her breath, laughing. "Chicken and Stars," she told him. "Campbell's, right? Red and white can?"

Zachary nodded uncertainly. "I think so. I don't really remember. I was just thinking of it the other day, how I've never had that soup since I went into foster care. I guess... none of my foster families ever had it. I don't know why. Or maybe they did, and I just forgot about it. But I can remember eating it at home. Joss making it for us."

"I'll have to ask her what else you guys ate. I can get Chicken and Stars. Is that it, then? Just a can of soup? You'll want to eat more than that during the week."

He chuckled. "I assume you're going to get all of the usual stuff too."

Kenzie rolled her eyes. She would get the usual stuff... if she knew what they were out of and what he would want to eat. Sometimes she felt like it was a losing battle. "Okay. Back to work with you. I want you to be all done when I get back, and we'll have lunch together. Chicken and Stars. With crackers. Did you guys eat it with saltines?"

Zachary nodded slowly, his eyes back on his laptop screen. "Yeah. Sometimes."

Kenzie was on her way, knowing that her shopping list wasn't complete, but she wanted to go a number of places, so it was probably best if she didn't have too long to spend at the grocery store anyway. Zachary could make another grocery run during the week while she was at the morgue, once he'd figured out what he wanted to eat that they didn't have.

Planning out her route, Kenzie figured she'd better hit the grocery store last so that the frozen stuff wouldn't thaw. She filled the tank with gas, made a couple of other stops, and then hit the grocery store.

While working her way up and down the aisles and checking items off her list, Kenzie found herself unaccountably anxious. She was sure it wasn't over forgetting to get something they needed. And there wasn't anything that she was really worried about.

Tyrrell's job at the foundation was on her mind, but she wasn't *that* worried about it. Hillary would like him, and he would like the job, and he would have at least a few months before there was any danger of his falling off the wagon. He would be on his best behavior for the first little while. It wouldn't be until several months or a year had passed that he would start feeling the pressure of the job and the temptation to go on a binge. So it really wasn't that.

Maybe it was the remnants of her concern over Joseph Howard and all of the elderly people in home care and nursing homes like Sunshine Care. There were a lot of people who needed care, and instead of receiving the comfort and compassion that they deserved, they were being abused and neglected. Even when someone like Kyle Howard was doing the best he could to provide what his father needed. She was concerned about the investigation, but she believed that Donald and the multi-disciplinary team they had organized were capable of taking care of it and were on top of things. She would have to check the news later to see if anyone was reporting on the multiple arrests that Donald had promised. It felt good to know that they were proceeding, so she wasn't sure what it was she was so anxious about.

She continued working her way through her shopping list and the aisles of the store. She realized that she had just passed the canned soup in a fog and turned back around to grab Zachary's Chicken and Stars. A man coming toward her turned abruptly and hurried to the end of the aisle, then disappeared around the corner.

Kenzie looked after him for a moment, then went on. Like Kenzie, he had obviously forgotten something and turned around to get it. Something that every shopper must do at least once during each shopping trip. She searched the shelves to find the Chicken and Stars and also grabbed a couple of other varieties of soup she might eat for her lunch or possibly expand Zachary's palate to include. She turned around again to continue shopping.

She looked at the list on her phone before entering the next aisle. A few more things, and then she would be done. Hopefully, she could check out quickly, as the store was still pretty quiet. Then she had a few things she wanted to get done around the house.

Looking up from her phone as she rounded the next aisle, Kenzie saw a figure flit around the other end of the aisle. The same man she had just seen turn and walk away from her on the last aisle?

But that was the way it was when she was shopping. *Everyone* was going up and down the aisles, and she was bound to pass the same people over and over again as they made their way through the store. The same as when she made a long trip on the highway and kept passing and being passed by the same vehicles, seeing them at the gas station or restaurant along the way.

Kenzie grabbed a bottle of salad dressing without paying any attention to the label. She kept her eyes on the end of the aisle to see if the man made a reappearance. She was sure it was nothing. She was already anxious, so she had started looking for something to explain her anxiety. It happened all the time. Human brains liked patterns and logical explanations.

Throughout the rest of the grocery shopping, she did not catch a clear glimpse of the man again. He had probably finished his shopping and checked out. It had only been a coincidence that she had seen him turn away from her a couple of times. She was still feeling the aftereffects of someone having broken into her house. It was only natural to experience paranoia and hypervigilance after such an invasion of the space she had previously thought safe and secure.

As she reached the last aisle, completing her list, Kenzie had a gnawing feeling of dread. It dragged at her, pulling her back when she needed just to check out and then she could go home. The elusive man was nowhere in sight. She was perfectly safe in her local grocery store on a quiet Sunday morning. There weren't many places she was less likely to be attacked.

Kenzie's phone was hot in her hand. She looked down at it,

expecting a text or call to come in from Zachary. He would sense that something was wrong and want to know when she would get home. But he didn't call. She thumbed her home button and then the phone icon.

The phone rang several times and, remembering how focused he had been on his work before she left, Kenzie worried that he wouldn't hear it and wouldn't pick up at all. She would get home and find him still staring at his laptop screen, notifications of missed calls on his phone screen.

"Kenzie, hi."

"Hi." Kenzie sighed out a breath, grateful that he had answered. "How are things going?"

Zachary paused, probably trying to figure out why she had called him to ask that. He was just doing his normal work. Nothing that had any impact on Kenzie or was likely to interest her.

"Things are fine." His voice ended in an upward note. A question. Wanting to know why she had called. When she didn't say anything, he went on. "How about with you? How are the errands going?"

"Good. I'm just about done. Just need to check out, and then I'll be on my way."

"Uh-huh."

Kenzie gave a little groan, trying to figure out how to say what she had to say without upsetting him. "I'm just... feeling a little anxious."

"What's wrong?"

"Nothing, I don't think. It's probably just because of the break-in. It's only natural that I would feel some anxiety after that, right?"

"Definitely. Perfectly normal."

"So I'm sure it's just that. But..."

He waited. "But...?"

"This is so stupid. I'm worried that someone might be following me."

"Really." In her mind's eye, Kenzie could see Zachary straightening up, going on the alert like a dog being called to hunt. He didn't echo "following you?" in a disbelieving voice. He didn't brush it off. "Where are you? The grocery store?"

"Yes."

"I'll come over."

Kenzie protested weakly. "You don't need to do that. I'm sure it's just an overactive imagination. You are followed at the grocery store all the time, aren't you? Because everyone is doing the same thing, going up and down the aisles, following the same path. Following the same path isn't following or stalking. It's just... going to the same place."

"I'd feel better about it if you weren't there alone. I'll come and meet you. We'll drive home together so I can make sure you're not tailed."

"Really? Do you think that's necessary?"

"Probably not," he said in a reassuring tone. "It's probably overkill. But I'm going to do it just to be on the safe side."

He hadn't said that he wanted to do it, or asked if she wanted him to do it. His words were definite. He was going to do it. There was no point in Kenzie expressing any more reservations about it. It probably was nothing. It probably was just another shopper. Not the guy who had threatened her. Not anyone else from Sunshine Care. No one intent on getting their revenge on her. But either way, Zachary would be there to ensure she wasn't followed home. They weren't going to get her again.

"Okay," Kenzie told him, feeling relieved. "I'll check out and load up the car, then I'll wait for you. It will only take you five minutes to get here."

"Less," Zachary said, and she knew by his tone of voice that he was wearing his speed-demon smile. She chuckled.

"See you in a few minutes, then."

Kenzie felt better after terminating the call. It was probably nothing. Zachary agreed. But he would come anyway and make sure that she was not at risk. They would drive back home, he would help her to unpack the groceries and put them away, and they would have Chicken and Stars for lunch. Her feet were not so heavy, and she was able to drag herself out to an available till and start placing her items on the conveyor belt.

She had expected Zachary to be there by the time she was finished paying for her purchases. Not just waiting beside her car, but standing inside the store, waiting impatiently for her to bag her groceries and get out to the car. Assuring her that he had not seen anything suspicious, and he would make sure that she got home safely.

But it did take longer than five minutes to make the trip safely. And he would need to pull himself away from his computer, put on his shoes, and get out to his car before that. Something might have distracted him. He might have had to go to the bathroom first or stopped to run a brush through his short, stubbly hair. Kenzie sighed and pushed her cart out to her car. She would have everything in the car and ready to go once he got there. Then they could just drive home. She was beginning to feel a little silly about calling him in the first place. Did she really think that she had a stalker?

It was laughable. The man who had broken in and attacked her was on the run. He had left town. He wasn't dogging her at the grocery store, checking up on what brand of soup she bought. No one had an ax to grind against her. No one knew that she would be at the grocery store at that moment. She had run a series of errands and hadn't seen anyone following her at any of the other stores or on the road.

It was just silly.

Kenzie's eyes caught on something on the pavement, and she leaned down for a closer look. A couple of quarters. She reached to pick them up.

50

Something hit the back of her head. Kenzie slapped her hand to her head, turning to look, her brain jumping to the conclusion that a bird had run into the back of her head. She remembered how it had felt when, as a child, she had bent down to look at and pick up a baby bird she thought had fallen from its nest, and the parent birds had dive-bombed her, smacking her in the back of the head with their wings.

But it wasn't a pair of protective birds. Large hands grasped her, pulling her off balance before she could straighten all the way up and dragging her beside the store, out of sight of anyone she might call out to for help. Kenzie stumbled and tried to pull away from him, trying to twist her arms out of his grasp.

"Stop it! Leave me alone!" she protested. "Let me go!"

She couldn't see him at first. Everything was a blur and he moved quickly, wrestling her into the alley beside or behind the store, shoving her against the concrete-block wall. She didn't know if she was being mugged or molested, kidnapped or murdered.

Kenzie braced herself against him, pinned in place, and tried to focus on him.

Kyle.

Kyle Howard.

Why would Kyle Howard be attacking her? She had done everything she could to help him find out the answers about his father, his stay at Sunshine Care, and what had killed him. She had been diligent in everything she had done. Yes, he had been angry about her not making her report and releasing the body to him earlier, but she had submitted her postmortem report and the body had been released to the funeral home so that he could bury his father and move forward in his grieving. So why was he angry with her?

"Kyle! Stop. What's going on? What's wrong? I don't understand!"

He spat curses at her, grabbing the collar of her blouse to hold her still when she tried to wriggle out of his grasp.

"It's your fault! It's all your fault! How could you do this to me?"

"What? I don't understand. I didn't do anything to hurt you."

"I told you what happened. Why wouldn't you believe me? Why are you telling everyone these lies?"

Kenzie was breathing heavily. She swallowed and shook her head slightly as she tried to comprehend what he was saying. "I don't... I didn't..."

"I did not kill my father! You said that I tied him up and allowed him to strangle to death. That isn't what happened!" Kyle twisted his hand, tightening Kenzie's shirt collar around her neck. "I did not neglect my father! I loved him and took care of him. I took him out of that place! That horrible, terrible place that dared to call themselves 'home.' Sunshine? Care? It was the darkest dungeon of a place that I could have sent him to. He didn't deserve to be there, and I rescued him. I wasn't like these other people who just let their loved ones suffer there, who never go to see them and to see that there is something wrong with the place. I went to see him all the time, almost every day, and I saw that they were not helping him. That he was getting worse under their care instead of better. I helped him!"

Kenzie nodded. She couldn't swallow and didn't think she

should try to talk. She felt like any sound she made would encourage him to tighten his throttlehold on her more so that she couldn't get any air at all.

"You want to know if he had the posey on when he died?" Kyle demanded. "Of course he did. Do you think I wanted him wandering around at night and getting into trouble? Setting the house on fire? Falling and breaking a hip? Once these old people break a hip, it's the end of the road for them. Do you know how many times I have heard someone say, 'he was just fine until he broke his hip'?" He twisted Kenzie's collar tighter. "I was taking care of my father. Making sure that he got all of the care that he needed. Doing it *myself* to ensure that he was properly taken care of. Everybody said that I should just leave him in that home. That I should quit trying to control everything or do everything myself and let them take care of him." He stared into Kenzie's face, eyes blazing. "Did you see how they treated people there? Have you seen?"

Kenzie nodded again. She wished that he would let her talk. She could reassure him that she believed he had done everything he could and had not meant to accuse him in her report. The Cause of Death was listed as accident, not homicide. She hadn't told the police to investigate Kyle and to arrest him if they could find evidence that he had used the posey. It was a tragic accident, no one's fault. But that obviously wasn't how Kyle had read her findings. The guilt of losing his father that way had overwhelmed him.

Kyle tightened his grip again. Kenzie panicked, unable to draw any further breath. She clawed at him, trying to scratch him, to gouge his eyes, to do whatever it took to loosen his grip. She was not an old man like Joseph Howard. She was younger than Kyle, in her prime, and she was sure she was stronger than he was. But the lack of oxygen weakened her, making it harder to think without getting muddled. She needed to get his hands off of her. She needed to loosen the twisted collar and draw deep, unfettered breaths again.

She had never realized how wonderful it was to just breathe without restriction. How had she never realized how much of a blessing it was just to breathe air?

His hands loosened slightly. Kenzie tried to writhe away from him. She flailed and kicked, and one of the kicks caught him hard and unexpectedly. He released her to grab at his own injury, cursing away. Kenzie stepped back from him and blinked to clear her fading vision.

Long, deep breaths to try to get enough oxygen to recover her brain cells and figure out how to get away from him without getting caught again.

Where was help when she needed it? Where was Zachary? Where were the police who used to walk a beat every day? Did cops still do that? Did they drive their routes? She could just see them checking their phones when they were supposed to be looking out at the street, missing vital information—failing to save someone like Kenzie, fighting for her life. Not that they would be able to see her if they drove by on the street. The alley was well hidden from any traffic.

Kenzie ducked behind a dumpster, waiting for the opportunity to run past Kyle while he was distracted. He was howling with pain and with the rage of having lost her. Too pained by his own injury to catch her again yet. But in another minute or two, he would recover and be intent on capturing her again and punishing her for his father's death. For the fact that he hadn't been able to save his father even after taking him out of the nursing home where he was being abused. For the fact that he had died from a device that was supposed to keep him safe.

Had Joseph Howard died by accident, or had a hand twisted the posey, as it had twisted Kenzie's shirt collar, cutting off his breath? He had been a frail old man, not young and healthy like Kenzie. The posey would have prevented him from being able to escape as Kenzie had. Even if he had been able to fight, it would not have been for long.

"Get back here!" Kyle raged, as if he were the parent and she was a recalcitrant child who had run away to escape a legitimate punishment. "You need to pay for what you did! How could you say those things about my father? He was a good man. Private. He wouldn't have wanted that filth splashed all over the paper."

Kenzie wondered if she had misheard him or if her brain had somehow skipped a track. She couldn't understand what he was talking about. She could understand the protest that he hadn't killed his father, but the rest of what he was saying didn't make any sense to her.

"Hey!"

There was a shout. A male voice. Kyle looked around and saw the source of the voice, then sought an escape route. He ran away, farther down the alley, away from the storefront, the parking lot, civilization. Kenzie tipped her head back, taking deep breaths, opening up her lungs further to take in more air. More oxygen.

There were footsteps, running, chasing. Kenzie thought she caught sight of a police uniform as someone ran by them, shouting at Kyle to stop. But she was afraid that he had too much of a head start. The cop would have to be pretty quick to catch up to him.

"Kenzie." Zachary was at her side. "Are you okay? Where did he hurt you?"

"I'm just…" Kenzie swallowed and tried to slow her breathing. "I'm fine. He just scared me."

"You should have waited inside. I was trying to get here. I'm sorry. I took too long."

"Traffic," Kenzie gasped, acknowledging that it had been out of his control.

Zachary shook his head. He stroked her head and briefly touched her carotid pulse. "I got pulled over."

Kenzie laughed, her voice too high and strained. "You got pulled over? *You?* I thought you were the one who never got caught."

"Well… I don't usually."

Kenzie put her arms around him and held herself close, safe against his body, warm and protected. "Did you get a ticket?"

"Not yet. I convinced him to come with me. Said that you were in danger. Finally got him to believe it." Zachary motioned in the direction that the uniformed cop had run.

Kenzie could hear approaching sirens. Backup for the traffic cop. A manhunt to try to catch Kyle before he got away.

"It was the guy who broke in?" Zachary asked. "Someone from the nursing home?"

Kenzie shook her head slightly, their foreheads against each other. "No, it was... it was the son of a man that I autopsied. He was raving about the autopsy report. About something else... I'm not sure what. Something to do with me saying stuff about his father in the paper. But I never talked to the papers; I have no idea what that was all about. He was... I guess he was so upset about his father's death..."

She thought about his twisting her collar, tightening it around her neck. She put her fingers to her throat to pull away the fabric that lay against her skin and to feel for any marks.

"Are you okay?" Zachary asked, tilting his head and leaning in to get a closer look at her neck. "What happened?"

"He was strangling me with my shirt. Had it pulled tight and..." Kenzie swallowed. Her throat was not swelling. There was barely even an ache. Not enough damage for anyone to see. But her breathing *had* been cut off.

"Is it okay? You should have a doctor look at it."

"No, it's okay. Is there even a mark?"

Zachary shook his head. "Maybe a little redness. No ligature mark. No bruising yet."

Just like Joseph Howard. Just a small mark on his throat. Hardly worth noticing. Accidental, as she had put in her report?

"We'll wait here a bit to see if they need you to give a statement or something, and then we'll go home," Zachary told her. "Take it easy the rest of the day."

"Yeah."

It was a few minutes before the uniformed cop came back. As Kenzie had feared, he had been left in Kyle's dust. He wasn't exactly a young man, but he apparently had what it took to run when the chips were down. Maybe he had been a track star in school, and it was all still there in his muscle memory.

"Are you all right, ma'am?" he asked Kenzie. "Do you need an ambulance?"

"No, no. I'm fine."

"He choked her," Zachary told the cop. "It's a good thing we got here when we did."

He looked at Zachary, face impassive, lids slightly lowered. "She'd gotten away from him by the time we got here. She probably would have been okay."

"Good thing we didn't have to find out."

"Yes." The cop rolled his eyes and shook his head slightly. "Fine. No ticket. But this is a warning. If I pull you over again, I won't be so generous."

"I don't usually go that fast in the city," Zachary said agreeably. "This was a special case. An emergency."

"When there is an emergency, you should be calling 9-1-1, not drag racing across the city and putting children and other pedestrians in danger. There is a speed limit for a reason."

Zachary looked down at his feet. While he looked penitent enough, Kenzie suspected he didn't feel the least bit bad for what he had done. He had been justified in his mind by the fact that Kenzie had, in fact, been in danger. She had been assaulted and could have been killed. If the assailant had used a weapon or had been able to hold on to her while he strangled her, there would have been a far different ending to the story. It was a good thing that Zachary and the policeman had gotten there when they did.

The cop nodded, apparently satisfied by Zachary's apologetic demeanor.

"Let's go back to the car," Zachary suggested. "That's where he attacked you? You should have stayed in the store until I got here."

"I didn't know how long you would be, and I talked myself into believing that I had just been imagining things. I just thought… I would get out into the fresh air to clear my head, load the groceries into the car, and be ready to go by the time you got here."

He shook his head. Kenzie snorted. Like he would have done anything else. Zachary was the impulsive one. A hallmark of his ADHD, but also, Kenzie thought, something to do with his traumatic upbringing. With never being able to trust the adults in authority over him. His automatic reaction, particularly in a life-and-death situation, was to do the opposite of what he was told.

The three of them walked back to Kenzie's car. It seemed like a long way from the alley where he had dragged her. It was hard to believe that he had pulled her across that distance before she had managed to recover enough even to get a look at his face. She had been surprised by the attack. She shouldn't have been. She had already been suspicious. She should have been looking all around for any danger. She should not have been distracted by something shiny.

Zachary bent down and picked up the quarters. "You must have dropped these when he grabbed you."

"No. I think *he* dropped them there to distract me. So that I would be looking down and he could get the drop on me."

Zachary looked at the coins in his palm in disbelief. He muttered an appropriate curse under his breath. He displayed them to the policeman. "Do you want these? For evidence?"

"You've already touched them. I don't think they will be any help to the detectives who follow up on the case. It's clear that he attacked her. The coins don't prove anything. You already know his identity, right?" He looked at Kenzie, who nodded. "So they're not going to need fingerprints."

Zachary shrugged and slid them into his pocket. He put the last bag of groceries sitting in Kenzie's shopping basket into the trunk and closed the lid. Kenzie sat down inside the car, sideways in the driver's seat with her feet out the door. She felt better in her own car, safe in its familiar bucket seat. They talked a little and waited while the cop communicated with his backup and whatever detective they were calling out to deal with the case. Kenzie knew a few of the detectives, Donald not the least of them, but she wasn't sure who would be assigned to the assault. Despite Kyle's connection with Sunshine Care, the attack was really not related to Donald's investigation.

Zachary jingled the change in his pockets. Kenzie looked at him.

"Sorry. I'll stop," he said immediately.

"Can we buy a paper?"

He looked surprised at the idea. They normally got their news off of the internet, like everyone else. But Kyle had been talking about the newspaper. What had that been about?

"You want me to go back in...?" He motioned to the grocery store. "Get a newspaper?"

"Yes, if you don't mind."

"Okay." Zachary shrugged. "Whatever you like."

51

Kenzie didn't get a chance to look at the paper until she had spoken to several law enforcement officers in the grocery store parking lot, their names and ranks a blur as she spoke to one after another, retelling her story, unable to explain why Kyle had been so angry about the autopsy report. If he had felt guilty about his father's accidental death—or if he had intentionally caused his death—then he should have been relieved that she had found it to be an accident. He could go on with his life without looking over his shoulder all the time thinking that the police might be on his trail. Or wondering what people around him thought. Because of course, people would think him a killer if Kenzie had come back with a ruling of homicide.

Eventually, she was all talked out and they seemed satisfied with the story. Kenzie suspected that there would not be much more activity on the file. They would put out a BOLO for Kyle, maybe stop by his home a couple of times to see if he returned there. But it wasn't like he was a serial killer. He had been angry, they had prevented him doing Kenzie any harm, and he would probably never do anything like that again.

Kenzie heated the Chicken and Stars while Zachary put slices of bread in the toaster. Kenzie spread out the newspaper, breaking their rule of not bringing anything distracting to the table while they ate. But it was to do with a case and, if autopsy reports and notebooks were exempted from the rule because they both enjoyed talking shop over dinner, then the paper should fall under the same category.

The headline screamed *18 Arrested in Nursing Home Bust.* A photograph showed several law enforcement officers escorting staff members out of Sunshine Care. Kenzie skimmed through the story, which listed the charges that had been laid against the group, though individual breakdowns were not set out. If anyone really wanted that information, it was a matter of public record. Kenzie was surprised to see that the list of charges included sexual assault. So either someone had named names, or there had been enough caught on video for the police to substantiate the accusations Kyle had made.

That should make him happy.

So why didn't it?

"Why was he upset about this?" Kenzie asked Zachary as they sipped their soup. "I would think that he would be delighted that the police were able to find enough to charge all of these people. That he was right, and they were going to put a stop to it. It verifies that he was right to get his father out of there."

Zachary considered this, gazing into the distance. "What exactly was it he said?"

"Something like... his father wouldn't have wanted that to be in the paper."

"Was he... attached to someone at the nursing home? Maybe he wouldn't have wanted everything to come out the way it did because he wanted to protect someone. A nurse that treated him well... someone who looked after or protected him."

"Kyle never said anything like that. He didn't say that there was anyone at Sunshine that had looked after his father. He had acted like they were all predators."

"Can I see?"

Kenzie turned the paper around and let Zachary look it over. He was a slow reader, so she picked up the next section and started browsing through it rather than watching him and making him feel like he had to hurry up and read it and come up with an answer. She found her own name on the second page of the section, announcing her ruling of accidental death in the case of Joseph Howard. Some reporter had done his research and added, "Mr. Howard was a former resident of Sunshine Care," and referred the reader back to the front-page headline. Kenzie grimaced. Kyle probably hadn't appreciated that his father's name had been attached to all of the splashy coverage about the nursing home. If his friends hadn't known that Mr. Howard had been a patient at Sunshine Care before, they did now.

Zachary glanced up at her. She must have made some noise when she had read the line. Kenzie shook her head. "Sorry, didn't mean to interrupt you."

He lowered his eyes to the paper again. Kenzie scanned the various headlines and turned to the Society section. Her eye was immediately drawn to a picture of her mother. A portrait was kept on file with the papers, which they pulled out whenever they wrote an article that involved Lisa Cole Kirsch that they didn't have an event photo for. Lisa looked as regal as a queen. That was how Kenzie had always thought of her when she was little. Queen over all she saw. Lisa had that poise, that polish, that made everyone stop and look twice. It made people who didn't even know who she was stop and listen to her when she made a request or gave a gentle command.

Kenzie looked at the headline and at the story.

"Oh, boy."

Zachary looked up again. "What?"

"It's... dang." Kenzie stopped, rereading the story. Zachary waited. "Well... the family foundation has been making donations and lobbying for legislation on elder care."

Zachary nodded. "Well, considering all that you've found out in the last couple of weeks and the arrests made at Sunshine Care,

I'd say the timing was pretty good. Having it line up with the arrests was lucky."

Kenzie didn't say anything.

"Is this something your dad is helping with the lobbying for?"

"No, he's probably recused himself from having anything to do with the foundation's efforts on this. He's usually against government regulation, and this is asking for more regulation."

"Oh. Okay. Then what's the problem?"

"One of the things they are trying to do is to get home care regulated. To make rules about what practices are and are not allowed in the home."

"So, not just nursing homes."

"They want social workers to monitor what is going on at the same level as foster parenting. Anyone who wants to take care of an elderly parent would have to be approved and to undergo a home study, training, random checks to make sure they were following all of the new regulations."

"Wow. Good luck with that. How would they even identify who was taking care of their parents?"

"Guardianship, for one. For someone to become the guardian of their parent, they have to go through the court system. But in the cases where someone is just helping out, or has power of attorney, and they never get guardianship... I don't know. I guess home care nurses would probably be required to report to the Department as well."

"So that covers everyone trying to take care of their elderly parents legally and with appropriate help. What about those who just tie grandma to the bed?"

Kenzie opened her mouth and couldn't find the words at first. He was right, however bluntly he had put it. "I guess it's the same as your client who was kept locked in the basement as a child. Nothing. There will always be people who flagrantly break the law and get away with it. No amount of regulation is ever going to catch them."

Zachary nodded. His eyes drifted back to his newspaper, then back to her again. "But that isn't what you were concerned about. I thought you would be happy about them trying to regulate home care. That's one of the things that you were worried about. They can set out guidelines for things like restraints. Train people in when they are or are not required and how to use them properly. How often they have to check on the person to make sure they are okay."

Kenzie smoothed the crease in the paper that ran through the article about the foundation. "Here's the thing. First, we have that article." She pointed to the front page about the arrests at the nursing home. "And then we have this article," she turned to the one about her autopsy report. "Saying that I ruled Mr. Howard's death to be an accident and that he was a resident of Sunshine Care. So anyone who reads it can connect Mr. Howard to those practices. And then we have this article, with 'Kirsch' written all over it, saying that home care regulations need to be tightened up because of the possible neglect and abuse going on when people take care of their own family members."

Zachary was always quick to make a connection. "Someone reading those two articles," he pointed to Kenzie's section, "might get the idea that you were involved in the push to regulate home care because you believe that Mr. Howard's death was preventable and that the son was guilty in his death, even if he couldn't be charged with anything."

Kenzie nodded. "And we've got a long list of the kind of abuses and neglect being perpetrated against the elderly."

"And any of the abuses listed in this article," Zachary tapped the Sunshine Care headline, "could have been going on in the Howard home as well."

"Yeah. So I can see why the son targeted me. Because it looks like I am saying he was guilty of abusing and ultimately killing his father."

"Yikes." Zachary shook his head. "I guess things looked pretty bad to him when he read the paper this morning."

"Especially if he was already feeling guilty. And I'm sure he was. Anyone would have."

"Do you remember what he said that his father wouldn't have wanted in the paper? Was it to do with one of those two articles?" Zachary indicated Kenzie's paper.

"No... it sounded like something else. Something his father would have been ashamed of." Kenzie closed her eyes and tried to hear Kyle's words again. "Filth. That *filth* being spread in the paper."

Zachary's eyes dropped to the Sunshine Care article. Kenzie started flipping through the remainder of hers in case something else might have set Kyle off.

"It's the sexual abuse," Zachary said, certainty in his voice. He swallowed and went on, his tone flat and unemotional. "That's the only thing someone would qualify as being *dirty*. Sexual abuse of boys and men is taboo to talk about. People don't want to admit that it happens, especially at the rates it does. Your victim didn't ever admit to any sexual abuse, did he?"

"No, I'm sure he didn't. His son suspected it, just because of his behavior, but he didn't have any evidence."

"And the son didn't go back to Sunshine Care and ask for it to be investigated. He didn't go to the police about it. He kept it quiet until after his father died, and then confided in you."

"And what he told me in confidence ended up in the paper," Kenzie said with a sinking feeling in her stomach. "And the article about my ruling references the Sunshine Care article, as if I had pointed them in that direction. I never said anything about Sunshine in my postmortem."

"So he thinks that you outed the sexual abuse of his father. Announced it all over the papers for all of his friends and family to see."

"And that I am crusading to regulate people like him who are taking care of their elderly parents because I think that he's responsible for the death of his father."

Zachary widened his eyes at Kenzie. "It's a good thing he didn't have a gun."

52

K enzie had been making notes to herself, trying to figure out what she was going to say to Dr. Wiltshire about the fact that it looked like she was using her position at the foundation to further the agenda of the Medical Examiner's Office. Or using her position as an assistant medical examiner to lend weight to the foundation's efforts to push far-reaching legislation through the senate.

She somehow had to explain to him that she hadn't been aware that what was going on at the foundation and at the Medical Examiner's Office would intersect and both appear in the newspaper on the same day. Kenzie had a sneaking suspicion that there would be further articles written to strengthen the connection between the two. Kenzie's role in both organizations would be repeated and enlarged on. They would try to twist the words of her postmortem report to show that she was using her influence at one office to further the agenda of the other. Whichever way they wanted the responsibility to flow.

She needed to be able to prove that she hadn't been aware of the foundation's lobbying efforts until after the news articles came out.

Kenzie sighed and tapped Lisa's contact number on her phone.

She gritted her teeth through the pleasantries and broached the subject as soon as she was able.

"Mother, I wanted to talk to you about this campaign to regulate home care and how it could look like I was involved in it at the same time as I was working on a home care death at the Medical Examiner's Office."

"Yes," Lisa agreed. "I was surprised that you didn't mention that to me at the time. I guess you can't, with the confidential nature of your work. But it was an *interesting* coincidence."

"Do you think you could make a statement indicating that I wasn't aware of the foundation's efforts at the time?"

"Well…" It was clear that Lisa didn't like this idea. She was probably happy with the news coverage linking the two isolated events. "I can't do that, MacKenzie."

"I know it's a lot to ask, but I don't want my family business and Medical Examiner business to be connected in any way."

"You *were* aware of the campaign. I can't deny that. There is a paper trail."

"What paper trail?"

"You signed a number of documents with respect to the campaign."

"No, I didn't."

Kenzie remembered her father's request that she read her emails with a sinking feeling. Kenzie had been doing more for the foundation, but that mostly involved signing documents. And Kenzie didn't read through everything that she signed. It was more of a formality, adding her as a second signatory to a document. Kenzie assumed that Lisa didn't want to be chasing down Walter for his signature all the time and wanted her daughter to have more involvement in the foundation, and that was why they were pushing for her to sign more documents. With Kenzie's busy job at the Medical Examiner's Office, she couldn't read everything they emailed her, so she skimmed through memos, signed where she was told to sign, and didn't pay much attention to new campaigns they were considering. They had done just fine in picking out programs to sponsor in the past; it wasn't like they needed her help or input on that.

Walter had even said they were trying to focus more on mental health issues after seeing the issues Zachary was dealing with. And she might have missed the opportunity to get Tyrrell the job at the foundation if she hadn't asked at just the right time. They had probably copied her on a memo about it at some point, and she hadn't even read it or clued in that it might be a good fit for Tyrrell. "Read your emails," Walter had told her. "We have been trying to keep you in the loop on what we are working on and future directions. It's not helpful if you never read them."

"MacKenzie," Lisa said in a slow, patient voice. "We did tell you what we were doing with this campaign, and you did sign documents concerning it. If there are potential conflicts between the foundation and your job, you need to inform us and recuse yourself."

"Umm... I guess so. I never saw the possibility of a conflict before. What the foundation does and what I do at the ME's office are worlds apart..."

"Until they are not. I had you as the second signatory on those documents because your father did not want his name on anything to do with more government oversight. If you have similar issues or conflicts with your work or your conscience, you need to tell me. How would I know otherwise?"

"You're right. You're right," Kenzie agreed, defeated. She knew that she had not been as diligent as she should have been and hadn't paid attention to what the foundation was doing. She had thought that just putting her name on a piece of paper was enough.

"I'm sorry if this has caused you any difficulties," Lisa offered. "But I can't tell anyone that you were not involved in this campaign when your name is on all the documents."

"No, you can't." Kenzie swallowed. "I'm sorry about that."

"Me too. We will try to avoid this happening again in the future."

"Okay. I'll pay more attention."

"Perhaps come to a board meeting or two. Our weekly stand-up meeting. These would help to keep you in the loop and would not take a lot of extra time."

Kenzie had in her mind that board meetings ended up taking all day, between the pre-meeting prep, the meeting, dinner, and follow-up drinks. But maybe that wasn't true. Lisa was efficient, and perhaps she kept her board meetings moving forward at a brisk pace.

"We meet by video," Lisa said. "You wouldn't have to drive here or stay for supper or overnight. Just an hour or two every couple of months. And the weekly stand-up is rarely longer than half an hour."

"Okay," Kenzie sighed. "I'll try to get to the next one."

53

Kenzie tried to tell herself that explaining what had happened to Dr. Wiltshire would not be a big deal. She had informed him what had happened by phone shortly after the attack by Kyle. After all, Kyle had escaped, and what if he decided to go after Dr. Wiltshire next? Dr. Wiltshire had been quite upset that she had suffered the assault due to doing her job and had told her to take a day off if she needed it.

That had been before she and Zachary had read through the newspaper and identified the stories that had presumably set Kyle off. Before Kenzie realized the apparent connection between her work at the ME's Office and the foundation.

But Dr. Wiltshire would be understanding. He would see that she had not intended to create a conflict of interest between the two organizations. That any correlation between her work at each of them was a complete coincidence, and she had not used the ME's Office to further the foundation's cause. She would be more careful in the future so that there could be no question of a conflict of interest.

But however many times she told herself that it would be fine and would not affect her position or Dr. Wiltshire's opinion of her, she couldn't rid herself of the lump in her stomach and heaviness in her chest.

When she arrived at the office, she saw a yellow sticky note on her monitor. Kenzie got close enough to read it.

Come see me as soon as you get in.

Dr. Wiltshire's writing, of course. And he was in before she, which was a bit concerning. He was rarely there in the morning before she was, unless he'd been attending at an early-morning scene of death. He left her to get everything organized and ramped up to go.

She put down her things, picked up a notepad and her phone, and walked to Dr. Wiltshire's office. The hallway seemed much longer than usual.

"Ah. Kenzie." Dr. Wiltshire looked up from his work and took off his glasses. "Come in. Have a seat."

Kenzie sat in her usual chair and positioned her notepad at the ready.

Dr. Wiltshire picked up a small stack of papers from beside them and placed them in front of her. Kenzie looked down at the documents and her mouth dropped open.

It was a set of documents she had signed for the foundation regarding the campaign for regulating home care. They were only vaguely familiar to her as she paged through them, hearing again Walter's gentle admonition that she had not been reading the materials they sent her. It was all there. A memo setting out the case for increased regulation of home care. The money that the foundation would put into the efforts. Directions of payment to the partner companies that would move it forward.

"Where did these come from? How did you get them?" she asked Dr. Wiltshire.

"They were on your desk."

Kenzie frowned, trying to figure out how they had gotten there. She must have printed them off to sign them at work. Walter had told her that they were important or urgent and she needed to get them back to Lisa. But then the day had gotten away from her, and she had ended up printing them again at home, signing them and sending them to her mother. What had happened to the copies she had printed at work? She couldn't remember tossing them into the recycling. Had she set them aside with some filing? Accidentally attached them to a lab report she had printed off before or after that? She couldn't remember pulling them off the printer and handling them after that.

"I'm sorry... I just found out about this yesterday," Kenzie said. "After the attack... Zachary and I discovered that the Kirsch family foundation was involved in this campaign... or spearheading it... I didn't know before that. It was in the paper, and I'm sorry that it might have given Kyle the idea that I had some kind of agenda against home care or for regulating home care."

"Kyle Howard or anyone else," Wiltshire pointed out.

"Yes. I'm really sorry about that. Like I said, I didn't even know. I just printed those here so I could sign them, but then other things happened and I put them to the side. I didn't even read them."

Dr. Wiltshire raised his brows. "So you didn't sign these?"

"Uh... no, not then." Kenzie flipped to one of the signing pages and showed off the blank signature page. "But... I did sign them later, after I got home."

"So you do, in fact, have a conflict."

"I don't really think that there is a conflict," Kenzie objected. "The foundation was working on this *before* I did the autopsy on Joseph Howard. It isn't something I put them on to because of what happened to him. Because I was upset and thought there needed to be regulation of poseys and other restraints in home care. It wasn't that at all."

"Instead, it looks like you were involved in this campaign, and then went looking for a body that bore out the premise."

Kenzie found herself with her mouth hanging open for the second time in the conversation. "No! No, I would never do something like that. You know that with Mr. Howard, I just followed where the clues led me. The mark on his neck, the engorgement of his organs, the home care worker's confirmation that they used restraints at times…"

"There is something called confirmation bias. Finding what you are looking for. Because that is what you are looking for. It prevents you from looking at other possibilities. You shut your mind to the things that don't fit and make the circumstances fit."

"It wasn't like that at all. I didn't read the documents before the postmortem. I didn't even read them when I signed them. I know that's a terrible business practice, but I was in a hurry and didn't want to deal with it. My mother had prepared everything and was the initial signatory, but she wanted a second signatory to seal the deal. I didn't even know what I was signing."

"That cannot happen again."

"No. I know. I've talked to my mother, and I will be more diligent about making sure there are no conflicts or correlations between my work here and what I see or sign at the foundation. I've learned my lesson."

"I'm concerned about this making it to the papers. Both your postmortem ruling and the piece on the Kirsch foundation sponsoring this campaign. The same day. That doesn't seem like a coincidence."

"It was." Kenzie shrugged. "Just bad luck…"

"Are you sure?"

"What other possibility is there? I didn't tell anyone about either one. I wasn't even aware of the foundation campaign. How could anyone else be?"

54

D

r. Wiltshire's mouth was a thin, straight line. "These documents were printed here," he said, tapping the pages. "I am concerned that someone saw them and made the connection to Howard's postmortem."

"And… passed it on to a reporter?"

Wiltshire nodded. Kenzie's mouth was dry.

"You think we have some kind of leak or spy? Someone who has access to my computer?"

"Or at least your desk."

Several people were through the Medical Examiner's Office every day. Staff who helped to move or process bodies, janitorial, and temporary help. And Kenzie's desk was public facing. People came to her to make requests for copies of documents. Who had seen it on her desk?

"I'll… I'll think about that and try to think of who it could have been," Kenzie told Dr. Wiltshire. "I still think it might just have been a coincidence."

"And there will have to be some consideration of… the consequences of this breach and this conflict of interest occurring and not being disclosed."

Kenzie had already been warned that her investigation at Sunshine Care, inadvertently masquerading as an employee of the Department had been grounds for dismissal. Now, close on its heels, the revelation that she had not disclosed a conflict of interest on the same death investigation.

"What consequence?" she asked, her voice suddenly squeaky.

"I will need to talk to my bosses." Wiltshire ran his fingers through his thinning hair. "See what they will agree to. I'm sorry, I can't just give you a pass on this. It may seem like a little thing, but any actions that negatively impact the reputation of this office could have far-reaching consequences. Your visit to Sunshine Care did not make it to the media, since no one there wanted to advertise the fact of the ongoing investigation, but this has gotten out. And while it may not be overt, it is out there for anyone to see and we can't make it disappear."

Kenzie rubbed her temples. Her eyes were burning, but she tried to look understanding and sympathetic to his dilemma.

"Okay."

"I'm hoping I can get away with a short suspension. You take a little vacation; I can show that I slapped you on the wrist, and then we get back to work."

Kenzie nodded. "Right. Sure."

"I am sorry, Kenzie."

"And I'm sorry that I brought this all down on you. I never intended to do anything unethical. I just... wasn't paying close enough attention." Funny that she was always the one irritated by Zachary's attention difficulties, even though she knew it was caused by a recognized disorder. Now here she was in trouble because she had not paid attention to something that she should have. "Whatever you think is appropriate... I'll take my consequences."

Not that she would have any choice. But hopefully, if she showed contrition, he would not feel the need to do anything more drastic.

"It will depend on what I can wrangle with the State's Attorney. I will make what I consider a reasonable recommendation and, hopefully, we will see eye-to-eye on it." Wiltshire nodded slowly, thinking things through. "You have your parents' reputations on your side. They are both well-known and liked in political circles, they do a lot of good with their foundation, so I think the powers-that-be will be satisfied that there was no intentional wrongdoing."

"I don't want to be seen as hiding behind them. Being protected by them. I haven't asked anyone to cover for me."

"I will be careful how I bring them into it."

"Maybe you shouldn't at all." Kenzie's stomach clenched. "Do you need to? It will be seen as trying to trade favors."

Though her father would see absolutely nothing wrong with that. Trading favors was his bread and butter. But it wasn't Kenzie's. She didn't want to feel like she owed anybody anything.

"I'm going to have to mention the Kirsch family foundation," Dr. Wiltshire pointed out with a smile. "That is inevitable."

"Right. I guess so." Kenzie cleared her throat. "I could step down, you know. From the family foundation. If you think that would make a difference."

"That... is your legacy. I couldn't do that to you."

"I want my legacy to be the search for truth. Someone else can run the foundation if my mother dies while I'm still working in this office."

"Well." Dr. Wiltshire shook his head, giving her a fond look. "I will keep that in mind. But I do not think it is necessary. It's the nature of politics and policing that sometimes conflicts will arise. You just need some more experience in dealing with them. It was an easy mistake to make. It just demonstrates your inexperience, not malice."

Kenzie suddenly felt very vulnerable. She was too old to be given a pass for inexperience.

"We'll work it out," Dr. Wiltshire promised. "For now... you can go home. You should have taken an extra day after the attack anyway. Rest and recreate. Talk to a therapist. This has been a tough investigation. Take some time to relax. You'll be glad you did."

55

Kenzie and Zachary walked back to the Petersons', with Zachary stopping to take occasional pictures. Kenzie didn't usually go with him on these new nature photography walks. She tended to get bored and impatient as he had to stop every so often to take a picture, adjust his settings, take another picture, move to a new angle, adjust some more settings, and take another picture... But it was a quiet, lazy day and she didn't have anywhere she had to be until Monday. It was good for them to spend time together out of doors, enjoying physical activity, without any pressure on either of them to talk or to be somewhere or working on a deadline. It was something that often got lost in their busy and sometimes stressful jobs.

"You got some good ones today," Kenzie suggested.

Zachary nodded. "I won't know how good they turned out until later, but yes, I think they will be!"

Kenzie moved a bit closer to put her arm around him as they walked, making sure as she did so that he wasn't getting ready to take another picture. But he also put his arm around her and gave her a little squeeze.

"How are *you* doing? Feeling... okay?"

"Yes. I'm fine. I'll be glad to get back to work."

He nodded his agreement. Kenzie had cleaned the house top to bottom over the past week, done some improvements that she had been planning for months, and frequently gotten in Zachary's way as he was trying to work. She was sorry to get in his way, but glad that he'd been around so that she wasn't trying to spend her week off work finding things to do around the house all by herself. It was much nicer to have someone home with her, at least during those times that he wasn't out running errands or meeting with clients, or whatever onsite investigations he needed to do. It was good not to be alone the whole time.

Zachary didn't press for more details about her feelings. They'd talked enough about it over the past few days, and she had nothing more that she wanted to share.

Lorne opened the door as they walked up the sidewalk, anticipating their arrival.

"Good timing! Pat is just finishing the gnocchi. I was afraid I was going to have to call you home early from your walk."

"Here we are," Zachary offered.

They let go of each other and entered the house separately. Kenzie saw Lorne smiling at the two of them. He liked seeing Zachary happy, and the two of them walking down the street arm-in-arm was bound to give him a boost. Zachary's relationship with Bridget had been very rocky and contentious. Kenzie suspected that it hadn't included a lot of leisurely walks to take nature pictures.

Pat was putting the serving dishes on the dining room table, so they all washed up and assembled in their usual places. Zachary went straight for the garlic bread, which was a surprise to no one.

Lorne sat down with a sigh and arched his back, hand pressed to his lumbar region.

"Did you hurt yourself?" Kenzie asked.

"No. Nothing particular. It just gets sore by the end of the day. Too much sitting. Or standing. Or walking. I don't like to take anything for it, but sometimes I need to."

"Have you seen your doctor?"

Lorne nodded. "He says I'm getting old. Can you believe the nerve? If they would stop letting junior high students into medical school... you can't believe the baby-faced kids that they are graduating as full-fledged doctors these days. And they get younger each year."

Kenzie laughed. "Yes, they do," she agreed. "When I went back to school, I didn't think I'd stand out that much. I didn't feel older. But they were calling me 'Mom' instead of Kenzie; they were all so young."

"I'm sure you didn't look that much older than them," Zachary said, tearing off a piece of bread and popping it into his mouth. "You *aren't* that much older than them."

"Old enough," Kenzie said, shaking her head.

"Don't talk to me about getting old," Lorne warned. "Getting old is for the birds! Tell me, what do you think is the best way to handle it when you get too old to live by yourself anymore? Is home care really a viable solution? A nursing home? Something else?"

Kenzie looked at Zachary, startled by the introduction of this topic. He must have said something to Lorne about what Kenzie had been investigating and dealing with. Zachary shook his head. "Not me."

Kenzie looked back at Lorne. "Well, it's very individual. It depends on what your needs are. Some things can be dealt with effectively in home care, and some can't. But whichever way you decide to go... you really have to do your research. Check out the backgrounds of the care workers. The reputation of the nursing home. Get a tour, and not just a short one. Talk to other people who have used that person or gone to that home. Really dig down and find out."

Lorne nodded. He pointed at Zachary. "No problem. I'll sic Zachary on them."

Kenzie smiled and nodded. "Yeah. He'd be happy to help."

"You're not going anywhere," Pat said, putting his hand on his partner's shoulder. "Not as long as I'm around to take care of you."

"As long as you *can*." Lorne pointed out. "And I don't want to be a burden to you. If it's too heavy a load…"

"Never," Pat vowed.

But Kenzie knew that was what he hoped, not what would necessarily be the outcome. Trying to care for a grown man who'd had a stroke or had Alzheimer's and grew violent was very different from just picking up after an elderly partner or feeding him. It could easily become too much for him.

"Make sure you know the law if you're ever considering some kind of home care," Kenzie said, addressing the remark to both Pat and Lorne equally. Even with Pat being a decade younger, something could always happen to him first. A blood clot. A car accident. A degenerative disease. "There may be some new legislation coming into play that would affect it. It may become highly regulated."

"Taking care of a partner or family member?" Pat asked, his brows drawing down. "How could they regulate that?"

"They could," Kenzie said. "There are things that *should* be regulated." She looked at Lorne curiously. "Did you read something in the paper?" she asked. "Is that what prompted these questions?"

Lorne shrugged and shook his head. "No, just something I've been thinking about since you were here last. Who has the time to read the paper?"

Zachary chuckled and tore off another bite of garlic bread.

Did you enjoy this book? Reviews and recommendations are vital to making a book successful.

Please leave a review at your favorite book store or review site and share it with your friends.

Don't miss the following bonus material:
Sign up for mailing list to get a free ebook
Read a sneak preview chapter
Other books by P.D. Workman
Learn more about the author

Sign up for my mailing list at pdworkman.com and get Gluten-Free Murder for free!

PREVIEW OF DEATH OF A CORPSE

CHAPTER 1

"You sure you're ready to go back to work?" Zachary asked.

Kenzie looked up from her phone to meet his gaze, uncertain whether he was serious. With his anxiety, it was not outside of the realm of possibility that he was worried about whether she was ready to go back to work. He sometimes worried about things she thought trivial or obsessed over some issue that was adjacent to what she would have expected him to worry about, as if he were trying to avoid the real problem.

But when she looked into his face, she saw the humor in his eyes and knew he was teasing. He knew very well how difficult it had been for her to relax and enjoy being away from the Medical Examiner's Office for the past week. Not that it was a vacation that she was supposed to enjoy. It was a suspension, not a reward for doing a great job on the autopsy of Joseph Howard. But she had tried to treat it like it was a break she had planned, taking the opportunity to give the house a deep clean and get to some projects she had been putting off.

Zachary would probably be happy to have her out from underfoot. He was used to being able to work alone during the day. Sometimes he was on the phone or out talking to clients or subjects face to face, but much of the work he did was from the computer, and he didn't like having to move from one place to another because Kenzie was vacuuming or distracting him with some other job. While he was capable of hyperfocusing on a file or task, he had been anxious about Kenzie's suspension and how she was feeling, so he was alert to every movement she made. Even across the house, she could sense him monitoring what she was doing, listening for anything that might indicate that she needed his help.

They had both been on top of each other too much, tiptoeing around in an effort not to bother each other, and then snapping at each other when it got to be too much. Couples stuff. Kenzie knew it wasn't anything serious, and that things would go back to normal once she was back at work, but Zachary had already been through one failed marriage and was constantly worried that Kenzie was going to turn on him like Bridget had, unable to stand his shortcomings any longer.

"I'm pretty sure, yeah," Kenzie agreed dryly.

"Anxious to get back to your patients?"

"Probably more anxious than they are for me to get back."

He chuckled. "I'm sure they'll open up to you once you get started."

Kenzie groaned. That was a new one. "How long have you been saving that?"

He shrugged, suppressing a smile. "I figured I had to get some new material. The old stuff was a little *cold* and *stiff*."

Kenzie shook her head. "Give me some of that coffee. I don't think I can take you uncaffeinated this morning."

He had a mug ready for her. Kenzie sat at the table, putting her phone away so they could visit undistracted. Zachary had made an effort to have breakfast on the table once she was out of the shower and dressed, and a glance did not reveal anything he had missed. That told her that he had put a lot of effort into it because he usually would miss at least one essential element.

Kenzie picked up her knife and the jar of marmalade and started to spread the marmalade on her buttered toast.

"What will your day be like today?" she asked him as he unwrapped his granola bar. She noticed he was wincing and tried to figure out what was bothering him.

"After I finish crying over you going back to work? I don't know; the whole day is pretty much a write-off after that. I don't know how I'll be able to focus on anything else."

He was still teasing, though. He might be a little anxious about her returning to work, but if he was, he wasn't letting it seep into their conversation. Once Kenzie was gone, she was sure he would throw himself into his email or another task, and wouldn't have another thought about her until she got home that night. Or maybe at lunch, if his growling stomach reminded him to take a break and eat. Sometimes he called her at lunch to touch base.

"Working on that missing teen?" Kenzie prompted.

"Yeah, that will probably be most of my day. With any luck, I'll be able to get a good lead on her. Maybe get a chance to talk to her and encourage her to go back home."

"Do you think so?"

"On a preliminary review, I think there's a good chance. It's the first time she's run away. It was after a fight. Chances are, she'll wake up and regret it and be looking for a way to return home without losing face. She's probably on a friend's couch."

"That doesn't sound too bad, then. She's not an addict or off with a gang banger boyfriend, or a victim of trafficking?"

"I don't think so. Not this time. There *might* be a boyfriend. That's one thing that I'll be trying to find out. But from what I've found so far, I don't think she's that mature."

"Kids can surprise you."

He nodded and munched on his granola bar. "I know that. I'm not saying the parents don't think she was mature enough for a boyfriend. I've looked at her social media, friends, school stuff, and searched her bedroom. I don't see any sign that she's interested in having a serious boyfriend right now or anyone else romantic. I don't think she'll be able to stay away from school for long, even if she doesn't want to go home. That's where her friends are. She spends most of her free time on team sports. She's going to be missing that connection."

"That's good." Kenzie washed down a bite of toast with a swig of hot coffee. "It should be a happy ending, then."

"Always nice to be able to bring a kid home. *And* get paid for it."

Kenzie reached for her phone, then pulled back her hand. They had a pretty strict "no phones at the table" rule to help them focus on each other instead of the constant pull of technology.

"I'm guessing that won't be the case for Elysse Allen," she commented.

Zachary sighed and nodded. "I'm glad I wasn't called on to investigate that one—way too much media attention. I wouldn't be able to make a move without an entourage following me. I think she's almost as popular as Brittany."

Brittany Blake was a social media darling that they ended up stranded with in a mountain resort. She had rented one of the other cabins. Kenzie had known how popular Instagrammers and other social media moguls could be. Still, she hadn't really understood the phenomenon until meeting Brittany, and after everything that had happened while they were there. It was astounding. And Zachary was right about Elysse Allen. If she hadn't achieved Brittany-level fame before her disappearance, the report that she was missing had certainly catapulted her into internet fame now.

She was everywhere you looked. Or her face was, anyway. Kenzie could barely turn on her phone or computer without seeing Elysse's face below a news item, on TV, in a social media feed, or in her inbox. Even without turning on a screen, she could see Elysse's face on newspapers, billboards, and flyers everywhere she went. Vermont was a small state, and they had adopted Elysse Allen as *their* cause. Vermonters would not rest until she was found.

"We'll leave that one to the police," Kenzie agreed. "Let them take any flak for her not being found yet."

Zachary was a private investigator and, while he sometimes crossed paths with the police, they preferred that he not have anything to do with any case they were actively investigating. So he ended up with smaller cases like the disappearance of the schoolgirl, which the police might have looked into but hadn't found anything significant on. They would keep their eyes open, but had not found any evidence of foul play or that the girl was in any danger. As Zachary said, she was probably sleeping on a friend's couch and would come home sooner or later. She had left voluntarily and would likely return in a day or two without incident. Not something the police wanted to put a lot of manpower into.

"Well…" Kenzie popped the last corner of toast into her mouth. "I guess I should probably be getting on my way."

Zachary bounced out of his chair, leaving his granola bar half-eaten. "What do you want for lunch? I was going to make you something to take with you."

Kenzie was notoriously bad for wanting to have something good and healthy for lunch, yet not making anything and then relying on the vending machine in the basement of the police station, full of stale sandwiches and unappetizing snacks. She glanced at the time displayed on the microwave.

"I really should be heading out soon."

"We can get you something that's quick." Zachary turned toward the cupboard and fridge, pursing his lips thoughtfully. He had prepared a lunch for Kenzie once before, assembled out of his various packaged snacks. But she didn't think that would do it for her this time. Zachary looked at her and raised one eyebrow. "Chicken and Stars?" he suggested.

It was a childhood favorite he had just recently reintroduced into his diet. But it wasn't Kenzie's favorite. She rolled her eyes. "Not Chicken and Stars."

He put his hand over his heart. "I'm wounded that you don't appreciate my culinary skills."

"It's not your culinary skills; it's just what's in the can." Kenzie waved the issue of lunch aside. "We'll get something for lunch next time. Today I'll just grab something at work."

Zachary wrinkled his nose.

"Not something *at* work," Kenzie clarified. "Something *near* work. A sandwich shop or diner."

"I don't think you want to be eating out of the work refrigerator."

Kenzie shook her head. "No. Not out of the big one," she agreed. She put on her shoes and grabbed her purse. "See you tonight. Have a good day!"

"Okay." He kissed her, held her for an instant longer than expected, and then released her. "You have a good day too. Don't kill anybody."

"All of my patients are already dead."

"You hope."

"They'd better be!"

CHAPTER 2

T he only person watching the clock was Kenzie herself. There wasn't anyone at the office making sure that she arrived at exactly the right time. She didn't have to clock in and out. She just showed up and got a start on the work on her computer and desk. She tried to time her arrival so that she got there ahead of Dr. Wiltshire, so that she had time to review the emails, lab work, and any new remains that had been checked in overnight, and have everything organized by the time he got there.

Sometimes he foiled her by being there early, however. Kenzie knew she probably should have expected him to be there ahead of her on her first day back after the suspension. Some kind of procedure to acknowledge that she had been away for disciplinary reasons, but was now back after serving her time.

"Let's have a quick meet," Dr. Wiltshire offered as soon as he saw her walk up to her desk. "We'll grab the boardroom. You'll still be able to see if anyone comes to your desk."

Kenzie's desk was the public face of the morgue. At the reception area, she gave people forms to fill out when they had requests. She answered phones and emails. She redirected people when they took the wrong elevator down and were looking for the cafeteria.

Even though she would never recommend that anyone eat at the cafeteria.

As long as she kept all of those things under control, and any other administrative duties, she could also join Dr. Wiltshire in autopsy, sometimes performing postmortems on her own as she grew more experienced and needed to call on him less. She was still supervised, but it wasn't like she would get any complaints from the patients.

Kenzie smiled her acknowledgment and sighed as she put her purse into the desk drawer and locked it. She didn't like going directly into a meeting without having checked her email or phone messages. She liked to know what was going on before she did anything else.

She followed Dr. Wiltshire into the boardroom. A box of donuts and a carafe of coffee were already on the table. Kenzie eyed the donuts. "I just had breakfast…"

"Well, you probably didn't have very much. If you're not hungry, you can wait until later. Have one for lunch."

Kenzie remembered how she had told Zachary that she would get something healthy for lunch today. She really did need to be careful of baking. She liked sweets a little too much.

"Later," she acknowledged. She would see how long she could hold out. Maybe she could get through the day without sampling the tasty pastries.

"Have a seat." Dr. Wiltshire sat down himself. He looked at her over the rims of his rectangular glasses frames for a minute, then took them off. "Glad to have you back. Things just don't run as smoothly here without you."

"Thank you. I'm glad to be back too."

"I'm sure you are. I hope you didn't drive Zachary crazy during your 'break.'"

"Well… yeah, I did."

Dr. Wiltshire chuckled. "We'll have to make sure he gets a break then, won't we?"

"I am not going to say or do anything that will reflect poorly on this office," Kenzie assured him. "I'm sorry for everything that happened, and it won't happen again."

"I'm sure it won't. We have to remember that the eyes of the public are on us. They expect us to act with the proper decorum and not to say or do anything that would worry people or make them distrust our findings."

"Yes."

Dr. Wiltshire nodded. "I'm sure I don't need to belabor the point."

Kenzie put her hand on the table, readying herself to stand up and return to her desk.

"Have you been watching the developments on the Elysse Allen case?" Dr. Wiltshire asked.

"Well… trying not to, actually. But it's everywhere. I wonder what her family thinks of all of the publicity. I suppose they like it, because the more people know what happened to Elysse, the better the chances of finding her."

"Yeah, they don't seem to shun the limelight."

Kenzie nodded her agreement. They definitely did not avoid any opportunities to talk to the media. It seemed like someone in her family was always talking to the reporters, trying to keep everyone not just informed, but engaged, almost frantic. A bunch of people running around like chickens with their heads cut off wouldn't help the investigators much. They needed to be able to do their jobs.

"Well, in case you haven't seen everything that's been on the news lately, they're bringing in dogs to join the search and rescue team today."

"That's a good idea. I'm surprised they haven't had any in earlier."

"They have had several scent dogs in to check out the various places she might have been and to see if they could get a trackable trail on her."

"Oh." Kenzie raised her brows. "What's going on now, then?"

"They're bringing in cadaver dogs."

"To see whether she died and is buried somewhere close by?"

Dr. Wiltshire nodded gravely. "Yes. The search has been ongoing for several days, and the police are not very optimistic about being able to find her alive. If she is in the wilderness, lost, injured, or detained by some third party, she's running out of time. Or has already run out of time. It's time to switch the focus of the search from search and rescue to recovery."

"Oh, dear. Her poor family." Kenzie had known that it would be coming. They couldn't keep a rescue mission going on forever. They needed to be realistic and accept that she was probably gone. It had probably been too late when they started looking for her. By the time her boyfriend had decided that enough time had passed and he needed to file a report with the police. If Kenzie understood the headlines correctly, he had waited until she had been missing for several days before getting the police on to it.

Was it any wonder he was the prime suspect?

"They will have to accept reality sooner or later," Dr. Wiltshire said.

Kenzie nodded and again prepared to stand. Talking about stories in the news was small talk, and she needed to get back to work and make sure everything was whipped back into shape.

"I'm telling you this," Dr. Wiltshire said slowly, "because the prime search area is just a few miles away."

Kenzie's heart beat harder as she processed this. "In Roxboro?"

"Within our jurisdiction."

"So if they find her remains, she might be brought here."

"She will be."

Kenzie tried to think of all the consequences of such a case. Media and politicians calling her. Psychics. Who knew who else? Maybe people trying to sneak in to get a picture of the remains themselves.

They would need to place Elysse's examination at the top of the list. There was no way the public would let anyone else ahead of their darling. Dr. Wiltshire should do the post on it, or at least lead. Kenzie would have to be careful how much information about the postmortem she said to anyone.

"This will be quite the media circus," Dr. Wiltshire said, nodding his agreement with what he read in her face. "We must be very careful every step of the way."

"I won't say anything to the reporters."

"Or to *anyone*. Not someone riding the elevator that you think is a law enforcement officer. Not someone who invites you over for a drink. An old friend who touches base and wants to know what you've been doing lately."

"No. I understand."

"Good. At the moment," Dr. Wiltshire pushed himself up from the table, "we know nothing. We have no statement to make. We are just waiting to see what happens."

"There isn't any guarantee that they'll even find anything."

"No. They could be wrong. She could be absolutely fine."

But it wasn't very likely. More than likely, Elysse Allen was dead.

Death of a Corpse, Book #7 of the Kenzie Kirsch Medical Thriller series by P.D. Workman can be purchased at pdworkman.com

ABOUT THE AUTHOR

P.D. Workman is a USA Today Bestselling author, winner of several awards from Library Services for Youth in Custody and the InD'tale Magazine's Crowned Heart award, and has published over 90 mystery/suspense/thriller and young adult books, including stand alones and these series: Auntie Clem's Bakery cozy mysteries, Reg Rawlins Psychic Investigator paranormal mysteries, Zachary Goldman Mysteries (PI), Kenzie Kirsch Medical Thrillers, Parks Pat Mysteries (police procedural), and YA series: Tamara's Teardrops, Between the Cracks, and Breaking the Pattern.

Workman loves writing about the underdog, who the reader may love or hate. She has been praised for her realistic details, deep characterization, and sensitive handling of the serious social issues that appear in all of her stories, from light cozy mysteries through to darker, grittier young adult and mystery/suspense books.

> P. D. Workman, does not shy from probing the deep psychological scars of childhood trauma, mental illness, and addiction. Also characteristic of this author, these extremely sensitive issues are explored with extensive empathy, described with incredible clarity, and portrayed with profound insight.
>
> — —KIM, GOODREADS REVIEWER

Some of Workman's titles have been translated into Spanish, French, Portuguese, German, and Italian.

Workman began writing at an early age and is a prolific reader as well as writer. She is also passionate about teaching and learning, expresses her creativity through art and cooking, and loves exploring the Calgary parks and green spaces where the Parks Pat Mysteries are set. She was a legal assistant for many years and has done extensive charitable work.

Workman was born and raised in Alberta, Canada, and is married with one adult son.

Please visit P.D. Workman at pdworkman.com to see what else she is working on, to join her mailing list, and to link to her social networks.

If you enjoyed this book, please take the time to recommend it to other purchasers with a review or star rating and share it with your friends!

tiktok.com/@pdworkmanauthor

facebook.com/pdworkmanauthor

twitter.com/pdworkmanauthor

instagram.com/pdworkmanauthor

amazon.com/author/pdworkman

bookbub.com/authors/p-d-workman

goodreads.com/pdworkman

linkedin.com/in/pdworkman

pinterest.com/pdworkmanauthor

youtube.com/pdworkman

Find P.D. Workman's books at

PDWORKMAN.COM

Scan the QR code below